RETURN

to

LOST CREEK JUNCTION

Dale Thele

Published by

Fountain Literary Press
a unique approach to publishing
Austin, Texas, USA

Copyright © 2025 by Dale Thele

ISBN: 979-8-9857557-9-4   (pbk)
ISBN: 979-8-9930718-1-7   (ebook)
ISBN: 979-8-9930718-0-0   (hc)

ASIN: B0FVWZGNZY

First Digest Paperback Edition: October 11, 2025
First Hardcover Edition: October 11, 2025

15 16 17 18 10 22 23 24 25

*Dedicated to those who believe in
ghosts, witches, and curses.*

"Don't matter if you believe
in them or not. If they're there,
they're there."

~ *Joan Lowery Nixon* ~
"The Haunting"

RETURN

to

LOST
CREEK
JUNCTION

a fictional tale

Dale Thele

Tuesday, May 14, 2019

Have you ever had one of those mornings when it feels like the universe is out to get you? The stars are misaligned, the planets are off-kilter, and your astrological sign is passing through the wrong house. No matter what you do, nothing seems to go according to plan. If you say 'no', then you're either not being honest or you're like an ostrich with its head buried in the sand. Let me tell you about my morning—it was a classic case of *Nothing Going as it Should*.

There I was, caught in a classic predicament that we've all experienced: running late for something important. In my case, it was a class at Xavier University of Louisiana. The clock was ticking, and anxiety was setting in. First things first, I couldn't find my keys. I turned the apartment upside down—checked under the couch cushions, rummaged through kitchen drawers, and even looked in the fridge (don't ask). No luck. Just when I thought things couldn't possibly get worse, my cell phone started ringing. Great! Except I couldn't find that either. It felt like I was playing a frustrating game of hide-and-seek with my own belongings. The phone was beeping somewhere deep within the apartment, but all I could think about was how late I was going to be for the final class of the semester. It was a comedy of errors, and I was the star, providing unintentional entertainment for anyone who might have been watching.

If this crazy episode had been a movie, the scene would have frozen on a frantic college student desperately searching for his cell phone. A voice-over might have made a hilarious remark to the audience at that moment. Yep, that frazzled college student would be yours truly—Taylor Greene. And just to be clear,

'Greene' is spelled with three E's, because why not make things a little more complicated?

In the corner of that frozen moment, you might have spotted my roommate and boyfriend, Giles Broussard. We've been together for almost a year now, which is quite a milestone in college years. I also brought a 6-year-old into the relationship— my fawn Great Dane, Beau. He stands 32 inches tall, and eats like a horse. Beau has been part of my life since he was a puppy, and his presence has added a whole new level of chaos to my already hectic morning. But hey, who doesn't love a bit of chaos, especially when it comes in the form of a 170-pound over-grown puppy who thinks he's a lapdog?

As I searched for my lost things, tossing couch cushions and rummaging through backpacks, I was also trying to keep Beau from stealing my lunch. The scene was pure anarchy. While Giles chuckled amusedly and Beau gave me enthusiastic slobbery kisses, it felt like I was stuck in a slapstick comedy. Who would've thought that losing a phone and a set of keys could turn into such an epic quest? But hey, that's college life for you—full of unexpected twists and turns, even when it comes to something as simple as looking for a cell phone and keys. The unpredictability of college life never ceases to amaze me. Looking back, I can definitely say it was a hilarious mess, a scene that could've come straight out of a Laurel and Hardy comedy flick.

With Giles' help, and what felt like an eternity, I finally found my keys *and* my phone—thanks to a random pile of laundry. By that point, I was already behind schedule, feeling the urgency of the moment. You know that feeling when you're racing against time? It was like being in a movie where every second counts. Where was the swelling background music? If you've ever had one of those mornings where it feels like the universe is conspiring against you, you're definitely not alone— we've all been there. I can't express the wave of relief that washed over me when I finally found my keys and held my cell phone tightly in my hands.

"Hello?" I shouted into the phone, letting out all my pent-up frustration. "Sorry, it's been one of those days," I added, softening my voice.

"Who is it?" Giles whispered in my ear.

I swatted at him like he was an annoying fly buzzing around my head. "Yes," I nodded towards the phone, turning my back to Giles in the hopes that he'd take the hint.

"Yes? What?" Giles asked, circling around me like a buzzard eyeing its next meal. Seriously, could he be any more annoying at that moment?

I turned away from him to focus on the voice on the other end of the call. "We'd love to," I said with a smile, feeling a spark of excitement.

"We'd love to what?" Giles asked, trying to lean closer and press his ear against the phone as if it were some top-secret briefing.

"Okay," I responded firmly. "We'll see you next week. Bye." I hung up.

"What's this about next week?" he pleaded like a child on Christmas Eve, eager to unwrap at least one gift.

I couldn't help but laugh. "How would you feel about taking a road trip next week?" I asked.

So, that's where my story begins. I won't reveal everything all at once; you'll have to experience it for yourself as the narrative unfolds. However, I assure you it's not at all what you're expecting. My story features ghosts, witches, curses, and plenty of things that go bump in the night. Buckle up, because all of us—yes, including you—are in for one incredible, unexpected adventure.

Dale Thele

ARRIVAL

Monday, May 20, 2019

The sun rose into a cloudless sky, as it often does during early summer mornings, casting a golden hue over the landscape. The sky is a crisp blue, and the green grass sparkles with dew droplets, giving the impression that overnight, fairies sprinkled the fields with tiny diamonds. However, for Giles, Beau, and me, this morning feels different. It marks the beginning of an exciting chapter filled with promises of unlimited adventures waiting for us to explore. We've set out on an unexpected road trip to Lost Creek Junction—a destination that wasn't until last week, on our immediate Bingo card.

Rachael's mysterious phone call sparked an impromptu adventure, prompting us to abandon our plans and embark on a spontaneous road trip. The thrill of the unknown filled the air as we packed our suitcases and climbed into my Jeep, ready for whatever lay ahead. With each mile we cover on the open road, our anticipation grows, like the fizz of a freshly opened soda pop on a hot day.

As the landscape whizzes by—a blur of trees and colorful billboards—I sense the excitement building. Laughter fills the Jeep as we share stories and dreams under the clear early summer sky, each mile bringing us closer to the unknown. What secrets await us in Lost Creek Junction?

One thing is for sure: this road trip's shaping up to be one we could possibly remember for years to come, even though we're unaware of the unexpected twists and turns that lay ahead.

As I turn the steering wheel of the Jeep into the driveway, a mix of excitement and urgency fills the air as we have arrived at our destination. Before I can even switch off the ignition, Beau leaps out to crouch on the grass at the edge of the brick driveway. Giles and I follow suit, already in motion, performing our own version of the *Pee-Pee Dance*. Our hearts racing, our adrenaline pumping, as we race to the porch with an undeniable sense of urgency.

I bang on the front door with my fist, our impromptu jig adding a playful rhythm to the air. We impatiently await entry, our bodies moving in sync with anticipation. Rachael opens the door with a bemused smile, but we're already in motion. Giles and I dart past her like two playful tornadoes, our destination clear: the bathroom—any bathroom!

I glance back as I dash through the parlor, my urgent call echoing, "We need to pee! We'll be right back!" The excitement of our little adventure fuels our uncontrollable giggles. For a moment, we're transported back to our carefree childhoods, bursting with laughter as we sprint toward the nearest bathroom, the need for relief immediate and pressing.

A few moments later, Giles and I reemerge into the parlor, a sense of relief washing over us as a huge weight is lifted from our minds. The tension from the previous predicament melts away like ice cream on a hot summer day. Giles, with a sheepish grin, zips up his pants while I decide, in a moment of spontaneity, to fully embrace the carefree spirit of summer. I let my shirt tail hang loose, a physical manifestation of my newfound relaxation. After all, comfort is key during summer break.

Rachael stands at the door, holding it open for Beau, who strolls in with an air of triumph. He has just transformed Rachael's front lawn into a surprising water park, a sight that leaves everyone, including Rachael, in delightful shock. His confidence reflects his pride in this unexpected and hilarious transformation.

"How was the drive?" Rachael asks, her eyes sparkling with curiosity.

"Oh, you know, the traffic was so-so," I reply, unable to suppress a chuckle. In an instant, Giles, Rachael, and I burst into fits of laughter at the absurdity of the situation. If we weren't friends, the moment could have been awkward and quite embarrassing.

"I missed you guys," Rachael exclaims, her voice filled with joy as she wraps Giles and me in a warm, tight hug. The happiness radiating from her is infectious, and even Beau, my gentle giant of a dog, joins in the celebration with an enthusiastic bark—his way of worming himself into being part of the love fest.

As Rachael breaks away from our embrace, she squats down to meet Beau at eye level. With a tender smile, she wraps her arms around his thick neck, pulling him into a huge hug that conveys deep affection. If my dog could blush, I swear Beau's snout would be glowing a bright crimson right now.

"Rach, your invitation left me a bit puzzled. What's going on?" I ask.

Meanwhile, Beau, enjoying the attention, leans into Rachael's embrace, his tail wagging wildly. I can't help myself and chuckle at the sight.

Rachael stands up, brushing her hands as if she has just finished kneading bread dough. "Let us just say this involves two of your old *friends*," she replies, her voice tinged with frustration. "They have crossed the line and become downright abusive toward my bed-and-breakfast guests. I had no choice but to close the B&B for the summer, hoping to cleanse the house of those two destructive spirits. As you know, summer is my busiest season."

The weight of her words linger like echoes in an empty hall, reverberating long after they've been spoken. How could two ghosts cause such chaos? The thought sends shivers down my spine. What kind of turmoil have they unleashed upon unsuspecting visitors? I can almost picture it: guests checking in, excited for a weekend getaway, only to be confronted by cold drafts, eerie whispers, and perhaps even the occasional flying teacup.

"Seriously," Rachael continues, pacing the room. "One couple claimed they felt cold hands around their necks, as if invisible hands were trying to choke them. Another guest swore they were chased by a ghost in the middle of the night, wielding an axe." She throws her hands up in exasperation. "It is as if those two ghosts are on a mission to ruin my business."

"What do you think stirred them up?" I ask.

"Let us hold off on this conversation until the other guests arrive, shall we?" Rachael replies, her tone cautious and measured. There's something in her voice that hints there's more she's not revealing.

"Other guests?" I echo, my eyebrows raising in surprise. "You mean you've invited more people?"

Before she can respond, a knock at the door breaks the rising tension in the room. It's a sound that heightens my curiosity, making me wonder who it might be, while also leaving me anxious.

"The two of you make yourselves comfortable while I get the door?" Rachael says, glancing back at us before walking toward the door we entered just moments before.

I exchange a glance with Giles, who mirrors my confusion. The prospect of someone else joining us is a thrilling mystery that leaves me curious and hungry for answers. My mind is a whirlwind of questions, like dried autumn leaves caught in a gust of wind, as I settle back into the upholstered chair, bracing for whatever might unfold next.

As she swings open the door, a wave of excitement washes over me. Entering the house are Julie, Ryan, and some strange guy I don't recognize—a mystery wrapped in casual attire.

"Taylor! Is that you?" Julie squeals, her eyes sparkling with joy as she sprints through the parlor like a shooting arrow, straight into my open arms. Her warmth envelops me like a fleece blanket on a chilly evening.

I pull back and grin at her. "So, I see you've brought your new boyfriend?" I ask, trying to gauge the newcomer who has captured her heart.

"No, no, you've got it all wrong—" Julie begins to protest, but Ryan interrupts her with a confident smirk.

"This is *my boyfriend*," he declares, firmly taking hold of the hand of the stranger beside him. "Meet Ashton Wentworth, *my boyfriend*," he states with unwavering confidence.

A wave of realization washes over me. I understand exactly what Ryan is trying to do—he's playing a game, and I refuse to let him get under my skin with this *my boyfriend* nonsense. I glance at Ashton, who seems unfazed by the sudden attention. He has a laid-back vibe that suggests he's accustomed to being the center of attention without even trying. I'm determined not to let Ryan's game affect me.

"Nice to meet you, Ashton," I say, forcing a smile while mentally preparing myself for whatever maneuver Ryan has planned next.

Ashton returns a nervous smile, and I can't help but feel intrigued by him. This unexpected turn of events isn't so bad after all. The day is still young, and if Ryan thinks he can stir the pot without facing any consequences, he's in for a surprise.

Public display of his new relationship doesn't bother me; Ryan's the one who ended things between us, not me. However, as I watch this scene unfold, I can't help but wonder: What's his plan? Is he trying to make me jealous, or is this his awkward way of moving on?

I mean, come on. It's like he's trying to play a twisted game—a psychological chess match where the rules revolve around stirring up old emotions that I believed were long settled. But here's the thing: I refuse to participate. The drama and theatrics are completely unnecessary.

In this complicated mix of feelings and misunderstandings, one thing becomes crystal clear: the past has a strange way of creeping back into our lives when we least expect it. Just when you think you've moved on, bam! There it is, smacking you in the face with a curveball. However, I'm resolute in my decision not to let that upset me. I have my own life to live, and it doesn't include revisiting old chapters that should remain closed.

Let him do his thing while I stand firm in my resolve. I've moved on, and I'm focusing on what matters to me—my happiness and growth. After all, life is too short to get caught up in someone else's emotional circus.

What I'm about to do next is a twist that's sure to send Ryan into a tailspin.

"Rye, meet *my boyfriend*, Giles Broussard," I announce with a playful smirk, intertwining my fingers with Giles's as if sealing the deal on this little surprise. My glance at Ryan says it all: *I gotcha, bitch!*

The moment hangs in the air as I watch Ryan's bravado crumble like a house of cards. He offers a weak handshake to Giles, his confidence evaporating faster than morning dew under the hot Texas sun. It's priceless to see his expression shift from cocky to confused in seconds.

"Wait, what?" he stammers, trying to regain his footing. "You... you didn't mention you were dating anyone."

I chuckle to myself at the irony. Ryan's little attempt to get under my skin isn't working. Now he's floundering like a fish out of water, and it's downright hilarious.

"How could I have mentioned it? I haven't seen you since last summer when you left me," I reply, enjoying every moment of his discomfort.

"So, here we are," Giles says, leaning in with a grin that lights up the room. "Nice to meet you, Ryan. I've heard a lot about you."

Ryan swallows hard, his bravado replaced by awkwardness as he realizes that his attempt to show off his new boyfriend has backfired. He has no idea what I may have told Giles about Ryan's and my past. This unexpected twist is exactly what I want—a chance for him to experience a taste of his own medicine.

"Yeah, uh... nice to meet you too," Ryan mumbles, clearly thrown off balance. The tables have turned, and I'm savoring every moment. *Ryan should know better than to provoke a gay jilted former lover. He could benefit from brushing up on the rules in the Gay Agenda Handbook.*

Just when I think I have a handle on the situation, there's a sudden knock at the door. A welcome distraction, I think to myself. But who could it be?

Rachael opens the door with a bright smile, revealing Duncan and his female companion. I steal a glance at Julie, and it's clear she's seen Duncan and his date too. Her reaction is questionable; her shoulders tense up. This reunion is bound to be a minefield of awkward moments, especially since she ended things with Duncan just last summer.

"Taylor!" Duncan exclaims, his face lighting up with that familiar boyish grin.

"I'll be darned!" I call out, "Duncan!"

We wrap our arms around each other like long-lost lovers reuniting after years apart. Though let's be honest—Duncan is as straight as they come. Or so he claims.

The air is thick with swirling memories, but as we pull apart, I catch Julie's eye and can't ignore the uncertainty in her expression. Will she survive this reunion? Will she be okay sharing space with her ex and his new girlfriend? The answer remains to be seen. Stay tuned, folks.

"Great to see you, bud," Duncan exclaims, his tall frame towering over me, a wide and welcoming smile on his face. "I'd like to introduce you to my girlfriend, Isadora Schaeffler." Isadora, a woman of striking beauty with long, flowing reddish-brown hair and piercing blue eyes, stands beside him, her posture exuding confidence and cultured poise.

I force a smile, but the tension in the room is unmistakable. This impromptu reunion feels anything but casual. I reach out my hand for a shake, but Isadora's gaze is like a laser beam, slicing through the noise of the room and hitting me right in the heart. Her nose crinkles in disgust, as if she's just come upon something repulsive—a rotting carcass or worse. I quickly withdraw my hand, half-expecting her to chomp a chunk out of it like an angry snapping turtle.

With a glance around the parlor that could sour milk, she announces to no one in particular, "I hope you've completed the restoration on the rest of the house. This outdated mishmash simply won't do." Her words hang in the air like a pungent perfume at a family gathering, sticking to the walls and making everyone wonder who forgot to open a window—heavy and suffocating. Just what Rachael needs: a décor critique from someone who thinks she's too good for this place.

I briefly glance at Duncan, who seems unaware of the cold tension radiating from his girlfriend. He's still smiling, utterly oblivious to the fact that his introduction of her seemed more like a warning than a warm welcome. Like they say, *love is blind...* and in Duncan's case—deaf and mute too.

"Yeah, well, it's a work in progress," Rachael says, trying to keep the mood light while bracing herself for whatever Isadora might say next. This reunion has just become a lot more interesting—but not in the way I had hoped.

"Izzy, my dear," Duncan says gently, taking her hand with warmth in his voice. "This house is a remarkable time capsule, preserved in its original condition since it was built nearly two hundred years ago."

Isadora wrinkles her nose in distaste, her disdain for the historical house evident. "How utterly revolting. Dunkikins, can't we stay at a Four Seasons instead? Surely there must be something more... civilized in this town?"

Duncan sighs and shakes his head. "Unfortunately, there aren't any five-star hotels in Lost Creek Junction."

With a dramatic flair that only someone as pretentious as Isadora could muster, she exclaims, "I'll endure a four-star hotel if it means getting out of this house. Just get me out of here." Her over-the-top personality shines through every word she utters.

Duncan chuckles softly, aware that Isadora's idea of

adventure doesn't quite match dusty antiques and creaky floorboards. However, as he looks around the charming yet outdated home, he can't help but appreciate its history. His admiration for the setting is evident—even if Isadora views it as a nightmare.

"Izzy, darling," Duncan begins, "there's only one hotel in this town, and let's just say it doesn't even boast a one-star rating."

"Are you seriously suggesting we have no choice but to stay in this... dump?" Isadora replies, her brow furrowing as she surveys the less-than-appealing interior.

Rachael silently glares at Isadora. If looks could kill, Isadora would have multiple knives sticking out of her chest like a human knife rack.

"Come on now, darling, give this place a chance," Duncan urges, his voice filled with misplaced optimism. "After a while, you might find that it grows on you."

"That's precisely what I'm worried about—something growing on me," Isadora retorts with a dramatic flair. "Let's just hope for your sake that there's enough penicillin around to combat whatever I might contract here."

"I'm sorry, Rachael," Duncan says, turning to our host with a tone of genuine concern. "Izzy can be a bit... well, high-strung."

"High-strung?" Ryan interjects with a playful smirk, clearly enjoying the moment. "More like high maintenance. But hey, at least we'll have interesting stories to tell when we leave here."

Isadora rolls her eyes at Ryan's teasing. "Great! Just what I need—memories of bedbugs and questionable room service."

Duncan forces a chuckle and nudges her playfully. "Look on the bright side—if we survive this place, we can handle anything."

With a resigned sigh, Isadora finally relents. "Fine." Then she turns to Ryan. "I warn you, if I wake up with an extra limb or something crawling on me, I'm blaming you—little man—whatever your name is."

"Whatever," Ryan snickers in response.

Duncan shoots Ryan a sharp glare, his patience wearing thin.

The tension between them is as thick as dust whirls in a vacuum cleaner bag.

"Alright, boys," Julie interjects, stepping between them like a referee mediating a heated match. Her intervention brings welcome relief, like a cool breeze in a heated room. "That's enough from both of you."

Giles leans in, his voice barely above a whisper. "What's the deal with Duncan and Ryan?"

I can't help but smirk as I reply, "Those two are like oil and water—they just don't mix. It's all bickering and banter between them."

With a conspiratorial glint in his eye, Giles leans in closer. "If you ask me," he says, lowering his voice to an almost dramatic hush, "they're secretly in love with each other."

I burst into giggles, unable to contain my amusement. "Oh boy," I respond playfully, "now that would be the day."

"What are you two boys scheming over here?" Julie asks, her eyes sparkling with curiosity as she approaches Giles and me.

"I was just filling Gill in on the intricacies of our group dynamics," I reply, a hint of intrigue coloring my voice.

Julie leans in close so that what she says is within my earshot only.

"Is it my imagination, or does Ash seem unusually quiet?" Julie asks, furrowing her brow slightly. "He hasn't said much since we arrived. What do you think his story is?"

"Honestly, would you want to put yourself in the line of fire for ridicule, especially as the newcomer in this group?" I ask, raising an eyebrow at Duncan and Ryan, who are locked in a tense standoff.

Julie nods thoughtfully. "I suppose you have a point."

"Maybe Ash is just being cautious," I suggest. "I mean, who wouldn't be a bit freaked out by this group?"

Julie scoffs, momentarily breaking the tension. "Or maybe he's just shy. You know how some people are when they're suddenly thrown into a group of strangers. Looking back on our ride here, he hardly said a word. Maybe you're right. He must be shy."

"Right," I add, glancing back at Ash. "But do you think there could be more to him than meets the eye? Don't you feel like there's something... off about him?"

"Like what?" Julie asks. "Just because he's dating your ex doesn't make him suspicious."

"I didn't mean it that way," I reply. "There's just something about him that I can't quite put my finger on."

As we continue speculating about Ash's reluctance to get involved, the rest of the room buzzes with varied conversations.

Duncan approaches me, curiosity written on his face. "Taylor, do you have any idea why we've all been called here?"

"Before you arrived," I say, glancing at Rachael, who's deep in conversation with Giles, "Rachael briefly mentioned something about ghostly encounters."

Duncan's eyes widened. "Please tell me it's not Ezekiel and Abrahim?"

"I suspect it is," I reply with a nod. "But let's wait for Rachael to bring it up before jumping to conclusions. Does that sound good?"

"Fine by me," Duncan concedes, though his expression shows that he's eager for more details.

As the air thickens with intrigue and anticipation, one can't help but wonder: why has Rachael called all of us together after a year apart?

I wish to take a moment to reflect on our varied histories. I've briefly mentioned the group and our relationships: me and Giles, Duncan and Isadora, and Ryan and Ash. However, what you might not know is the drama that unfolded last summer. Ryan and I were in a long-term relationship, and later in the summer, Duncan and Julie got together. Unfortunately, their romance was short-lived. Ryan and I parted ways after a dramatic incident that occurred while I was away at a chess tournament in New Orleans. In hind sight, our relationships sort of seem like stuff soap operas are written, am I right?

Now that all of us are back together under one roof, the stage is set for a potentially explosive reunion among exes who haven't seen each other since last year.

Before I continue the story, I want to share some additional information about myself and my friends.

You already know my name, it's Taylor Greene, I'm an average twenty-one-year-old college student attending Xavier University in New Orleans. Just last week, I completed my third year of college. I transferred from the University of Texas at Austin last fall after winning a full scholarship and placing third in the National Collegiate Chess Tournament. Although third place didn't qualify me for the International competition, I was more than happy to accept the scholarship money as my prize.

I was born and raised in Beaumont, a small town in South Texas near the Louisiana border, about 250 miles southeast of Austin. Beaumont isn't just a location for me; it's a significant part of my identity. The rich and simple life there has profoundly influenced me, shaping who I am in ways I'm still discovering.

At first glance, you'll notice I'm quite ordinary—just another face in the crowd. However, my medium build, striking dark blue eyes that often reveal my emotions, and sun-kissed, long, straight ash-blonde hair distinguish me from others. Standing at 5 feet 10 inches tall, I easily blend into the backdrop at parties, which doesn't bother me at all.

Life hasn't always been easy for me. When I was sixteen, I faced one of the toughest challenges imaginable: I lost both of my parents in a car accident. This heartbreaking event changed everything. For the next two years, I lived with my grandma, who became my rock during that turbulent time. After that, I moved to Austin to share an apartment with my boyfriend, Ryan Bartlett—you'll learn more about him in a bit.

My best bud is an irresistibly adorable fawn Great Dane named Beauregard Winston Churchill Greene—quite a regal name, right? But let's be honest, I just call him Beau because his full name is a bit of a mouthful. I only use his full name when he misbehaves, which is amusing because he knows he's in big trouble at that point. That's when he pulls off his best hide-and-seek moves, darting away as if he thinks I can't find him. Despite his calm demeanor, Beau is surprisingly clever. I still remember the day I got him as a tiny, precious puppy—a Christmas gift from my grandma after I lost my parents. He filled a void I didn't even know existed, and he has been my best buddy ever since.

Then, there's my current boyfriend, Giles Broussard. Our story began in a unique way—we met in New Orleans during a chess competition last summer. He was the cab driver who picked me up at the bus station and took me to the host hotel, and we hit it off right away. By the end of the summer, we officially became boyfriends.

Giles and I share more than just a love for chess; we also have similar builds, which often leads us to share clothes. Although we are the same age, he appears older than I, because of his short, trimmed beard and cropped light ash-brown hair, which has a hint of premature gray at the temples. His complexion is slightly darker than mine since he's a native of New Orleans and has Cajun ancestry. Giles is a student at Xavier University, but he attends part-time while I go full-time. Unfortunately, he wasn't as fortunate as I was to receive a full scholarship, so he works full-time and takes classes part-time.

Next, there's my ex-boyfriend, Ryan Bartlett. Until we broke up last summer, we'd been inseparable since before elementary school, sharing countless adventures and laughter as next-door neighbors for years. However, life took a turn when I lost my parents and had to move in with my grandma across town.

During those challenging times, Ryan and I didn't let the distance or circumstances rip us apart. Instead, we grew even closer, overcoming the odds and becoming boyfriends.

Ryan has captivating emerald-green eyes that sparkle with mischief, and his curly coppery-blond hair adds a touch of warmth to his occasionally challenging personality. We're the same age, but he has the advantage of a few extra pounds. To be honest, let's call it what it is—he's developing a bit of a tummy roll.

Did I mention that Ryan is a student at the University of Texas? That's why we moved to Austin, where we shared an apartment for two years. Living with Ryan was an adventure filled with late-night study sessions and plenty of pizza deliveries.

Then there's my friend Duncan Campbell, who comes from the charming city of Charleston, South Carolina. His family may or may not own a soup company by the same name. All I know is that I don't know how wealthy Duncan's family is; however, rumors suggest they are pretty well-off. What really distinguishes Duncan isn't his family's financial status or prestige; it's his remarkable generosity that touches the hearts of everyone he encounters, along with his unwavering open-mindedness that makes each person feel respected and included.

We first met in an introductory class at UT, and from that moment on, we clicked. Our friendship grew stronger from there.

Duncan is a towering figure, standing well over six feet tall, which makes him noticeably taller than me. With his slender frame, you might mistake him for someone struggling with anorexia. However, don't be deceived—this guy eats like he has a tapeworm. Seriously, he never seems to gain an ounce. If only I could borrow some of his incredible metabolism.

Duncan is more than just his towering height and insatiable appetite; he's a captivating embodiment of nostalgia. Picture this: his long, sleek black hair falls over dark, mysterious eyes, which seem to hold countless secrets. He complements his look with a signature creamy beige straw fedora, a stylish nod to a bygone era that he wears with pride. Duncan effortlessly embodies a vintage surfer style, reminiscent of a character from a 1960s beach movie. His charm is so magnetic that even if he weren't as straight as they come, I could easily see myself falling under his spell.

And did I mention that he's a genius? We're talking Einstein-level intelligence here. His brilliance never fails to amaze me, and it's just one more reason why Duncan is annoyingly perfect in every way.

Duncan's new girlfriend is Isadora Schaeffler. While I don't know much about her, I assume she comes from a fairly wealthy family. Isadora's built like a runway model, standing at 6 feet tall, making her just slightly shorter than Duncan. Her long, wavy hair has dark reddish-brown tones, and her striking aqua-colored eyes are truly captivating. Isadora wears a lot of makeup, resembling a canvas created by a makeup artist, complete with bright red lipstick. Her wardrobe features exclusive designer pieces and bespoke boutique-style clothing—definitely high-end stuff.

I almost forgot to mention Ryan's current boyfriend, Ashton 'Ash' Wentworth. He's so quiet that I often forget he's around. I know very little about him, but from what little I've observed, Ash has a slim build and stands about six feet tall. He has deep-set dark eyes and light golden-brown hair, which I suspect is styled professionally every week, giving him a high-maintenance vibe. His clothes are impeccable, and he seems perfect in every way. This makes me wonder why he's with someone as imperfect as Ryan. I suppose opposites do attract.

I mustn't forget Julie Burris; if I do, she'd be furious with me. Julie is a wonderful friend I met in the same university class as Duncan. From the moment we connected, it felt like we were destined to be friends—especially since she had always dreamed of having a gay best friend. And guess what? I fit that role perfectly, proudly being her *gay bestie* until I moved away from Austin.

Julie's a striking natural blonde from Dallas, known for her captivating appearance that attracts attention. Her unique and eye-catching sense of fashion truly sets her apart while still reflecting her down-to-earth and approachable personality. With her shoulder-length hair, contagious smile, and mesmerizing blue-gray eyes, she possesses an undeniable allure.

Despite her affluent background, Julie is anything but

pretentious; she completely defies those stereotypes. While her family's wealth may not match that of the Campbell's, it comes close. Her mother's passion for luxury is evident in the extravagant gifts she bestows upon her only child—gifts that would make any girl envious. The Burris family fortune comes from a chain of sporting goods megastores that span the southern states.

Let me introduce one more friend: our hostess, Rachael Maguire, who owns the house where we're staying. She moved to Lost Creek Junction from Greenville, Maine, late last summer. Rachael's a 5-foot-8-inch, medium-built beauty with medium ash brown hair that flows down her back and striking pale gold eyes that seem to look straight into your soul. She's the kind of person who would give you the shirt off her back if you needed it; her kindness knows no bounds. Although my time with her has been brief, the moments we've shared have been truly precious and worthwhile.

Now you have a bit more insight into my friends. While I have many others, these are the friends I'm eagerly looking forward to spending part of my summer with at Lost Creek Junction.

As we gather around the dining room table for supper, I'm overcome by a wave of nostalgia. The aroma wafting through the air is absolutely divine. Rachael, with her culinary wizardry, has truly outdone herself. This evening's feast features succulent oven-roasted chicken, perfectly golden potatoes, flavorful carrots, and elegant translucent pearl onions that enhance the presentation. And lest I forget, the cornbread dressing, which is bursting with flavor and complemented by a variety of mouthwatering side dishes. Her skill in the kitchen never ceases to amaze me.

This delicious spread not only satisfies my hunger but also fills my heart with cherished memories. It takes me back to my childhood Sundays when my mom served similar meals after church. I can almost hear her bustling around the kitchen, preparing our Sunday meal, with her love and care infused in every dish. She'd place the chicken and vegetables in a covered roasting pan before we left for church, allowing them to slowly bake to perfection in the oven. Meanwhile, we would sing hymns and endure a lengthy sermon, all the while eagerly anticipating the delicious meal waiting for us at home.

Every bite of Rachael's meal feels like a delightful journey down memory lane. It's incredible how food can transport us back in time. As we begin to eat, I can't help but feel grateful for these moments—where flavors intertwine with stories from our past.

A tantalizing array of dishes is passed around the table, creating a delightful mix of flavors and laughter. The atmosphere is lively, filled with chatter as everyone enjoys their meal and savors each bite. Just then, Rachael taps her water glass with a dinner knife to get our attention. With a serious expression, she poses a thought-provoking question: "What, if anything, do any of you know about Ezekiel and Abrahim?"

Little does she realize the can of assorted worms she has just opened—one that is bound to stir up mixed memories for Julie, Duncan, Ryan, and me from last summer.

The room falls silent, and the atmosphere shifts as Julie's face pales, her fork halting mid-air. "Duncan and I were both kidnapped," she reveals in a soft-spoken voice. "But each incident happened on separate occasions."

Duncan nods solemnly, his eyes reflecting a deep understanding. "Neither of us remembers how we ended up where we were found—or even how we got there in the first place."

The weight of our shared traumas hangs heavy in the air, stifling the laughter and lively conversations that filled the room just moments ago. We are bound by a history that none of us ever expected to share with anyone outside of our close-knit circle.

Ryan and I exchange uneasy glances as the weight of Duncan's words settles in. It serves as a stark reminder that beneath our lighthearted meal lies a deep-seated history connecting Julie, Duncan, Ryan, and me—a series of horrific stories we never imagined we'd have to share. The tension in the room rises to another level.

"Who did this to you?" Giles asks, his eyes searching our faces for answers.

"It had to be Ezekiel and/or Abrahim," Julie asserts. "There was no one else it could possibly have been."

"Why do you suspect Ezekiel and Abrahim?" Rachael asks, her brow furrowing with curiosity.

"Who are Ezekiel and Abraham?" Giles interjects.

"It's Abrah*i*m—with an 'I' , not an 'A,' I correct him.

"So? Who are they?" Giles insists.

"They're a pair of angry ghosts that haunt this house," Duncan replies.

"Hey, wait a minute. Ghosts?" Giles interrupts. "You guys are talking as if Ezekiel and Abrahim are living, breathing people. What's going on?"

"In a sense they are real," I say.

"I'm confused. I thought you just said they were ghosts," Giles smirks. "Who gives ghosts names? Except for maybe Casper."

"Giles, the story of Ezekiel and Abrahim is complicated. We'll discuss the details later," Duncan replies, briefly glancing around the room at each of us, almost as if silently seeking our permission to continue.

"Rach," Duncan asks, "may I call you Rach?"

"I do not see why not. That is what my friends call me," Rachael shrugs.

Duncan lowers his voice to an urgent whisper. "Rach, to answer your question, let me tell you a little about Ezekiel and Abrahim," Duncan explains. "Shortly after we arrived here last summer, strange things began happening in this house—events we couldn't explain that ultimately led us to suspect Ezekiel and Abrahim."

"When we first arrived in town," Julie chimes in, "we were

firm skeptics. We thought ghosts were just stories told by the uneducated and the superstitious. But after everything we experienced in this house, our skepticism was shattered."

"What do you mean by 'everything' ?" Rachael presses, her tone reflecting the seriousness of the matter.

Ryan's voice cuts through the mounting tension, his words filled with nerves. "There was Duncan and Julie's kidnappings—just two of the many chilling incidents that made us question our beliefs."

"What about the strange men we saw in the house?" I ask. "We could never explain how they got in or out of this house without us seeing them."

"And what about Taylor getting caught in the mine cave-in?" Julie chimes in. "That was no accident," her voice trembling with the weight of her words.

"What cave-in?" Giles asks, his face a mask of confusion. "Taylor, you never mentioned anything about a cave-in."

I take a deep breath, steadying my voice despite the memories crashing over me like waves. "I was lucky—I didn't get hurt too badly. But I swear, just before the mine caved in, I saw either Ezekiel or Abrahim lurking inside the mine with me. To this day, I'm convinced those two ghosts had something to do with the mine collapse."

Isadora, Giles, and Ash huddle close together, their expressions a mix of disbelief and fear as Julie, Duncan, Ryan, and I recount the harrowing events of last summer in this very house. It's astonishing how quickly everything spiraled out of control, trapping us in a web of mystery and fear that we never fully unraveled.

"Did you really get trapped in a mine?" Giles asks, his voice barely above a whisper, curiosity etched on his face.

"I thought I was going to die," I reply, the memory flooding back like a chilling wave, sending a ripple of fear down my spine. "The mine caved in around me. That's when I knew for certain that I was a goner."

"You must've been terrified?" he presses, leaning closer as if trying to grasp the gravity of my experience.

"Probably the most terrified I've ever been," I admit. "But honestly? Last summer was a roller coaster of terrifying moments."

"Yet," Giles remarks, a hint of disbelief in his voice, "here you are, back where all that crazy stuff happened. Why would you come back here?"

"I guess you could say I'm here for Rach," I reply. "She reached out for help, and here we are—back in Lost Creek Junction to support her. That's what friends do—stick together through thick and thin."

"But I thought Rachael only knew you and I," Giles asks.

"Yes, that is true," Rachael answers. "However, last summer, I learned about Julie, Duncan, and Ryan from Taylor's amazing stories, after all of you had left Lost Creek Junction. The bond of your friendship is what prompted me to invite each of you back to Blackburn House."

This revelation leaves us all in awe as we realize the unexpected depth of our connections. Looking around the room at the faces of Julie, Duncan, and Ryan, I understand that despite the fear and chaos of last summer, we have all shown incredible resilience. This bond is what brought us back together. Sure, the mine experience was a nightmare, but it also taught me something important—we can face anything as long as we have friends.

"So, Rach, what do you think triggered Ezekiel and Abrahim's anger this time? Last summer, those two ghosts were furious at Taylor because they thought he was trying to take their gold mine," Julie says, her eyes sparkling with curiosity. "What could have possibly stirred them up again?"

"I'm at a complete loss," Rachael admits, furrowing her brow in confusion. "Everything was going smoothly. The bed-and-breakfast was thriving, and just when I thought things couldn't get better, a development company approached me with an attractive offer to buy the gold mine and build a resort."

"Approximately when did Ezekiel and Abrahim start acting

out?" I ask.

Rachael sighs, as she thinks back. "I'd say it began about the same time I decided to accept the offer to sell the mine and the surrounding property. Honestly, why hold onto an abandoned gold mine that has never produced any sizable amount of gold? It's just a patch of discarded land overgrown with weeds. They made me a generous offer, so why not seize the opportunity? It felt like the sensible thing to do—simple as that."

"Ah, there's your answer," I say.

"What answer?" Rachael replies, her brow furrows in confusion.

I take a breath, understanding the weight of my words. "By discussing the possibility of selling the mine, you've provoked the anger of Ezekiel and Abrahim. They won't rest until they get their mine back."

"Did you say, get 'their' mine back? What exactly do you mean by that?" Rachael asks.

"It's a long and complicated story for another time," I reply. "But believe me, those ghosts think they own the mine."

Rachael's eyes widen with concern. "What can I possibly do to appease those two restless spirits?"

"As long as you pursue the sale of the mine, Ezekiel and Abrahim will likely haunt you—long after any sale is finalized," I say.

"I had no idea that Ezekiel and Abrahim were so attached to that abandoned mine," Rachael exclaims, her eyes filled with realization. "If I had known there was a potential problem, I would never have considered the development company's offer. Tomorrow morning, I am going to call the company and tell them I have changed my mind—I will not sell to them or anyone."

"Ah, that should surely appease the restless spirits," I say with a wink, referring to the mysterious happenings that had plagued Rachael's bed-and-breakfast. "You can immediately reopen your bed-and-breakfast without worrying about Ezekiel and Abrahim scaring off your guests."

"Wow, that was surprisingly simple," Rachael exclaims, a hint of embarrassment creeping into her voice. "Now I feel silly for inviting all of you to come here."

"Ghosts, curses, witches?" Giles asks. "Are you all out of your minds?"

"Gill," I reply, "you were born and raised in New Orleans, and you believe the local legends of vampires and witches."

"Okay," Giles concedes, "maybe I believe that local folklore makes for interesting stories, but..."

"Trust me," I insist, "there are some things that defy logic."

With a mix of disbelief and curiosity, Giles glances around the room at the faces staring back at him, at the moment, he seems at a loss for words.

Isadora's nervous energy is apparent, her discomfort evident as she shifts in her chair and her eyes dart around the room. "Dunky," she begins hesitantly, "can we please go home now?"

Duncan, always the voice of reason, responds thoughtfully, "Let's give Rachael a couple of days to be absolutely sure the ghost situation is settled. After all, we wouldn't want to leave any unfinished business behind... again, right?"

"Oh shoot," Isadora shivers. "This place gives me the creeps—especially after hearing those scary stories."

Duncan's smile is reassuring, and his steady voice acts as an anchor in the room. "This place isn't so bad. Give it a chance," he says, his calmness a balm to the unsettled atmosphere.

Rachael, our host, looks at each of us with a mix of relief and excitement. "I want to thank all of you for coming all this way. If I had known about the circumstances surrounding Ezekiel and Abrahim beforehand, I could have saved us all a lot of trouble. But now that you are here, I would like to extend an invitation—feel free to stay until I get the bed-and-breakfast back up and running."

"Hey," Julie chimes in, her eyes sparkling with enthusiasm. Her excitement is infectious, filling the room with a renewed sense of energy. "I have an idea—we can help you prepare for the reopening."

"Really?" Rachael asks, her voice filled with surprise and gratitude. "Would you really do that for me?"

"What are friends for if not to lend a helping hand?" I reply with a grin, feeling the trust and camaraderie among us, like an inviting cup of cocoa on a winter's night, enveloping us in warmth and indulgence.

"But aside from Taylor and Giles," Rachael continues, "the rest of you hardly know me."

"I trust Taylor's judgment," Julie says. "If he vouches for you, that's enough for me."

Rachael beams at me, her heart swelling with appreciation as she glances around the room at her new friends.

Just then, Isadora pipes up with her childlike voice, soft yet creepy and insistent: "Dunky, can we please go to bed now?"

"Of course," Duncan replies, rising from his chair with an easygoing smile. Together, he and Isadora head upstairs to their shared guest bedroom.

Julie, Giles, and I quickly spring into action, clearing away the supper dishes and then washing them. The clinking of plates and our teamwork create a warm and comforting atmosphere. Meanwhile, Ryan and Ash head to their guest bedroom upstairs.

Once the last plate is washed, dried, and neatly put away, an unexpected commotion erupts from the floor above.

"You can't just leave Julie and me stranded here," Ryan pleads, desperation evident in his voice as he and Ashton make their way down the staircase. Ashton is in front, clutching his suitcase tightly—an obvious sign that he's leaving. His knuckles are white from his grip. Ryan, shoulders slumped, follows closely behind, his steps heavy with the weight of the situation.

"I have to go back," Ashton replies with unwavering determination. "It's my job, my responsibility."

A defeated Ryan leans against the wall, arms crossed, frustration bubbling over. "But how are Julie and I supposed to get home? We rode here in your car."

Ashton raises an eyebrow, a smirk creeping onto his face. "Didn't you mention that last summer you took a bus back home after Taylor broke up with you?"

"Correction," I interject, my voice sharper than I intend. "Ryan broke up with me, not the other way around." The tension between us is obvious, a remnant of our past relationship that we've never quite managed to resolve.

"Whatever," Ashton mutters, dismissing my comment as he moves toward the front door. He turns to Rachael, who is watching the scene unfold with confusion. "Thank you, Rachael, for your hospitality. But I really must get back to Austin—my boss called, and my job... well, you understand."

"Of course," Rachael replies, her tone warm and understanding. "It was truly a pleasure meeting you, Ashton. I understand how important your job is."

"But Ash, we had an agreement!" Ryan whines.

"All bets are off. I'm not refunding the money you paid me to pretend to be your boyfriend," Ashton states firmly.

"Oh my God!" I nudge Julie with my elbow and whisper, "I was right. Ash isn't what he seemed to be."

Ashton steps into the night, and the door clicks shut behind him, echoing like the final note of a song fading away.

Ryan lets out a dramatic sigh and runs a nervous hand through his hair. "Great. Now what?" he mutters to himself, so self-absorbed that he doesn't realize he just admitted to Julie, Rachael, and me that his relationship with Ashton was a lie.

Julie shrugs, glancing at me with a raised eyebrow. "I guess Rye and I are taking the bus back home."

I can't help but laugh at the absurdity of it all. Life, with its unexpected twists and turns, can be quite entertaining. Sometimes it throws curveballs when you least expect them, but without those surprises, life would definitely be boring.

Ryan stands frozen against the wall, his expression a mix of confusion and curiosity as he surveys the room filled with expectant faces. The atmosphere buzzes with unspoken questions, each one a piece of the puzzle in the drama unfolding before us.

"Well?" Ryan finally breaks the silence, raising an eyebrow.

"What's everyone staring at?"

Honestly, my heart aches for Ryan, but I feel even more sympathy for Ashton. Their relationship, or lack thereof, was a tangled web of unspoken truths. This situation raises so many questions: Was Ryan merely using Ashton as a pawn to settle a score with me? Was he trying to show off his so-called ability to move on? If that's the case, I can't feel sorry for him—only disappointment at how petty he has become. Poor Ryan. What happened to the vibrant person I once knew? It's disheartening to see someone transform into a shadow of themselves, driven by jealousy and insecurity. It's a stark reminder of how relationships can change people, for better or for worse.

Haven't we all been there? Watching someone we care about lose their way in the pursuit of validation can be difficult. It makes you wonder: what does moving on really mean? Is it about finding someone new, or is it more about healing and growing from past experiences? In this moment, surrounded by expectant faces, it feels like Ryan is trapped in a situation of his own making. He's trying to appear calm, but I can see the cracks forming beneath the surface. This reminds me that moving on isn't just about filling an empty space; it's about finding peace within yourself first. I hope Ryan figures that out before he loses himself completely. I also see the potential for growth in him—the opportunity to emerge from this stronger and wiser. It's a reminder that even in the most challenging times, there's always the possibility for personal growth.

As the night falls, a peaceful calm settles over the big house on the hill, enveloping each of us in our own little worlds. Ryan has taken a room for himself now that Ashton is returning to Austin, and he seems to be relishing his solitude. I can almost picture him sprawled out across the bed, perhaps reading a comic or lost in his thoughts.

Julie, on the other hand, is likely cozied up in her familiar space—the same bedroom she enjoyed last summer. For her, it probably feels like a time capsule filled with memories and comfort. Meanwhile, Duncan and Isadora have claimed the charming bedroom that Duncan used during last year's visit. I can imagine the laughter and late-night conversations echoing off the walls once again.

Giles and I find ourselves sharing the same quarters that Ryan and I enjoyed at this time last year. Each creak of the floorboards brings back a flood of memories—late-night snacks, light conversations, and all those moments that felt significant at the time. This serves as a powerful reminder of the importance of this shared space.

As we settle into our respective areas, there's an undeniable warmth in knowing we're all together again, even if we're tucked away in our own corners of the big house on the hill. It's this warmth that makes our togetherness so comforting.

All of this unfolds on the second floor, but let's not forget Beau, who has made himself quite at home on the plush green velvet settee in the downstairs parlor, embodying the very essence of comfort. Seriously, if there were a contest for relaxation, he would win it hands down. Meanwhile, Rachael has retreated to her bedroom on the third floor, most likely soaking up her solitude like a cat basking in a sunny windowsill. Her room has become a sanctuary of tranquility.

Rachael's decision to move out of the garage apartment was because she wanted to be closer to us, her guests who flocked to her like biblical locusts (minus the destruction, of course). However, she confided in me that her true reason for moving back into the house is to keep a watchful eye on everything. This revelation has added a complex layer to our household dynamics, highlighting the depth of our situation.

So here we are: Beau lounging like royalty on the ground floor, us on the second floor, while Rachael keeps an eye on all of us from above. It's a quirky setup, but it feels right—like the perfect blend of comfort and caution within our little group of friends.

DAY TWO

Tuesday, May 21, 2019

As the morning sun rises like a radiant orb in the sky, it gently spreads its golden rays through the gap in the bedroom curtains. It gently nudges me awake from my dreams, filling the room with warmth and light. I take a moment to breathe in the tranquility around me as nature awakens outside. Each ray reminds me of the beauty of new beginnings and inspires me to seize the day ahead.

On the opposite side of the bed, Giles lies blissfully unaware. His gentle snores create a soothing rhythm that fills the room. With a soft yawn and a stretch, I slip out of bed, the anticipation of my morning routine settling in. I put on my clothes and pad down the hall in my socked feet. Each step brings me closer to the heart of the house—the kitchen—where the rich aroma of freshly brewed coffee beckons me like an old familiar friend.

After descending the stairs, I pause to check on Beau, who's peacefully sprawled along the length of the parlor settee. Should I wake him? Not yet. I'll let him enjoy his sleep. Soon enough, he'll be begging for his morning romp outside. I can't help but smile at the good memories we've shared over the years.

For now, my senses guide me to the kitchen, a warm and inviting space where Rachael and Julie are already seated at the table. Their laughter fills the air, adding to the cozy atmosphere as they sip coffee from mugs and nibble on decadent sweet rolls—an unspoken invitation to join their cheerful morning ritual.

"Good morning, ladies," I announce eagerly as I pour myself a steaming mug of coffee. The rich aroma envelops the kitchen.

"You two are up bright and early."

"It is really not that early," Rachael replies with a playful roll of her eyes.

"Any time before noon is considered early for college guys on summer break," Julie teases with a carefree smile, setting a lighthearted tone for the morning.

"You've got that right," I respond, blowing gently on my hot coffee to cool it down, fully immersed in the moment and the company around me. The worries of school, lectures, and responsibilities momentarily drift away, replaced by the simple joy of friendship and shared moments over coffee. It's these little rituals that remind me how sweet life can be, especially when you have good company to enjoy it with.

"What's this I hear about getting something right?" Duncan asks as he strolls into the kitchen, adjusting his fedora with a flourish of a rock star.

"Oh, it's nothing much," Julie replies with a smirk, clearly enjoying the playful banter.

"No way! You're not pulling that Rye nonsense on me," Duncan declares firmly, his eyes narrowing with playful defiance. "Come on Taylor, fess up, who got what right?"

I roll my eyes, a smirk creeping across my face. "The girls were hinting that all of us college guys are too lazy to get out of bed before noon during summer break. Can you believe how absurd that is?"

"What's absurd?" Ryan mumbles as he shuffles into the room like a sleepy bear emerging from hibernation, his hair resembling a bird's nest in desperate need of some good old-fashioned TLC. I stifle a giggle at his disheveled appearance.

Duncan chuckles and says, "Oh, you know, female stuff."

"Ah," Ryan nods sleepily, avoiding our conversation as he pours himself a steaming mug of coffee. The rich aroma fills the air, momentarily dispelling his drowsiness.

"Seriously, though," I continue, "who needs to be up early when there are no classes to attend? Summer vacation is our time to perfect the art of sleeping in."

"Exactly," Duncan chimes in, raising an imaginary trophy. "Gold cup in snoozing," he adds, following it up with an attempt to recreate the sound of a cheering crowd.

Julie shakes her head, laughing. "You guys are hopeless. But hey, at least you're entertaining."

The kitchen is filled with laughter and the unmistakable sounds of college life, where getting things right often comes down to having fun and enjoying each other's company.

"Duncan," Ryan begins, a mischievous glint in his eye, "where's that *lovely lady* of yours hiding?"

"She's getting her beauty sleep," Duncan responds with a grin.

Ryan takes a leisurely sip of his coffee, leans back with an exaggerated sigh, and says, "I don't know about the rest of you, but honestly? That girl of yours seems like a real bitch."

"Rye," I interject firmly, "that's not exactly kind—especially since you just met her yesterday afternoon."

"Excuse me? Who said anything about being kind?" Ryan retorts, his tone sharp. "Didn't any of you notice how stuck-up and rude she was?"

"Easy there, Rye," Duncan responds calmly. "Sure, Izzy can be demanding and a bit abrasive at times."

"At times?" Ryan exclaims, raising his eyebrows in disbelief. "Dude, yesterday she rolled her eyes at me when I asked if she wanted some iced tea."

"Okay, maybe she wasn't in the mood for tea," I suggest, trying to defend Izzy. "We all have our moments."

"Moments? That was more than just a moment—it's her entire vibe," Ryan scoffs, shaking his head.

Duncan chuckles, clearly enjoying the banter. "Look, she's not everyone's cup of tea, but she has her reasons for being the way she is."

"I understand where you're coming from," Ryan concedes, "all I'm saying—if you're dating her for her personality, you might want to reevaluate your standards."

"Or perhaps you should try to get to know her better before

making snap judgments," I counter.

"I guess time will tell." Ryan shrugs and takes another sip of his coffee. "Just don't say I didn't warn you."

"Now, listen to me," Duncan implores, his eyes earnest with conviction. "Her behavior isn't entirely her fault—it's a reflection of how she was raised."

"Raised? Really?" Ryan interjects, skepticism etched across his face. It's clear he's not buying what Duncan is selling.

Julie shakes her head, crossing her arms like a referee ready to call a foul. "Duncan, how someone is raised doesn't excuse being difficult and unkind. Rachael, don't you agree?"

"Leave me out of this," Rachael asserts with a hint of exasperation. "I am not taking sides. This is not my argument."

"I couldn't agree more with Julie," Ryan chimes in, his tone unwavering as if he's just delivered the final verdict.

"Come on, guys, give Izzy some slack to adjust," Duncan suggests thoughtfully. "She's simply not used to mediocrity."

"Mediocrity?" I retort, incredulous. "I never imagined I'd see the day when Duncan Campbell would let wealth cloud his judgment."

The room falls silent for a moment, the tension thickening. It's one of those times when everyone is waiting for someone to crack a smile or throw in a joke to lighten the mood. But instead, we find ourselves debating whether upbringing can genuinely excuse someone's behavior or if it's merely a cop-out.

As I glance around at my friends, each displaying their own mix of skepticism or support, I realize that this conversation is no longer just about Izzy; it's about how we perceive people and their choices. Perhaps that's the real issue we're dealing with.

"Okay, I realize now that I could have chosen a better word than 'mediocrity'. What I meant to convey is that Izzy comes from a wealthy, ultra-conservative family. She's been pampered her entire life by servants who did everything for her, and from childhood, she received everything she ever wanted. As a result, it's not easy for her to step outside the luxurious lifestyle she's accustomed to."

"In other words," Ryan snaps back, frustration bubbling over, "she's a spoiled rich snob who thinks she's better than us."

The tension around the table is obvious as his words linger in the air, resonating with unspoken truths. Is it fair to judge someone based on their background? Or do we all carry our own biases that shape how we perceive others?

Not a word is spoken as we exchange glances around the table, a subtle hint of unspoken camaraderie hangs in the air.

Suddenly, Duncan snickers, breaking the silence like a clap of thunder.

"What a ridiculous conversation to have over morning coffee," Duncan muses, shaking his head in disbelief. Just like that, the weight of judgment lifts, replaced by the lightness of shared humor and understanding. After all, isn't life too short to let misunderstandings ruin a good cup of coffee?

Just then, Beau trots in with an air of regal authority, shaking off the remnants of sleep as if he's shedding yesterday's worries. He casts me a sidelong glance that clearly says, *Are you going to open the door for me, peasant boy?*

"Alright," I concede with a chuckle. "You win, your grace." I rise and swing open the back door for him to step outside before returning to my chair at the table.

"Don't you ever worry that he might run off?" Rachael asks, her brow arched in concern.

"Who? Beau or Giles?" I snicker at the thought.

"Beau, of course," Rachael giggles.

"Nope," I respond confidently, savoring another sip of my delightful coffee.

"Beau is far too set in his ways to run off," Ryan asserts, a hint of exasperation in his voice. "Besides, if he did decide to make a break for it, who would feed him? Let's be real—Beau isn't stupid—he knows exactly where his next meal is coming from."

And there it is—the undeniable truth about my furry overlord. Beau may strut around like he owns the place, but deep down, he knows where the good stuff is. So while we joke about his potential for adventure, we all know he's not going anywhere anytime soon. After all, why would he leave when he's got me wrapped around his paw?

Rachael raises an eyebrow, intrigued. "So, Rye, how exactly did you become an expert on Beau?"

Ryan rolls his eyes dramatically. "Duh! Taylor and I were together as a couple before Giles swooped in and stole the spotlight. Besides, I've known Beau since he was a pup."

"Oh, right," Rachael nods knowingly. "You broke up with Taylor because of Giles."

"Do you have to phrase it like it's some kind of scandal?" I interject, feeling the tension rise.

"If it looks like a duck and walks like a duck..." Ryan mutters under his breath, trailing off with a smirk.

"Okay, Rye, that's enough," Julie gently chides, but her tone is firm.

I notice Julie and Duncan exchanging a quick, unspoken glance. Could there still be a spark between them?

A thick silence blankets the conversation as we reflect on the complexities of pets and loyalties.

"I have never had a pet," Rachael admits, her brow furrowing in curiosity. "So, are all dogs as well-behaved as Beau?"

"Ah, Beau is a special case," I reply with a smile. "He was trained as a puppy and took to it like a fish to water. I believe much of it comes down to the bond you share with your pet."

"Training was not a challenge for you?" Rachael asks, raising an eyebrow in playful skepticism.

I can't help but laugh. "With Beau, it was like he trained me," I say, recalling the endless lessons in patience and persistence— on my part.

Just then, Giles strolls into the kitchen, wearing that trademark amused grin on his face. "Training, you say? You must be talking about me," he chimes in, clearly enjoying the friendly banter.

I chuckle and shake my head playfully. "Not at all, Gill. You were already well-trained by the time I met you."

Meanwhile, Ryan is doing his best to steal the spotlight by sticking his finger in his mouth and pretending to gag. In another time, he might elicit a chuckle or two from the others, but at this moment, his antics go unnoticed by everyone except me.

I see a twinge of jealousy in his eyes towards the bond that Giles and I share. It's puzzling how one person can feel so left out while trying so hard to get attention through silly stunts. This is a classic case of sibling rivalry, even if we're not related by blood. But that's just how it goes in our little circle—filled with laughter, lighthearted jabs, and a dash of envy now and then.

"Alright, everyone," Rachael announces with an inviting smile, "this kitchen is not large enough for all of us. Let us move this party to the dining room so I can make breakfast for everyone."

The promise of delicious food hangs in the air, making it hard not to feel excited about what's next. As we transition from the cramped kitchen to the spacious dining room, I can't help but wonder: will Ryan ever realize that there are better ways to connect than through childish pranks? Sure, his antics can be funny at times, but they often leave us rolling our eyes more than laughing.

Shortly after we settle into our chairs around the dining table, the aroma of sizzling bacon and hot biscuits began to fill the air. I glance over at Ryan, who's eyeing the stack of empty plates probably imagining they are full of eggs, bacon, and toast. Maybe today will be different; perhaps he'll find joy in sharing a meal instead of plotting his next prank. With laughter bubbling around us and the clatter of utensils creating a cozy symphony, I can't help but feel hopeful. Perhaps this breakfast gathering will be just what Ryan needs—a chance to connect. After all, isn't sharing good food one of the best ways to bond?

As Rachael serves breakfast, I take a deep breath and smile. Today feels promising, and who knows? Maybe Ryan will surprise us all and leave the childish antics behind... at least until lunchtime.

After a delightful breakfast, we linger around the table, savoring our refilled mugs of coffee. Just as the warmth of conversation envelops us, Rachael speaks up, her voice filled with curiosity. "I would love to hear how you all first learned about Ezekiel and Abrahim, if you do not mind my asking," she says, her eyes sparkling with intrigue.

Silently, Duncan, Julie, Ryan, and I glance at each other, waiting for someone to take the lead. Finally, Julie breaks the silence. "Oh, it all began on our very first full day in this house," she begins, her voice dropping to a conspiratorial whisper. She pauses for effect, allowing the suspense to build. "That morning, before breakfast, I found a skeleton key wedged between the doorframe and the wall in my bedroom. Can you believe it? The key was unlike anything I'd ever seen—ornate and mysterious. Naturally, I couldn't resist turning it into a pendant on a satin ribbon that I wore around my neck."

As she speaks, I remember that morning and the tarnished key dancing against her delicate collarbone.

"During breakfast," Julie continues with a grin, "I proudly revealed my find to the guys."

"The conversation took a turn when someone suggested we explore the house—after all, it was going to be our summer home away from home," I exclaim.

Ryan chimes in, "We split into pairs to explore this place."

"Exactly! Rye and I ventured into the garage and even checked out the upstairs garage apartment," I add.

Duncan grins as he shares, "Julie and I checked out the cellar."

"After Rye and I wrapped up our exploration of the garage, we made our way back inside, eager to share our findings."

"I don't remember if it was Taylor or me who called out for Duncan and Julie when we realized they weren't in the kitchen," Ryan says.

"When I heard Taylor call my name, I called up for him and Rye to join Julie and me in the cellar," Duncan recalls.

"Rye and I cautiously descended the rickety stairs, each creak echoing my apprehension as we joined Duncan and Julie in that dimly lit space," I add. "It felt like we were walking into a horror movie, and besides, I'm not a fan of confined spaces."

"While we were down there, knucklehead Taylor knocked over a ceramic container," Ryan interjects, shaking his head at the memory.

"The lid flew off, unleashing a terrible stench that clung to our hair, clothes, and everything around us," Julie shudders, her face contorting in disgust as she remembers the foul aroma that assaulted our senses. We all gagged a little; it felt as if a pack of skunks had decided to make that place their permanent home.

"Julie found the lid and quickly placed it back on the container, but that terrible smell lingered in the air, wrapping around us like a thick cloud," Duncan recounts, his voice tinged with unease. "We had no choice but to retreat upstairs."

"Then, during the night, a fierce thunderstorm erupted," Ryan adds, his eyes wide with remembrance. "Both Taylor and Julie claimed they each saw eerie faces of an old man in the shadows of the house."

Duncan leans in closer, urgency creeping into his tone. "We feared there might be intruders lurking in the house, so I called the cops."

Julie shakes her head in frustration. "When the police arrived, they were no help at all. They just told us we were victims of *overactive imaginations*."

"A few days later, we discovered an old journal hidden in the house. It told the story of a witch who sold her gold mine to two miners, only for them to meet a tragic fate during a cave-in," I explain.

"The townsfolk unearthed the miners' bodies, but before they could give them a proper burial, something strange occurred: the bodies vanished into thin air," Julie interjects.

"Wait, what?" Rachael asks, her eyes widening. "They just disappeared?"

"Yup," I nod, feeling the rising tension in the room.

Duncan lowers his voice to a whisper as if afraid someone—or something—might be listening. "Legend has it that the witch didn't let them rest in peace. No, she decapitated them and trapped their souls in a ceramic container hidden away in the cellar of this very house. Their spirits were doomed to linger there for eternity unless someone dared to open that container and set them free."

"Later, Julie had an unexpected encounter that changed everything. She spoke with a small girl ghost who came with a warning: *Beware of Ezekiel and Abrahim*," Ryan recounts, referring to the restless spirits that Taylor inadvertently unleashed when he toppled the ceramic container in the cellar.

"So, that's how you learned the names of the ghosts?" Giles asks.

"Yep," Julie answers with a nod.

Rachael interjects, her eyes sparkling with curiosity. "The girl ghost you mentioned—could her name have been Arabella?"

"Wait, you know about Arabella?" Julie asks, intrigued by Rachael's words.

"Yes," Rachael says eagerly, her excitement evident. "Arabella was Mrs. Scruggs' niece, or so I have been told. She supposedly traveled from the East by train and then by stagecoach to live with her aunt, but tragically passed away shortly after arriving here."

Julie furrows her brows as she processes this new information. "You've heard of Mrs. Scruggs?" she asks, her interest deepening.

"Yes," Rachael responds thoughtfully. "Mrs. Scruggs was either a distant aunt or a cousin—I do not know the exact relationship. All I know for sure is that my being here is somehow tied to being related to her."

"Wow," Julie shakes her head in disbelief. "What a small world we live in. Mrs. Scruggs is the witch mentioned in that old journal."

"Duncan," Rachael interjects, eager to steer the conversation back on track, "please continue with what you were saying before we got sidetracked."

"Right, where was I?" Duncan muses, tapping his chin as he gathers his thoughts. "Ah, yes. Ezekiel and Abrahim—those two ghosts were nothing but disembodied heads. Strangely enough, there were no records of their bodies ever being found. As ghosts, they were absolutely furious because, when they managed to escape from that ceramic container, they still believed they owned the mine." He pauses for dramatic effect, letting the tension build. "But here's the twist: when the miners perished in that cave-in, the witch swiftly reclaimed ownership by putting her name back on the deed to the mine. Thus, the ownership of the mine was passed down within the family from generation to generation, until Mrs. Blackburn willed it to Taylor, breaking the family succession."

"But, Taylor—," Rachael starts. I abruptly interrupt her by shaking my head. "Not right now."

"What do you mean by *not right now*?" Julie asks.

"Later," I reply. "Go on, Duncan. What were you saying about the gold mine?"

"Like I was saying, the ghosts had no idea they had been trapped inside that unassuming ceramic vessel for two centuries, and their thirst for vengeance against the witch who cursed them had grown over time. Over the years, ownership of the mine shifted like sand in an hourglass until it finally landed in Taylor's lap along with this house," Duncan says, his voice low and dramatic.

"That made Taylor the new target for the ghosts," Ryan interjects, adding humor to his words. "You know how these things go—new owner, new problems."

"And then Mrs. Blackburn showed up—" I begin, but I'm swiftly interrupted by Julie's gasp.

"What? Mrs. Blackburn showed up? That's impossible! She's dead! She willed you this house!" Her eyes widen in disbelief, a mix of shock and fear washing over her.

"Yeah, but let me explain," I say. "Mrs. Blackburn wasn't

really dead. She faked her death."

"Why am I just now hearing about this?" Julie demands, her anger bubbling to the surface like a pot of water on the verge of boiling over.

"This all happened after you guys left last summer," I reply defensively.

"Duncan," Julie asks, "did you know about this?"

"This is the first I've heard of it," Duncan says with a shrug.

"So, Taylor, did she tell you why she left everything to you?"

"Yep," I nod, feeling the weight of the moment.

"Well? Don't keep us in suspense. Seriously, man—why did she leave everything to you?" Duncan presses, his curiosity apparent.

"Turns out Mrs. Blackburn is my aunt," I reveal, my heart racing at the unexpected twist.

"Wait, did you just say she's your aunt?!" Julie exclaims, her eyes wide with surprise. "You need to spill details right this minute!"

"I promise I'll explain everything later," I assure her.

"So, how does Rach fit into this whole situation?" Julie probes.

"She's the current owner of this house and the mine," I say, trying to keep things simple. "Trust me, Julie, and I'll fill you in on all the details later."

"Rach?" Julie's eyes widen. "You're involved in this?"

"Hold on, Julie," I respond. "Don't take this out on Rachael. It wasn't her choice. As I said, we'll explain everything later."

"You had better do that," Julie demands.

"Rach, now that you own the mine and this house, it seems the ghostly heads are determined to haunt you. They'll do everything in their power to stop you from selling their precious mine to that development company," I explain. "And that's, in a nutshell, the story of Ezekiel and Abrahim—and their gold mine."

"But wait, you left something out," Julie interjects, her eyes sparkling with excitement. "While we were exploring the cellar,

I stumbled upon an ancient leather-bound cookbook."

"That's right," I reply with a nod. "I forgot all about that book."

"It was inscribed in a foreign language," Julie continues, "and filled with intricate hand-drawn sketches that suggested it was a book of recipes."

"What did you do with the cookbook?" Rachael asks.

Julie chuckles and leans back in her chair. "For a while, I kept it close at hand—studying its pages like they were a treasure map," she admits, a hint of nostalgia creeping into her voice. "The recipes looked like they were written in some ancient language, and I was convinced it held the key to culinary greatness. But after countless attempts to decode its secrets left me frustrated and confused, I finally returned it to its dusty shelf in the cellar," Julie sighs dramatically.

Dale Thele

DAY THREE

Wednesday, May 22, 2019

The morning starts off like most any other—sun shining, birds chirping, you know the drill. But by late morning, things aren't going so well for Rachael.

"Hey, Rach," I call out as I enter the kitchen. "We're getting a game of Monopoly together. Want to join us?"

Rachael stares out the window over the sink, lost in her thoughts. She seems almost entranced, her gaze fixed on something beyond the glass pane.

I peek over her shoulder and look out the window, intrigued by what has captured her attention so completely. Outside, there's nothing unusual—just her backyard with grass, trees, and a small patch of overturned dirt, perhaps remnants of a once-dreamed garden.

"Rach?" I try again, hoping to snap her out of her odd state of mind.

She blinks and slowly turns toward me, giving me a blank expression.

"Are you alright?" I ask.

"Of course I am," she replies, but there's something off about her tone. It's too quick, too distant. "Why wouldn't I be?"

"For a minute there, you had a weird expression on your face," I say gently, trying to gauge what's going on with her.

"I suppose I have a lot on my mind," she admits, her eyes drifting back out the window as she absentmindedly squirts dish soap into an empty sink, without water or dishes. It feels as though she's trying to wash away more than just dirty dishes.

I can't shake the feeling that something is bothering her. The usual spark in her eyes is dim today.

"Do you want to talk about it?" I offer, not wanting to push her but also reluctant to let her slip away into the thoughts clouding her mind.

She takes a deep breath and finally turns to face me fully. "Maybe later," she responds, a faint smile touching her lips, though it doesn't quite reach her eyes.

"Rach..." I say gently, taking the bottle of dish soap from her hand.

Her eyes follow my movement as I set the soap down. Suddenly, as if jolted from a daydream, she exclaims, "Oh my," blinking rapidly like someone emerging from a trance. Her gaze is fixed on the pool of dish soap in the sink. "This is a disaster. What have I done?"

I put my arm around Rachael's waist, guiding her to a nearby kitchen chair and help her sit down.

"What's going on with you?" I ask, pulling up a chair beside her.

There's a moment of silence as Rachael tilts her head, contemplating my question like Beau does when he's trying to figure something out that doesn't make sense to him.

"Taylor," she finally says, her voice tinged with worry, "I have no idea what I am going to do."

"What are you talking about?" I ask, genuinely puzzled.

"I have got myself tangled in a mess I never saw coming," she admits, nervously wringing her hands. "What I thought was a promising deal with the development company has become my worst nightmare."

"Why do you say that?" I probe further.

"Earlier this morning," Rachael begins, her tone tinged with anxiety, "I called the development company and told them that I had changed my mind about selling the mine. I made it very clear that I do not want to sell the mine or the adjacent land." Her words linger in the air like autumn leaves caught swirling in the wind.

"And then what happened?" I ask, leaning in as Rachael

shares her frustration.

"They would not take no for an answer," she replies, her voice thick with disbelief. "They doubled down, acting like a group of bullies on the playground. Their threats were blunt and aggressive—if I dared to back out of the deal, they said they would file a lawsuit against me so quickly it would make my head spin."

"I'm so sorry, Rach," I say, gently patting her folded hands. It's hard to watch my friend be steamrolled like this.

"I cannot believe it," she continues, shaking her head. "I thought this deal with the development company was based on mutual respect, but now it feels like I am stuck in a bad movie where the villains will not quit. With each passing hour, their pressure weighs down on me, and all I want is to reclaim my peace of mind and protect what is mine. So here I am, navigating a minefield of intimidation and greed, trying to stand my ground."

"I'm sure there's something that can be done," I try to comfort her, though I feel the heaviness in her words.

"At this point," Rachael sighs, "it seems like a losing battle. The development company will win, and I will lose the bed-and-breakfast to Ezekiel and Abrahim."

But just then, a spark of inspiration hits me. "I've got an idea," I say, my mind racing. "Mr. Andrews, the attorney I used last summer, might be able to help. It couldn't hurt to go see him."

Rachael raises an eyebrow, a flicker of hope breaking through her despair. "Do you really think he can do something?"

"Absolutely! He really knows his stuff and isn't afraid to stand up to bullies."

Her grip tightens around my hand as she considers my suggestion. "Okay, let's do it," she says, determination returning to her voice. "I will not let them walk all over me without a fight."

Sometimes, all it takes is a little encouragement to turn the tide.

After an hour, Rachael and I find ourselves in Mr. Andrews' waiting room. The atmosphere feels like that of a cranky old lioness' lair, and the receptionist's people skills are akin to those of a starving grizzly bear emerging from hibernation. She eyes us suspiciously, as if we've just walked in wearing nothing but our underwear and clown shoes. Her behavior begins to irritate me, and before I know it, I react in a way that surprises even myself—I stick my tongue out at her, just like I did to Janell Simpson back in grammar school when she really got on my nerves.

The shocked receptionist gasps and swivels her chair around faster than I can blink, abruptly turning her back to us. Meanwhile, Rachael is lost in her own thoughts, completely oblivious to my little act of defiance. I really wish Ryan were here. He would have laughed at my antics. But this isn't about me—it's about Rachael. She has a dark, heavy cloud of worry hovering over her, clinging to her like plastic wrap. I truly hope Mr. Andrews can help her because she deserves far better than the treatment she's receiving from that large corporation.

"You may go in now," the receptionist coldly announces, resuming her typing as if we never existed.

"Do you want me to come with you?" I ask Rachael, trying to offer encouragement.

"Please," she replies with a crooked smile that makes my heart ache even more for her situation.

As I swing open the office door, Mr. Andrews is waiting for us like a seasoned captain ready to navigate a ship through choppy waters. His combination of authority and unmistakable small-town charm makes him both reassuring and intimidating at the same time. He welcomes us inside his office and gestures for us to sit, his voice steady as he gets straight to the point.

"Just so you know, Miss Maguire," he says as he walks around his desk, "Taylor filled me in on your situation over the phone earlier." He clears his throat and sits down in his chair behind a cluttered desk, which is stacked with manila folders, loose papers, and a couple of dog-eared paperback mystery novels. "My dear," he continues in a soothing and empathetic tone, "I must advise you not to hinder the sale. You've made a verbal agreement to sell, and that in its self is considered a legally binding contract." One thing about Mr. Andrews is that he doesn't mince words.

Rachael's eyes widen as her mind races through the implications of his words. I can practically see the gears turning as she grapples with the reality of her situation.

"Is there any way for Rachael to back out of this deal?" I ask.

Mr. Andrews leans back in his chair, taking a moment to consider my question as if it were a puzzle he's trying to solve. "Well, there are always options," he replies slowly, choosing his words with care. "But it's complicated. Breaking a verbal contract can lead to legal repercussions."

The air in the room feels thick with tension as Rachael processes what that could mean for her. It's not just about the gold mine; it's about her future and the choices she hoped she had.

The weight of his words lingers like an old winter coat hanging on a chair—familiar yet suffocating, reminding us both of what lies beneath its heavy fabric. I glance at Rachael; her expression is a mix of hope and dread. She's caught in this tangled web of legalities and emotions, and all I want is to see her free from this burden.

"Are there any other options?" I ask, trying to sound more confident than I feel. I want to ensure that all possible angles are considered because I want the best outcome for her.

"Unfortunately, it's unlikely," Mr. Andrews replies, sighing in a way that reflects our shared disappointment. "While there have been cases where the legality of verbal agreements has been questioned, pursuing this route could result in years of litigation and significant expenses, with no guarantee of a favorable verdict. My best advice is to accept their offer and move on."

Rachael's shoulders slump at his words, the weight of the situation pressing down on her.

"I'm so sorry, Rach," I say softly as I reach over to pat her hand reassuringly. "I really hoped Mr. Andrews would find a way out for you."

She nods slowly, her eyes filled with uncertainty and tears. It's difficult to watch someone you care about struggle, especially when the solution seems simple yet feels out of reach.

We sit in silence for a moment, both of us feeling the weight of the situation settling around us. But I believe we'll find a solution together—no matter how daunting it seems right now.

"May I ask," Mr. Andrews continues thoughtfully, "when does the buyer want a definitive answer from you?"

"Midnight tonight," Rachael replies, her voice barely above a whisper.

Back at the house, time slips through our fingers like sand on a summer seaside beach. What choice will Rachael make? As the clock ticks down to midnight, we realize the stakes are high. It's not just about the pending deal; it's about what it means for Rachael's future—specifically her chance to be free from two out of control ghosts. The weight of this decision sits heavily on her heart, and I can't help but wonder if there's a way to turn things around. For now, all we can do is wait. With each passing minute, the tension in the house thickens. You can practically feel the electricity in the air as we exchange glances, each one filled with unspoken questions. What if she makes the wrong choice? What if this deal doesn't just determine her fate but also leaves her haunted by ghosts?

I lean back in my chair, trying to project calmness, even though my heart is racing.

"Hey, Rach," I say lightly, hoping to ease some of the pressure. "Whatever you decide, we're here for you. No ghosts are going to scare you away from your future."

She smiles faintly, but I can see the uncertainty still clouding her eyes. Midnight is creeping closer, bringing with it the weight of her choice. Will she break free from the ghosts or let them linger forever? All we can do is wait and hope that she finds clarity before the deadline approaches.

The grandfather clock in the upstairs hall strikes midnight with a resonant chime, marking a pivotal moment. An air of overwhelming tension envelops the Blackburn house. With a heavy heart, Rachael makes the fateful phone call to announce her decision.

"Rach, what did you decide?" I ask as she returns to the parlor, the air thick with anticipation. Duncan, Ryan, Giles, Julie, and I are all waiting for her verdict, our nerves on edge.

"I had no choice but to sell," Rachael says, tears welling in her eyes.

"You did what you had to," I reassure her, understanding the complexity of her situation. I see the strain in her eyes, a mix of relief and regret swirling together like storm clouds. It was a tough decision, but sometimes you have to do what needs to be done.

"Now what?" Rachael asks, her voice barely above a whisper as she stares into the darkness of the parlor, where memories linger like afternoon shadows.

"We wait for Ezekiel and Abrahim's response," Duncan remarks thoughtfully, his brow furrowed in contemplation. You can tell he's already considering what this means for all of us—what's next after making such a weighty decision.

"It's late—there's nothing more we can do tonight," Ryan interjects. "I'm heading to bed." He stretches and yawns, clearly ready to escape the tension that lingers like smoke after a fire.

"Agreed," Duncan replies. "That seems like the most sensible course of action." He shakes his head in disbelief at his own accord with Ryan. "It's a strange feeling, finding common ground with Rye after all the back-and-forth we've had," he says as he makes his way up the staircase toward the bedroom he shares with Isadora.

Ryan chuckles softly as he follows Duncan, a flicker of camaraderie sparking between them despite their disagreements.

It's amusing how quickly things can change; one moment, you're at odds, and the next, you're nodding in agreement like old friends.

As the rest of us reach the landing, the weight of the night settles in—decisions loom ahead, but for now, all we can afford is rest. The world outside is quiet, yet inside our minds, thoughts race like wildfire. What will Ezekiel and Abrahim do? Only time will tell, but for tonight, it's time to embrace sleep and not worry about what tomorrow may bring.

As each of us retires to our respective rooms for the night, the great house gradually surrenders its light. One by one, lights flicker out, casting shadows that stretch and dance across the walls, leaving behind an enveloping darkness thick with uncertainty. It's a sharp contrast to the bustling energy of the day—a quiet moment that invites reflection and perhaps a little worry. What will tomorrow bring? Will Rachael's big decision prove to be a game-changer, or will it be just another bump in the road? Questions echo within me like distant thunder rumbling across the horizon, hinting at storms of insight yet to break upon the shores of understanding. I can't help but wonder if we're on the brink of something amazing or if we're setting ourselves up for another round of confusion. It's funny how one choice can ripple out and change everything or potentially change nothing at all. I guess we'll find out soon enough. For now, though, I'll let the darkness cradle my thoughts, hoping for clarity with the dawn.

Lying in bed with Giles peacefully sleeping beside me, I can't shake off the restless energy coursing through my veins. It feels like I'm wired, even though the night is quiet and still. However, that peace is just a facade, because lurking in the corners of my mind are the shadows of two vengeful ghosts. They aren't just figments of my imagination; they are real, and their anger has likely been simmering ever since Rachael made that fateful phone call to the developer.

I glance at Giles, his face relaxed and serene, completely

unaware of the storm brewing just beyond the veil of sleep. Lucky guy. Meanwhile, I'm wide awake, caught in this strange limbo between the living and the dead. I can almost hear the whispers of the ghosts, their rage apparent in the air around us. It's not a matter of if they'll strike back; it's a question of when. Every creak of the house feels amplified, like a ticking time bomb counting down to some inevitable confrontation. I know Rachael tried to do the right thing, but these spirits? They don't care about intentions or right and wrong. They want revenge, and here we are, trapped in their web of intensifying fury.

I take a deep breath, trying to calm my racing heart. Maybe if I focus on Giles' steady breathing, I can drown out the noise of my own anxiety. But deep down, I know this isn't over. The ghosts are waiting for their moment, and I can only hope we're ready when they finally come.

The grandfather clock tolls twice, slicing through the stillness of the night and waking me from a light sleep. Then, there's nothing but dead silence. It's as if someone hit the mute button on the world, leaving me in this eerie, soundless void. Everyone else is fast asleep, probably dreaming about sunshine and rainbows, but I'm stuck in this thick veil of dark silence that feels heavy, like a fog smothering any flicker of light.

Just when I think it can't get any creepier, BAM! The night becomes unhinged. Lightning cracks the sky wide open, momentarily illuminating everything like a scene from a horror movie. Shadows dance about, and for a split second, I swear I see something lurking just out of reach. Then comes the thunder—rumbling like an angry beast ready to pounce. And the rain? It's not just falling; it's pounding against the house like it's trying to break down the walls to come inside.

The relentless rain feels like a warning, a reminder that nature doesn't mess around. I curl up under the sheet for protection, my heart racing as chaos unfolds outside. This night is anything but ordinary—it's a wild mix of silence and storm that has me on edge.

Wow, what a storm! The lightning is incredibly bright, like staring into a million flashbulbs at once—my retinas must be getting fried. And the thunder? It crashes so hard I swear I can feel it in my bones, like a wild percussion concert happening right inside my chest.

Outside, the rain pours down in blinding sheets, turning everything into a chaotic water park ride gone wrong. It feels as if I'm stuck on an amusement park attraction that's far too intense, with no idea of when it will end. The wind howls like a pack of hungry jackals on the hunt, adding to the unpredictability of the situation. You know that eerie sound that makes you want to peek out the window, yet also makes you want to curl up in a ball under your blankets? Afraid to look outside, worried that whatever is lurking there might be watching you? That's exactly what's happening right now.

The old house trembles with each thunderous boom, its wooden boards creaking as if expressing their discontent with the storm. It feels as though the house is a living being, weary and irritable from enduring the wrath of Mother Nature. I can only hope to survive this tumultuous night without any unexpected surprises.

I pull the bed sheet up to my chin, seeking comfort in its fabric as I stare up at the ceiling above me, wishing it could shield me from whatever malevolent forces lurk in this old house. Seriously, it feels like every shadow has eyes and is watching me, and the air is thick with an unsettling vibe that makes me want to disappear under the covers. Each creak of the floorboards sends a shiver down my spine, as if they're trying to warn me about something I can't quite understand.

Suddenly, a heart-wrenching moan echoes through the hall— a sound so pitiful it seeps into my very marrow. It's not just a random noise; it feels like a cry for help from beyond. My heart races as I glance toward the partially closed bedroom door, which creaks ominously with each gust of wind slipping through the cracks around the windows. The door sways slightly between open and shut as if caught in some ghostly dance. I'm not sure what's worse—getting up to investigate or staying here, wrapped in my sheet like a burrito of fear. The house feels alive tonight, and I can't shake the feeling that whatever lurks out there is waiting for me to make a move.

Each time that door inches open, it feels like a scene from a horror movie unfolding before me. I can't help but anticipate something dreadful lurking behind it. The faint creak echoes through the room, mimicking the sound of footsteps, and my heart races as if I'm in a sprint. What's on the other side of the door? Is it just my imagination playing tricks on me, or is something even more sinister waiting there?

These old walls seem to breathe, as if they hold the whispers of long-lost souls. I can almost hear them—urging me to uncover their secrets or warning me to keep my head down and stay put. It's a mental game, a dance with curiosity. Am I being dramatic, or is something truly lurking in the shadows, waiting for me to take that leap of faith?

The thought sends chills racing down my spine. Who wouldn't feel a little freaked out? This old house has its fair share of stories, and I can't shake the feeling that one day I'll have to muster the courage to face whatever it has in store for me. But until then, I'll just be here, heart pounding and wondering if tonight will be the night I finally find out what's behind that door.

Without warning, there's a thunderous crash. The door bursts open, slamming against the wall as Beau rockets into our room like a missile. He does a belly flop onto the bed, scratching and clawing the bed sheets as he burrows headfirst beneath them, trembling in sheer terror.

"What's going on?" Giles demands, sitting upright in bed and rubbing the sleep from his eyes as if trying to shake off the remnants of a dream.

"It's Beau," I say over the howling wind and the relentless rain pelting against the house. "The storm frightened him."

"Oh," Giles replies, sinking his head into his pillow like a bear preparing for a long winter's hibernation.

Meanwhile, Beau is buried under the bed sheets, with only his twitching tail visible. It's almost comical how such a large creature can have such an over-the-top reaction to a storm. I can't help but chuckle at the sight—my brave guardian reduced to a quivering heap hiding from Mother Nature's tantrum.

"Come on, buddy," I coax gently, pulling back the sheets to reveal Beau's wide eyes staring back at me, filled with fear. "It's just a little thunder."

He lets out a soft whimper, and my heart aches for him. I reach down to give him reassuring scratches behind his ears, feeling his tension slowly ease. Like a timid little turtle peeking out of its shell, he inches forward, finally deciding that maybe it's safe to come out.

"Maybe I should turn on some music or something," I suggest to Giles, who is halfheartedly trying to find a comfortable position again.

He rolls over dramatically and lets out a sigh. "Yeah, sure. As long as it's not that awful jazz playlist you love so much."

I chuckle and pull out my cell phone, ready to drown out the storm with some soothing tunes. As the first notes fill the room, Beau relaxes beside me, resting his head on my stomach.

"See? It's not so bad after all," I whisper to him, my voice a gentle reassurance as Giles grumbles about the weather, beating a bed pillow into submission in hopes of finding the perfect spot to go back to sleep. Outside, the storm rages on, but inside our cozy little bubble, it's just another night filled with furry cuddles and relaxing melodies—complete with a very anxious pup who needs a bit of TLC to get through the storm.

Lying on my back with Beau nestled between Giles and me, I feel like I'm trapped in a horror movie. The lightning outside resembles a wild dance party, casting strange shadows that flicker across the ceiling. Honestly, it looks like ghosts are having a rave up there. I pull the sheet tight to my chin, hoping it will protect me from the storm's fury, but let's be real; it's just a flimsy barrier against the madness outside and whatever may be lurking inside. The storm's intensity makes me feel like a prisoner in my own bed, while Beau and Giles are lost to the raging storm, comfortably snoring like a well-rehearsed duet. Here I lie motionless, too anxious to sleep.

Every rumble of thunder sends a chill racing down my spine. It's not just the weather that has me on edge tonight; it's this old house. The way it creaks and groans makes it feel alive, as if it's whispering secrets I'm not meant to understand.

Then, out of nowhere, a scream slices through the dark—a frantic, desperate sound that makes my heart skip a beat.

"What was that?" Giles bolts upright, his eyes wide and panicked.

Beau perks up too, his ears twitching like antennae, trying to pick up the source of the noise.

"I don't know who it was," I manage to say, my voice barely above a whisper. "It sounded like one of the girls."

Panic creeps in as we exchange glances, both of us feeling the weight of something sinister lurking just outside our bedroom door. The storm rages on, but it feels as though whatever is happening in the hall is even scarier than the thunder crashing overhead. This old house is hiding something, and I can't shake the feeling that tonight it might reveal its darkest secrets.

"Should we go check?" he asks, his voice barely above a whisper.

I hesitate, biting my lower lip. The thought of facing whatever—or whoever—made that scream makes my skin crawl. But we can't just lie here. Not when someone might be in trouble.

"Yeah," I finally say, steeling myself as I swing my legs over the side of the bed. Just as I do, a second scream pierces the silence—sharp and desperate. My heart pounds in my chest as adrenaline surges through me. "We have to help her!" I exclaim, wrapping a robe around myself. It's not exactly heroic attire, but it's better than running around the house in just my pajamas.

"Who are we helping?" Giles mumbles, tying the belt of his terry bathrobe. Classic Giles—always opting for the most peculiar habits. He insists on sleeping in the nude because he says *clothes feel too constricting*. Yet, he cocoons himself tighter than a mummy in the bed sheets he hogs with reckless abandon. Isn't that just rich? Meanwhile, I stick to my tried-and-true routine: a comfy t-shirt and soft cotton pajama bottoms, a habit ingrained since childhood. But enough about our nighttime quirks; let's get back to the story.

As Giles and I step out of the comfort of our room, we find ourselves face-to-face with Duncan and Ryan in the hallway.

"Who screamed?" I ask, looking between Duncan and Ryan, hoping one of them has the answer to this mystery.

"I think it was Rachael," Duncan declares, his voice steady yet laced with uncertainty.

"Why do you say that?" Giles asks, his brow furrowing in thought.

"Both Julie and Izzy are safely tucked away in their rooms with their doors bolted tight," Duncan explains. "I instructed them to stay put until we figure out what's going on."

"Good thinking," I agree, nodding in approval. It's a smart move—safety first.

"So, by process of elimination, that leaves only one other person..." Duncan begins, but before he can finish, a loud bang echoes from the floor above, causing us all to jump.

"Rachael!" Ryan exclaims suddenly, his eyes wide with realization. The name hangs in the air like a fully filled balloon, ready to pop. We exchange glances; the tension is rising.

"What do you think is going on?" I ask.

Duncan shrugs, looking more puzzled than ever. "I don't know, but we need to check on her," he says, his tone shifting from casual to serious.

"I'm right behind you," Giles replies as we rush toward the stairs. The four of us sprint up, our hearts pounding as we reach Rachael's bedroom on the third floor. A sense of urgency grips us when we find the door locked, a strange lime-green glow seeping ominously from beneath the door.

"Rach!" Duncan calls, pounding his fists against the door.

"Are you okay?" Silence from the other side drapes over us like a heavy velvet curtain, muffling every sound while sparking our imaginations.

"Rachael!" I shout, desperation creeping into my voice. "Please answer me!"

Still no answer—just an eerie green glow pulsating from under the door.

"Step aside, boys. I'm going to break down the door," Duncan declares, determination shining in his eyes as he does his best hero imitation.

We quickly shuffle aside, adrenaline pumping through our veins like we're gearing up for a wild roller coaster ride.

Duncan takes a deep breath, his heart racing as he prepares for the potential horror lurking behind the stubborn door. He steps back to gather momentum, as if he is about to launch himself into the stratosphere. With a running leap, he charges forward. Just as his shoulder is about to slam into the wood, the door swings open on its own, catching Duncan off guard and leaving him struggling to regain his balance.

Peeking inside, the room shimmers with an eerie lime-green glow that feels almost alive, like stepping into a scene straight out of a science fiction movie. Thick threads of gooey green ooze drip from the ceiling like some otherworldly rain, coating every surface in a thick layer of shimmering slime. It feels as if a strange alien party has exploded in here. The furniture is covered in this gloppy substance, and the walls drip and glisten ominously under the strange light.

"Rachael?" Duncan calls from the open doorway, urgency in his voice. "Are you in there?"

"No," Rachael replies, appearing beside me in the dimly lit corridor outside her bedroom. She raises an eyebrow, curiously. "What's all the commotion about?"

Relief washes over Duncan as he turns to face her. "We thought you were in trouble."

"Why would you think that?" Rachael asks, her tone a mix of confusion and annoyance.

"We heard you scream," I interject, trying to get to the bottom of the situation.

"Twice, to be exact," Duncan adds, crossing his arms defensively.

"I didn't scream," Rachael exclaims, her eyes widening in disbelief. "Why on earth would you think I screamed?"

"If it wasn't you," I ask Rachael, "then who screamed?"

"Are you boys alright?" Rachael inquires, her brow furrowing with concern. "You're acting strange—even for you guys."

Duncan narrows his eyes, skepticism etched on his face. "If you didn't scream," he challenges, "then who did?"

"I have no idea what you're talking about," Rachael denies.

"Where did you just come from?" Duncan asks.

"From the kitchen. I grabbed a glass of milk and some cookies," Rachael replies nonchalantly. "I was in the mood for a snack. Is that a crime in my own house?"

Duncan and I exchange glances, half relieved and half bewildered. So, there were no ghostly screams or midnight horrors—just Rachael indulging in a late-night craving.

"Cookies at this hour? Seriously?" I chuckle, shaking my head.

Rachael shrugs with a mischievous grin. "What can I say? A girl's got to eat."

With the tension easing, we burst into laughter, realizing that maybe our imaginations had run wild after all.

"So?" Duncan presses, leaning closer with wide eyes full of intrigue. "You really didn't scream?"

"Read my lips," Rachael insists, her tone steady, "I-did-not-scream."

Ryan, ever the curious one, chimes in, "But didn't you hear someone scream?"

Rachael slowly shakes her head. "The only thing I heard was the storm raging outside," she states firmly as the wind howls ominously through the trees.

It feels like a scene straight out of a horror movie, and I sense the tension in the air thickening.

"Wait a minute, that doesn't make any sense," Duncan exclaims, shaking his head in disbelief. "We heard a scream, but you didn't?"

"How is that even possible?" I ask, my heart racing as confusion clouds my thoughts. It feels like we're trapped in a twisted version of a detective story where the main character is oblivious to the danger surrounding them.

"Maybe you guys are going crazy," Rachael replies with a sly grin. There's something about her smirk that doesn't seem quite right. Is she messing with us, or is there something more sinister at play? The storm rages outside, but it's nothing compared to the turmoil brewing in our minds. What really happened tonight, and why can't we all agree on what we heard?

As the wind howls and rain pelts against the windows like pebbles, I can't shake the feeling that we're being watched. The shadows in the corners of the hallway seem to stretch and twist, almost as if they're alive.

"Okay, let's just think this through," I say, trying to keep my voice steady. "We all heard something—"

"Or maybe we didn't," Rachael interjects, her eyes glinting with mischief.

Duncan rolls his eyes, clearly frustrated. "This isn't working. We need to figure out what's going on."

But how do you solve a mystery when the clues are scattered between reality and paranoia? As I glance around at my friends, their faces illuminated by flashes of lightning, I wonder if we're all just losing it together—or if there's something truly terrifying lurking just out of sight.

So here we are, hanging out in the hall outside Rachael's room. Then, out of nowhere, Rachael does something bizarre. She reaches up to her face and peels back her skin as if she's taking off some creepy latex mask. My heart nearly stops. I kid you not—it feels like I'm in the middle of a horror movie.

Beneath the peeled-back skin, there's an old man's face staring back at me—totally not Rachael. This guy's face is all wrinkled and twisted, and he's laughing like he just heard the funniest joke in the world. The sound echoes through the hall, reverberating off the walls in a way that sends chills crawling down my spine. Honestly, I'm torn between screaming and laughing because I have no idea what's happening.

He—or whatever it is—floats to the center of the bedroom, and honestly? It feels like something straight out of a twisted horror movie. The entire atmosphere is just off. There are two terrifying ghost heads swooping and diving around the bedroom, cackling. It's not the kind of laughter that makes you smile; it's sharp and awful, clawing at our ears like nails on a chalkboard. Just when I think it can't get any crazier, the ghosts vanish, the storm stops, everything goes dead silent, like someone flipped a switch. One second we're overwhelmed by this cacophony of madness—green, glowing, goo dripping from the walls of Rachael's room, ghosts causing chaos—and then? Nothing. Just an eerie stillness that wraps around us like a heavy blanket, making it hard to breathe.

Honestly, I can't shake the image of Rachael's face being ripped off like a snake shedding its old skin. And those insane laughs? They echo in my head like some twisted soundtrack I can't turn off. Am I going mad?

"What is going on?" Rachael inquires, her voice a mix of confusion and annoyance. She speaks from behind us. "Why are you guys standing outside my bedroom?"

"Rach, is that really you?" I exclaim, still trying to grasp the bewildering sight before me.

"Of course it is me. Who else would I be?" Rachael responds, her tone laced with exasperation.

In a moment of curiosity, Ryan pinches Rachael's cheek, causing her to squeal in surprise. "Ouch! What is the big idea?" she protests, swatting his hand away.

"Yeah," Ryan agrees, nodding emphatically. "It's definitely Rach."

Frustration mounts in Rachael as she crosses her arms, clearly fed up with our antics. "Will someone please explain what the heck is going on here?" Her eyes dart between us, searching for clarity amidst the chaos.

Duncan scratches his head thoughtfully, his expression a mix of concern and contemplation. "Rach," he begins hesitantly, "I'm not even sure how to start explaining what just happened. It's like something out of a bizarre dream."

"You are not making any sense," Rachael exclaims, her eyes wide with confusion as she darts her gaze between Duncan, Ryan, Giles, and me, trying desperately to piece together a puzzle with missing pieces.

"Rach," I reply gently, sensing the rising panic in her voice, "you need to sit down. We have something to tell you."

Ryan, Giles, and I follow Duncan as he escorts Rachael into her bedroom and toward her bed. I'm taken aback for a moment; my mouth drops open as I look around the room. Where did the green goo disappear to? Just moments ago, the room was drenched in lime-green slimy stuff, and now it's gone. Giles and Ryan seem just as stunned as I am, searching the room for any sign of it. Duncan is so laser focused on what he wants to say to Rachael that he doesn't notice how the room has returned to normal.

"What is it?" Panic creeps into Rachael's voice, her breaths quickening. "What is wrong?"

"Just sit down," Duncan urges, his tone steady but serious as he guides her to the edge of the bed.

The weight of the moment hangs in the air, thick with uncertainty. As she sinks onto the mattress, I see her mind racing, trying to catch up with our erratic energy.

"Okay, I am sitting. Now spill it," she demands, crossing her arms defensively.

Ryan flicks on the nightstand lamp, casting a warm glow over the room. However, as we settle in, a strange unease hangs in the air—where has that glowing green ooze gone? Just moments ago, it had seemed to cover everything around us. Even Duncan notices the change in the room but doesn't say anything; his eyes convey everything.

"You guys are starting to scare me," Rachael says, her brow furrowing deeper. "You are acting really strange—it is kind of weirding me out."

As we exchange glances, our bewilderment reflects hers. What just happened? The ooze had felt alive, pulsing with an energy that buzzed beneath our skin.

"Rach," Duncan begins, his voice laced with urgency, "what I'm about to tell you might freak you out even more than you already are."

Rachael raises an eyebrow, a mix of intrigue and apprehension in her gaze. "Okay, now I am officially weirded out."

"Earlier," Duncan continues, glancing at Ryan for support, "about an hour ago, all of us—except for you—heard a scream."

"Actually, it was two screams," Ryan interjects, his tone serious.

"That's right," Duncan agrees, nodding gravely. "Two screams. But here's the twist—they didn't come from either Izzy or Julie—they were both sound asleep. We—Ryan, Taylor, Giles, and I—rushed up here to check on you and found your door locked."

Rachael furrows her brow. "That is odd," she replies slowly, piecing together the unsettling puzzle. "There is no lock on that door."

Ryan examines the door, his brow furrowing in confusion. "Duncan," he calls out, urgency lacing his voice, "she's right—there's no lock on this door."

"Really?" Duncan replies, a hint of skepticism creeping into his tone. "That's strange. But still, the door wouldn't budge. I was just about to shoulder-shove it when—"

"It opened by itself," Ryan exclaims, excitement bubbling over.

Duncan's eyes widen as he continues, "And that's not even the craziest part. Your entire bedroom was drenched in this glowing lime-green slime. It dripped from the ceiling like some bizarre alien rain and oozed down your furniture and walls.

Everything was covered in that pulsing lime-green stuff."

"It kind of reminded me of that gooey stuff called *Slime* from when we were kids. You remember that stuff? It came in a plastic tub," Ryan rambles.

The vivid imagery of the encounter leaves us guys momentarily speechless. We stand awkwardly in Rachael's room, still trying to wrap our heads around what just happened.

"Green slime, you say?" Rachael asks, her brow furrowing in confusion as she scans her room for residual signs of the strange substance. "Where is the green slime now?"

"I have no idea," Duncan replies, curiously shrugging his shoulders. "It just vanished into thin air."

"Ok-ay..." Rachael says slowly, giving Duncan a skeptical look that clearly questions his sanity. "You expect me to believe that story?"

"After your door opened unexpectedly—from the open doorway, I couldn't see you in the bedroom," Duncan explains earnestly. "So I called out your name."

"Then *you* answered him," Ryan chimes in. His facial expression is like one of those cartoons where a huge question mark floats above ones head. "You were standing right next to Taylor, munching on a half-eaten cookie."

"Popping up unexpectedly as you did, I was just trying to determine where you'd been," Duncan protests, throwing his hands up in exasperation.

"You told Duncan you were coming back from the kitchen after grabbing milk and cookies," Giles adds with an uncertain tone.

"Then," Ryan interjects, his eyes wide with excitement, "just moments before, you ripped off your face like it was a cheap latex Halloween mask. But what was underneath wasn't you at all—it was an old, wrinkled ghost head."

Duncan leans in closer, lowering his voice to a conspiratorial whisper. "And that ghost head? It erupted into laughter. Suddenly, it floated into your room to swoop and swirl through the air with another ghost head. They joined each other in a cacophony of laughter, as they flew about your bedroom."

"The laughter grew louder and louder," Ryan recounts, his eyes sparkling with excitement. "Just when it seemed like it could go on forever, it suddenly stopped. In that instant, everything went dark—then you, Rachael, reappeared as if summoned by magic, and just like that, normalcy returned, with no ghosts or green glowing goo in sight."

Rachael remains silent for a moment, scrutinizing each of us with a piercing gaze. "You expect me to believe that outlandish tale?" she challenges skeptically. "How long did you all plan this little prank?"

We exchange confused glances, caught in disbelief.

"Oh, Rach! You're okay!" Julie chimes in, her tone one of relief as she breezes into the bedroom.

"Wait—you are in on this too?" Rachael shoots back at Julie, her eyebrows rise in disbelief.

"What are you talking about?" Julie asks, furrowing her brow in confusion. "In on what?"

"Are you seriously telling me that you and the guys did not just pull a prank on me?" Rachael's voice rises in disbelief.

"Prank you?" Julie replies, her eyes wide with shock. "Are you out of your mind?"

"So, let me get this straight," Rachael continues, her tone a mix of incredulity and curiosity. "You mean to tell me that the wild story you just shared actually happened? Swear to God?"

"Honestly," Duncan interjects earnestly, "everything we told you happened exactly as we said."

Rachael pauses, her mind racing. "Okay," she finally concedes, "maybe something did happen. But how do you explain it?"

"It had to be Ezekiel and Abrahim, I tell you," Duncan reveals, his voice low and tense. "They've unleashed their haunting as revenge for you selling their mine."

"But it is not *their* mine," Rachael protests, her eyes wide with disbelief. "That old mine has been abandoned for decades."

Julie rolls her eyes, clearly unimpressed. "We know that,"

she interjects, her tone steady yet firm. "But they refuse to accept the truth of the matter."

Rachael runs a hand through her hair, frustration bubbling up. "It is frustrating, to say the least. How can anyone—or any things—be so attached to a place that has long lost its purpose?" She takes a deep breath, trying to calm herself. "So what now? Am I destined to be haunted for the rest of my life by those two ghosts?"

The uncertainty in her voice is obvious. Honestly, who wouldn't be freaked out by the idea of angry spectral visitors constantly hovering about?

"Unless you have a secret method for banishing angry old ghosts," Ryan replies with a wry smile, though his eyes reveal his concern. He always knows how to lighten the mood, even when things feel heavy.

As we stand around surrounded by uncertainty, the weight of our situation hangs in the balance. One question remains: How do we confront spirits who refuse to let go of their past? Perhaps it begins with understanding them—acknowledging their pain and letting them know they are not forgotten. After all, everyone wants to feel seen, even if they have been trapped as spirits for centuries.

Maybe it involves helping them move on, such as giving them a proper send-off or revealing their stories so they can finally find peace. Imagine a ghostly book club where we honor their life stories and provide them with closure. Or perhaps it's something completely different—something we haven't thought of yet. Maybe we need to throw them a party. Who wouldn't want to celebrate their life, even after they've passed on?

Whatever it is, we'll figure it out together. Tackling ghosts is far more enjoyable with friends by your side, right?

Dale Thele

DAY FIVE

Friday, May 24, 2019

I'm not going to sugarcoat it: the house on the hill has officially become a battleground, all thanks to the two resident troublemakers, Ezekiel and Abrahim. These mischievous ghosts have stirred up a storm of chaos that is quickly becoming the new normal. Honestly, just thinking about it is exhausting. What can we do but brace ourselves for the wild ride and hope for the best? So far, luck has been on our side—no one has been harmed in this first spectral skirmish, which is a minor miracle considering the shenanigans those two may get up to in the near future.

But let's be real: we're just scratching the surface of these eerie encounters. We can expect each night to bring new antics that are bound to be even crazier than the last. Thank goodness for daylight. It gives us a much-needed break from their ghostly rambunctious carryings-on, allowing us to catch our breath and mentally prepare for whatever madness awaits us beyond sunset. As we gear up for yet another night of supernatural shenanigans, all we can do is keep our fingers crossed and hope that Ezekiel and Abrahim don't take things too far. Buckle up folks; it's going to be a bumpy ride. In the meantime, we relish the quiet that comes with daylight.

"Good morning, Rach," I call cheerfully as I step into the kitchen, the aroma of fresh coffee filling the air. Before indulging in my morning routine, I head to the back door and swing it wide open. In a flash, Beau dashes past me, eager to explore the backyard.

"How in the world did you know Beau wanted to go outside?" Rachael asks with a curious smile.

"It's his morning ritual," I reply with a wink. "What's the first thing you do after waking up in the morning?" I grin.

"Okay, point taken," Rachael smirks.

"As for Beau, I figure, why should I wait for him to beg for me to open the door when I can open it in advance and enjoy my morning coffee uninterrupted?"

"Speaking of which," Rachael says playfully as she hands me a steaming mug of rich coffee, "here's fuel to start your morning."

I take a sip, savoring the warmth that spreads through me as I settle into a chair at the table across from her. I take a moment to soak in the peaceful early hours. A fresh breeze whispers through the open door while birds serenade us with their soft chirping—a delightful symphony Giles and I rarely experience amid the bustling streets of New Orleans. This tranquil morning feels like a refreshing escape from the approaching sweltering afternoon, dominated by raucous cicadas and sticky humidity. As I take another sip of coffee, I can't help but feel grateful for these quiet moments that remind me to take a breather and enjoy life's simple pleasures. There's something magical about mornings like this, where time seems to slow down just enough for us to appreciate the little things—a warm mug in hand, the gentle rustle of leaves, and the promise of a fresh, new day ahead. It's easy to get caught up in the chaos of city life, but here, in this little pocket of tranquility, everything feels just right.

"I simply adore mornings," Rachael declares, almost as if she can read my thoughts. "They are so peaceful and serene. It is the perfect time to hear your own thoughts without interruptions."

"Morning, morning, morning," Ryan bursts in, his exuberance seeming wildly out of place for this early hour—especially for him.

"So much for peaceful and serene," I snicker, shaking my head. "Rye, why on earth are you so cheerful at this hour? And more importantly, why are you up before the sun has fully risen?"

"I've decided to make some life changes," Ryan replies, his grin widening.

"What kind of life changes are we talking about here?" I ask, raising an eyebrow. "Or do we really want to know?"

"Waking up earlier is one of them," Ryan declares as he pours himself a mug of coffee. The rich aroma of the coffee wafts through the air, inviting and warm. Outside, Beau's excited barks echo from the backyard, causing a fleeting smile to cross my face.

"What's got Beau all riled up?" Ryan inquires, a hint of curiosity dancing in his eyes as he leans against the kitchen counter, too lazy to turn and look out the window behind him.

"He's probably thrilled to be reunited with his butterfly friends," I reply with a playful grin.

Ryan raises an eyebrow, skepticism etched on his face. "Butterfly friends? Really?" His tone suggests he may think I've lost my marbles, yet, he swivels to peer out the window.

Just then, Duncan strides into the kitchen, drawn by the enticing scent that has now filled the room. "Is that fresh coffee I smell?" he asks eagerly, his eyes lighting up as he makes a beeline for the coffee maker on the counter. With deft hands, he pours himself a generous mug, the steam curling upward like a dream.

"Where's Isadora?" I ask.

"Oh, you know how it is with females—she's getting her beauty sleep," Duncan replies with a playful grin as he takes a seat at the table.

Rachael leans in, her eyes sparkling with curiosity. "You haven't shared how you and Isadora met," she nudges, clearly eager for some juicy early morning gossip.

Duncan chuckles softly, "Well, there's not much to tell, really. We met at a fundraising event toward the end of last summer in Charleston." His tone is relaxed, but I sense the fondness in his memory.

"So, Isadora is from South Carolina?" I inquire, picturing the charming streets, historic plantations, and that beautiful Southern hospitality. It seems like the perfect backdrop for a romantic spark.

"Not really," Duncan replies, a hint of amusement dancing in his eyes as he enjoys the moment. "She's actually from Atherton, California."

"Atherton?" Ryan asks, sounding skeptical. "You made that place up."

"No, I didn't," Duncan replies. "It's located between Menlo Park on State Route 82 and North Fair Oaks. Get me a map and I'll show you."

"No need," Ryan says, trying to shrink into the background.

I raise an eyebrow, surprised. "California? That's quite a leap from Carolina," I comment, suddenly curious about her West Coast home.

"Yeah, but she's got that charming Southern elegance down to a T," Duncan says, his grin widening. "It's part of what captivated me."

As we sit around the table, sipping coffee and listening to Duncan's stories, I can't help but feel the pull of their dynamic— two souls from different places coming together in unexpected ways. It reminds me that sometimes, the best relationships bloom from the most unlikely encounters.

Rachael leans in, her curiosity expanding. "What I want to know is, what was she doing all the way in South Carolina?"

"Visiting school friends before the fall term started," Duncan explains, his tone light and casual.

"So she is going to school in South Carolina?" Rachael asks, furrowing her brow slightly as she pieces together the puzzle that is Duncan's life.

Duncan shakes his head with a smile. "Nope! She attends the University of Texas in Austin."

"But you just said Isadora is from California," a confused Rachael says.

"She is from California, but she now lives in Austin,"

Duncan clarifies before taking a sip of coffee.

Rachael tilts her head, intrigued. "Why do I sense there is more to this story that you are not letting on?"

"Yeah, I guess there is," Duncan replies, a hint of nostalgia in his voice. "A friend from high school introduced me to Izzy at a fancy fundraising gala for a local hospital. It was one of those nights where everything just clicked. We met, we hit it off, and ever since that night, we've been inseparable." There's a spark in his eyes, suggesting that there's more to the story, but Duncan remains tight-lipped. To get personal information out of him, you have to pry it out, like a dentist pulling teeth.

I raise an eyebrow, intrigued. "Izzy doesn't seem like the type of girl I would picture you with," I remark.

"Why not?" Duncan asks playfully, a teasing glint in his eye.

Ryan chimes in with a smirk, "I think what Taylor means is that she can be a bit... difficult."

"Rye," I scold lightly, rolling my eyes. "Must you put words in my mouth?"

Duncan chuckles, shaking his head. "Izzy can be quite the handful," he admits with a knowing smile. "Since the day we met, our families have been nothing but supportive of our relationship. Izzy's family is well-off—though perhaps not quite as affluent as mine. But that's what makes us so compatible; we both come from wealthy backgrounds, and our parents are already discussing plans for our future together."

"Plans for the future?" I repeat, raising my eyebrow again. "Sounds serious."

"Sounds to me like your folks are eager to keep all that combined wealth within the family, huh?" Ryan interjects, raising an eyebrow.

"Could be," Duncan muses, a hint of amusement dancing in his eyes. "It's certainly better than the alternative—an arranged marriage." He takes a leisurely sip of his coffee, appearing completely unfazed by the complexities of his relationship with Isadora.

Rachael leans in and begins cautiously, "Duncan, I have just met you, and I do not want to sound rude, but there is something about Isadora that I cannot quite put my finger on."

Ryan chimes in with a smirk, "I can tell you what it is—she's a *bitch*."

"That is not what I meant," Rachael retorts, shaking her head. "There seems to be something... off about her. No offense, Duncan."

"Oh, none taken," Duncan replies with a casual shrug. "Izzy's one of those girls who's an acquired taste. Some people savor caviar, while others prefer shrimp cocktail."

"Speaking of shrimp cocktail—" Ryan begins, but he's abruptly cut off as Isadora glides into the kitchen, her presence demanding immediate attention.

"Look who it is," Duncan announces, unable to stifle a grin.

"God save us all," Rachael whispers, rolling her eyes as Isadora approaches.

"Dunkie," Isadora whines, her voice dripping with annoyance, "can you please silence that blasted dog? With all that barking, I can't get my beauty sleep."

I glance at her, feeling a mix of sympathy and amusement bubbling inside me. "I'm sorry, Isadora," I reply with feigned sincerity. "Sometimes Beau gets a little carried away when he's playing. I'll definitely have a word with him later about his rather selfish behavior."

Isadora shoots me a glare that could curdle milk. Taking a casual sip of my coffee, I feel a twinge of guilt for my callousness, but it feels oddly satisfying too. A giggle threatens to escape my lips, yet I know better than to let it slip. After all, who wouldn't want to poke fun at the queen of drama herself?

"Dunkikuns," Isadora says, her voice dripping with concern as she glares at me. "I don't think your friends like me."

"Don't be silly. Of course they do," Duncan replies, balancing reassurance with the kind of exasperation that only comes from being trapped in a sitcom-style moment. He shoots a stern look at Ryan, Rachael, and especially me, as if to say, *You guys are the reason for this drama.*

It's honestly hard to keep a straight face. The three of us exchange glances, struggling to suppress our giggles.

"Dunkie, darling," Isadora continues with an exaggerated sigh, "I'm going back to the room. Will you be a dear and bring me a cup of tea?"

As soon as she's out of earshot, we burst into laughter, tears streaming down our faces. The sheer absurdity of it all is too much to contain. Duncan barely holds back a snicker, and I can see a glimmer of mirth in his eyes as well.

"*Dunkie, darling. Be a dear and bring me a cup of tea,*" Ryan perfectly mimics Isadora, sending us spiraling into another fit of uncontrolled laughter.

"Alright," Duncan insists, a playful grin beginning to spread across his face. "That's enough. That's my girlfriend you're laughing at."

But truth be told, there's nothing quite like this ridiculous moment to lift our spirits. Isadora's theatrics may be over the top, but they've sparked a connection that makes us all laugh. Who knew a cup of tea could fuel such a hilarious episode?

"Boy, howdy," I exclaim toward Duncan, unable to hide my amusement. "Looks like she's got you whipped and wrapped around her little finger."

Duncan rolls his eyes, but I notice a hint of a smile tugging at the corners of his mouth. "It's not like that at all," he protests, his cheeks flushing.

Rachael jumps in with a teasing smile, "From where I am sitting, it seems like you are on a pretty short leash, my friend."

Duncan can't help but chuckle, the playful banter dissolving any defense he had. "Okay, okay, maybe I give in to her more than I should," he admits, which only adds to the humor of the moment.

"More than you should? Dude, it looks like you're practically her slave," I laugh, leaning back in my chair as Rachael smiles and nods in agreement.

"Hey now," Duncan retorts, holding up his hands in surrender. "I'm just trying to keep the peace here."

"Sure, keep telling yourself that," Rachael winks, clearly enjoying this little roast session.

Duncan's face flushes a deep crimson as he springs up from the table. With quiet determination, he walks to the sink and fills the tea kettle with water that sparkles in the warm morning light. When the kettle begins to whistle—a sharp sound shatters the silence—his focus sharpens. It's like watching a magician at work; every movement is not only deliberate but also precise, with each gesture reflecting his devotion to *Princess* Isadora. He selects the perfect tea bag and adds just the right amount of sugar and cream, along with a slight squeeze of lemon, mixing the ingredients along with his heart into that cup. Finally, he arranges everything on a serving tray, its surface gleaming with promise. Taking a deep breath, he steels himself for what lies ahead. He gracefully ascends the stairs, ready to deliver more than just tea—he's bringing a piece of himself along with it.

Moments later, I catch a quick glimpse of Beau trotting back into the house, his tail wagging with an unusual energy. I set my coffee mug down on the table, feeling a tingle of curiosity. Turning to Ryan and Rachael, I ask, "Did either of you notice anything peculiar about Beau when he came inside?"

Ryan shakes his head, his brow furrowing slightly. "Nope, I wasn't really paying attention. Why do you ask?"

Rachael shrugs nonchalantly. "I did not notice anything out of the ordinary."

A spark of intrigue ignites within me. "I'll be right back," I say as I rise from my chair, a sense of urgency propelling me toward the parlor. "Beau," I call out, my voice playful yet curious as I spot him sprawled comfortably on the settee. "What do you have in your mouth?"

He pivots his head ever so slightly, a guilty look flashing across his face as he conceals something from me. "Come on, Beau. I asked you a question. What do you have there?" His attempt to hide whatever it is only deepens my curiosity. Just before he can fully pull off the sneaky act, I catch a glimpse of something—a bone.

"Where did you get that bone?" I ask, half-expecting an elaborate explanation but mostly hoping he'll let go of his newfound prize. "Be a good boy and give it to Daddy." I extend my open hand.

Like a guilty child caught with their hand in the cookie jar, he hesitantly drops the bone. I chuckle at his sheepish expression; there's something undeniably charming about my pup's clumsy attempts to hide his treasures. As I pick up the bone from the floor, my curiosity is piqued. I turn it over in my hands, trying to make sense of its odd shape. Seriously, where did he find this thing?

Don't get me wrong; I'm in favor of him having something substantial to chew on, but when I don't know where something like this bone came from, I get overly protective. What exactly has he brought into the house? The smooth edges and bizarre shape don't suggest a normal *chew toy*—it practically screams *What the hell is this*, as if to say I should be worried about where he found it. As I hold it up to the light, the shiny surface reflects the sunlight, making the origin of this unusual bone even more of a mystery and the concern for Beau's safety more daunting.

Honestly, I feel like I should be wearing a detective's hat and embarking on a bone-hunting expedition. Each moment weighs heavily on my mind. What kind of adventures has my fur baby been up to while I wasn't paying attention?

With a deep breath, I decide this little mystery calls for some investigation. The kitchen is the perfect spot to begin to unravel its secrets. I need to know if this strange object has a story waiting to be told. Maybe it's a relic of a heroic dog escapade, or perhaps just a peculiar find from the neighbor's trash can. Either way, it's time to play Sherlock and uncover the tale behind my pup's curious new acquisition.

"Rach," I ask, holding up the bone in question as if it's Exhibit A in a murder trial. "Do you recognize this bone?"

"No, I cannot say that I do," Rachael replies, her brow furrowing in confusion.

"I wonder where Beau found it," I muse aloud, turning the bone over in my hands as I try to determine whether it's something I should be concerned about or if it's just a random dog treasure.

"Why don't you ask Beau?" Ryan chimes in, leaning against the counter with a smirk.

"Yeah, right. Like he's going to answer me," I retort sarcastically. "If you haven't noticed lately, he's a dog—dogs don't talk, genius."

"I know that," Ryan shoots back with a grin, his eyes sparkling with mischief. "But maybe he will *show* you where he found it."

"Actually, that is not a bad idea," Rachael agrees, her interest growing as she leans closer to inspect the bone.

"What's not a bad idea?" Duncan asks as he strolls back into the kitchen, clearly oblivious to our little mystery.

"Beau found this bone," I explain, sliding it across the table for Duncan to take a gander at. "But I have no clue where he got it."

"I completely agree with Rye," Duncan says, his fingers brushing over the bone as if it holds secrets of its own. "If you can persuade Beau to show you where he found this, it could answer your questions." With a furrowed brow, Duncan inspects the bone, turning it over with a mix of curiosity and concern.

"Hey, guys," he continues, his tone shifting to one of gravity. "This isn't just any ordinary bone—it's a human tibia. You don't come across bones like this every day. If there's a tibia lying around, there's likely an entire skeleton nearby." He pauses for effect, letting the weight of his words to sink in. "You really should get Beau to show you where he got this bone."

"Duncan, how do you know about this stuff?" Rachael inquires, her eyes wide with intrigue.

"Duncan knows *everything*," Ryan chimes in with a playful grin. "He's like Einstein—smart."

Feeling overwhelmed by Duncan's unexpected knowledge, I push back from the table and make my way to the parlor. "Hey there, Beau, my buddy, my pal," I say sweetly, trying to charm him despite our recent disagreement. After all, I did take away his new bone, and he isn't exactly thrilled with me at the moment. "Can you show Daddy where you found this bone?" I hold it up for him to see, hoping to spark some enthusiasm. Looking over my shoulder, I realize I'm not alone; Rachael, Ryan, and Duncan have followed me into the parlor. Their expressions are a mix of intrigue and amusement as they watch my attempt to win over Beau.

I sense the mounting tension in the air and worry that Beau might feel hesitant under the curious eyes of my friends. "Hey, everyone," I say, trying to keep my voice light and reassuring, "how about you wait for me in the kitchen? Having you all here might make Beau hesitant to show me where he found this bone."

As they retreat into the kitchen, I feel a wave of relief wash over me. Beau hops down from the settee, his movements graceful yet cautious, and I follow closely behind him through the kitchen and out into the backyard. Like a child's parade, Ryan, Duncan, Rachael, and I trail behind him as he makes his way across the sun-drenched lawn. Beau leads us to Rachael's future garden—a patch of earth still waiting to be transformed into a vibrant vegetable haven. The soil lies overturned and bare, a canvas of potential just waiting for seeds to be sown.

"Beau," I ask, "can you show Daddy where you found the bone?"

Hesitant at first, Beau tentatively begins to dig into the overturned soil of Rachael's garden. The four of us exchange glances, a mix of confusion and intrigue swirling in the air along with clumps of dirt.

"This can't possibly be where he found it," Duncan asserts, shaking his head. "If this were the case, Rachael would have unearthed that bone long before Beau got to it while tilling the soil. I think your dog has led us on a wild goose chase. Remember, tibia's come in pairs—like pieces of a puzzle forming a complete human skeleton."

"Beau," I gently scold, "stop digging up Rachael's garden."

He looks up at me with wide soulful eyes filled with innocence and confusion, as if to say, *What's the deal? I'm just doing as you told me to do?*

Rachael examines the hole Beau has made in her garden plot, her eyes sparkling with curiosity. "No," she says, her voice bright with anticipation. "Let him dig. Maybe he wants to show us something."

"Are you sure?" I ask, skepticism creeping into my tone. "I mean, he's probably just making a hole to bury his new prized bone."

"Trust me," Rachael insists, her enthusiasm infectious. "Let him dig."

"Okay, if you insist," I reply with a shrug, turning to Beau and giving him my permission with a playful grin. "Go ahead, buddy. Dig to your heart's content."

He pauses and looks up at me, his big, expressive eyes seeming to ask, *Are you absolutely sure this time?* I nod, offering a warm smile to encourage him—an unspoken bond of trust. He resumes digging with relentless fervor, each thrust of his paws sending clumps of dirt soaring into the air like confetti at a New Year's celebration. Just when I think we're in for just a typical late morning in the backyard, he halts, his eyes wide with excitement, tail wagging a mile a minute.

In a triumph only a dog can understand, he produces yet another bone from the depths of the garden and drops it right at my feet, tail wagging furiously. Curious, I lean down, scoop it up, and hand it to our resident bone expert, Duncan. "Is this another tibia?" I ask, excitement bubbling in my voice. It's not every day that we stumble upon such odd treasures.

Duncan takes the bone. Brushing off the dirt, he studies it like a detective examining crucial evidence. His brow furrows deeper with each passing second, and I can practically see the gears turning in his head. "Actually," he replies slowly, "this appears to be a fibula—a bone that's closely associated with the tibia."

Suddenly, he freezes in place, the atmosphere shifts. A pallor washes over his face as the realization hits him with all the subtlety of a freight train. "I think we should call the cops," he says, his voice dropping to a grave whisper. "There might be a body buried here."

Dale Thele

DAY SIX

Saturday, May 25, 2019

"I wasn't about to sleep in this morning," Julie declares, her eyes sparkling as she gently blows on her steaming mug of coffee while sitting at the kitchen table. "Yesterday, I overslept, and what happened? I missed all the excitement."

"Excitement? Really?" I chuckle, trying to downplay her concern.

"Okay, maybe there was a little bit of drama," Rachael admits, a wry smile playing on her lips. "I just cannot believe there are human bones in my backyard. What if someone is buried where I intended to plant my vegetable garden? What then?"

"Let's not jump to conclusions," Julie advises, her voice steady. "We don't know anything for certain yet."

"Exactly," I agree, nodding emphatically. "Let's wait for the police to figure out what's going on."

As we savor our coffee, our imaginations ignite like explosive dynamite sticks, fueled by the tension of Rachael's revelation. The idea of bones buried beneath the surface in the backyard has a strange allure—like something straight out of the mystery novels I so enjoy reading.

Our quiet moment of contemplation is suddenly interrupted when Beau bursts into the kitchen. His tail wags furiously as he scratches at the back door, whining impatiently and staring at it, eager for his morning outing.

"Sorry, Beau," I say, shaking my head as I rise from the table with a resigned sigh. "You can't go play in the backyard this morning—the yard is off-limits because it's swarming with police searching Rachael's garden."

Beau's head droops, and a soft whine escapes him; even his tail hangs limp, a clear sign of his disappointment. I can't help but feel a pang of empathy for him.

"Awe," Julie says sympathetically. "Poor Beau really wants to go outside."

"Come on, buddy," I encourage gently. "Let's go to the front lawn instead."

Encouraged by me, Beau perks up and wags his tail energetically once again. With an unexpected burst of enthusiasm, he dashes toward the front door, and I hurry after him. He doesn't linger outside; he quickly takes care of business and, showing a sense of responsibility, races back inside, leaving the allure of his butterfly friends behind.

As I walk back into the kitchen, where Julie is already waiting with a playful grin, she raises an eyebrow and says, "Well, that was a lightning-fast trip, wasn't it?"

"Yeah," I reply with a chuckle, "he hurriedly took care of business and seemed eager to come back inside. I guess the front lawn can't compete with the wonders of the backyard."

We exchange a knowing look, both understanding that for Beau, every moment outdoors is an adventure—whether he's chasing butterflies or simply exploring. In the end, however, the allure of home always wins.

Rachael shakes her head in wonder. "I cannot believe how much Beau seems to grasp our conversations. It is like he is part of every discussion we have."

"Absolutely," Julie nods enthusiastically. "Sometimes I almost forget he's a dog."

Just at that very moment, Duncan strolls into the kitchen, raising an eyebrow. "Who's a dog?" he teases. "I hope you're not talking about me."

"I'd never say that about you," Julie declares, her voice laced with playful mischief. "That's not to say that I might not think it."

Duncan chuckles, a grin spreading across his face. "Thanks

for the backhanded compliment," he says, pouring himself a steaming mug of coffee. However, as he takes a sip, his amusement fades, replaced by a sudden surge of curiosity as he glances at Julie standing beside the window. "Wait a second... Is that really how you feel?" Without waiting for a response, he turns his attention toward the window, pulling back the curtains to study the men digging in the backyard.

Outside, the bright morning sun casts a sharp contrast over the future garden plot, now outlined by ominous yellow crime scene tape. This once tranquil space has been transformed into a chilling reminder of the havoc that can erupt beneath the surface of everyday life. The presence of police officers milling about serves as a sobering indication that something unimaginable may have occurred here. One can reflect on the implications of such an unsettling scene, considering how secrets hidden in plain sight can disrupt not only a community but also the very fabric of trust and safety that we often take for granted, leaving us with a lingering sense of unease. What lies beneath the surface of Rachael's aspiring garden?

"Looks like the cops got an early start this morning," Duncan remarks, raising an eyebrow. "Any updates on what they've found?"

Julie shrugs, her eyes darting between the garden and Duncan. "Not yet, but this is definitely not the kind of morning any of us were hoping for."

Duncan takes another sip of coffee, his mind racing with possibilities. "Yeah, no kidding. Who would have thought this old house would turn into something out of a true crime television show?"

The two share a knowing glance, acknowledging the gravity of the situation outside.

Rachael joins Duncan and Julie at the window, her brow furrowed with concern as she scans the activity outside. "Honestly, do you think they will share any news with us?"

"I don't know, Rach. I really don't know," Duncan replies, shaking his head with a mixture of resignation and deep curiosity. "It seems they've declared your garden a crime scene—just look at that yellow tape. What a way to ruin a perfectly lovely morning."

"This time, my procrastination has actually paid off," Rachael exclaims, relief washing over her. "I would have been furious had they uprooted my live bell pepper and okra plants."

Just then, Ryan shuffles into the kitchen, his hair a wild tangle of bedhead, and a yawn escapes his lips. "Hey, what's all the commotion outside?" he asks, rubbing the sleep from his eyes.

"Gardeners are landscaping Rachael's backyard," Duncan replies with a sarcastic smirk.

"No, seriously, what's going on out there?" Ryan asks, peering curiously through the back door window.

"They're looking for more bones that might belong to the two Beau found yesterday," I explain, trying to keep my voice steady despite how unsettling it all is. "Remember when Beau brought that first bone into the house?"

"Of course I remember," Ryan says, pouring himself a steaming mug of coffee, his brow furrowed in thought. "But I didn't think the cops would make such a big deal out of it."

"What did you expect?" Duncan chimes in, raising an eyebrow as if he's just heard the most ridiculous thing. "You think the cops would take those two bones and leave it at that, calling it a day?"

"Not really," Ryan admits with a shrug as he takes a sip of his coffee. "But why all this fuss over a couple of old bones? It all seems a bit much, don't you think?"

"It wouldn't be such a big deal if the bones weren't human," Duncan replies, his voice steady but tinged with unease. "But since they're human remains, it changes everything."

Ryan leans against the counter, staring at the floor as if the weight of our conversation is pressing down on him. "Yeah, I guess you're right. But still... how did those bones end up there? It just seems strange, you know?"

"Welcome to small-town life," I say with a half-hearted

chuckle. "You never know what kind of drama will unfold next."

Duncan shakes his head, still looking out the window where the police are combing through the garden with shovels and rakes. "Let's just hope they find what they're looking for quickly and put this whole episode to rest, for Rachael's sake."

"Agreed," Ryan replies, worry seeping into his voice. "Honestly, this is all too creepy." A noticeable shiver runs down his spine as his thoughts manifest physically. The air grows thick with tension; every shadow seems to stretch and twist in the corners of our minds.

Rachael's eyes widen, a mix of disbelief and fear flashing across her face. "Do you think the cops will arrest me? Will they accuse me of killing and burying someone in my yard?"

The question lingers like smoke from a dying fire, obscuring clarity and muffling sound, choking off air, making it hard for Julie to breathe. She hesitates, her uncertainty evident. "No, I doubt that," she replies, though her tone suggests she's not entirely convinced. It's one of those moments where you want to be supportive but can't shake the feeling that things are spiraling out of control.

"You think I am guilty," Rachael snaps suddenly, turning on Julie with an intensity that catches her off guard. "You believe I killed and buried someone in my yard, don't you?"

"I didn't say that," Julie defends herself quickly, raising her hands as if to ward off the accusation. It feels like they're walking a tightrope, where one wrong word could send them both tumbling into chaos.

"But you thought it, didn't you? Admit it, the thought crossed your mind," Rachael retorts sharply, and the tension between them crackles like electricity. It feels like a storm is brewing— intense and unpredictable.

"To be perfectly honest, I haven't known you for very long," Julie replies, her brow furrowing with uncertainty. "I don't know much about you."

The truth is out there, and we're all feeling the weight of the unknown.

"Alright, that's enough out of both of you ladies," Duncan interjects firmly, his stern voice steadying the room. "Let's not jump to conclusions. No one actually believes Rachael has harmed anyone. You're letting your imaginations run wild amidst everything that's going on."

"I'm sorry, Rach," Julie apologizes, her cheeks flushed with embarrassment. "I don't know what came over me. Deep down, I know you're not capable of doing something like that."

"Thanks for having my back, Julie," Rachael replies with a faint smile. "If I were in your shoes, I might have had similar thoughts."

"Now, don't you girls feel better?" Duncan asks, relief evident in his voice as he glances between the two of them. The tension lingers as the girls exchange wary looks, each contemplating the weight of their earlier suspicions. The air is thick with unspoken truths and lingering doubts.

"What have I missed?" Giles asks, stepping into the kitchen with urgency etched on his face, his voice cutting through the lingering tension. The atmosphere shifts abruptly as he surveys the room, sensing the unresolved tension hanging over us all.

Rachael takes a deep breath, preparing to explain the whirlwind of emotions that has led to this moment. "It was just a little misunderstanding," she begins, trying to keep her tone light to ease the heaviness in the room.

Giles raises an eyebrow, intrigued but still cautious. "I hope it's nothing serious. We've got enough drama as it is without stirring up more."

Julie nods vigorously, eager to move past the awkwardness. "Yeah! Let's focus on what really matters."

"Gill, are you just now getting up?" Ryan asks, raising an eyebrow in disbelief.

"No, I've been awake for a while," Giles insists, his voice steady but tinged with tension. "I was looking out the upstairs bedroom window, watching the cops in the backyard."

Duncan leans forward, his curiosity aroused. "Did you notice anything we should be concerned about?"

Giles hesitates for a moment, carefully weighing his words. "I couldn't tell for sure," he begins slowly, "but it looked like they might have retrieved more bones."

A heavy silence falls over the room as the implications of Giles' words sink in, forcing us to confront a tense reality.

"Ah, there go my tomato plants," Rachael quietly mutters to herself, regret evident in her voice.

"What was that, Rach?" Duncan asks, curious about her sudden distraction.

"Oh, it was nothing," she replies with a dismissive wave of her hand, her attempt to downplay the situation. "I was just thinking about the vegetable garden. I could have lost my tomatoes had I planted them earlier."

At this moment, the weight of our conversation clashes with Rachael's seemingly trivial worries about her garden. It's a stark contrast—almost jarring—how life can throw us into disarray while our minds cling to mundane concerns like tomato plants, even when facing something much more serious.

Ryan casually glances around the kitchen, his brow furrowing in thought. "Hey Duncan, where's Izzy? Still getting her *beauty sleep*?"

"Oh no!" Duncan suddenly exclaims, springing from his chair like a startled cat. He rushes to fill the kettle with tap water from the faucet, his movements quick and urgent. "I promised Izzy a cup of tea before leaving the bedroom. How could I have forgotten?" He glances at his wristwatch. "Oh no, look at the time! She's going to kill me."

"Duncan," Ryan says, a hint of mischief in his voice, "you're in luck. When she kills you, the cops have made a fresh hole in the backyard just for you."

As Duncan brushes past him, he pops Ryan on the back of the head.

"Ow! That hurt!" Ryan protests, rubbing the spot where Duncan struck him.

"Good," Duncan retorts with a smirk, mischief dancing in his eyes. "Maybe that'll jump-start your brain." His jab at Ryan's wit brings smiles to everyone's faces.

"What did I say?" Ryan asks, acting innocent.

"Under the circumstances," I gently interject, "that comment probably wasn't the most appropriate thing to say. You have a tendency to speak before you think."

Duncan rolls his eyes, exasperated. "Now, if I can just make this tea before I meet my maker..."

As the kettle's water boils, the kitchen buzzes with a mix of apprehension and lackluster conversation—a dismal start to what should have been a gloriously lazy summer day... if only Beau hadn't discovered that first bone.

Meanwhile, Duncan strides up the stairs to his bedroom, carrying a tray of tea and toast, leaving behind an air of unsettled tension.

Just as I begin to settle into the moment, a sudden knock at the back door pierces the silence—sharp and insistent. Being the closest to the door, I walk over to answer it, curiosity bubbling within me. When I open the door, I find none other than my favorite cop, Sergeant Ramos, one of Lost Creek Junction's finest from last summer's stay in this house.

"Sergeant Ramos," I exclaim, my voice tinged with surprise and a hint of unease, making it sound more like I've bitten into a sour lemon than greeting an old friend. "To what do we owe this unexpected pleasure?"

He furrows his brow as he studies my face. "Do I know you? You look familiar," he replies, his mind clearly working overtime—like a hamster on its squeaky wheel, frantically searching for that elusive memory.

"Let me help you. Picture last year, around this time," I remind him, a hint of sarcasm in my voice. "You responded to our report of an alleged intruder."

"Oh yes, I remember now," Ramos says, a glimmer of recognition lighting up his eyes like a spark in the darkness. "You're the young fellow with the dog, am I right?"

"Correct," I reply with a nod, feeling a strange mix of familiarity and tension in the air. It's interesting how quickly memories can come flooding back, even amidst the unease lingering in the moment. "Oh my gosh! Gill, do you mind corralling Beau before he recognizes Sergeant Ramos' voice?"

"I'm on it," Giles says as he hurries out of the kitchen and heads for the parlor.

"Is Miss Maguire at home?" Ramos asks, his tone shifting to one of official business.

"Rach!" I call out. "It's Sergeant Ramos, here for you."

"Yes, officer," Rachael responds as she steps into view of the open door. Her expression is one of curiosity, like a child waiting for a surprise."

With a respectful tip of his uniform cap, Ramos replies solemnly, "Ma'am, we've reached a conclusion—there appear to be remains of at least two bodies in your yard. We've gathered sufficient evidence to hand this case over to the coroner for autopsies.

"Oh my," Rachael gasps, her hands instinctively flying to her mouth in shock. The severity of the situation hits her like a sudden gust of wind, leaving her momentarily stunned, trying to comprehend the implications for her and her home.

"Wait, what? Two bodies?" I blurt out, my mind racing with questions. "How did two bodies end up here?"

Ramos shifts uncomfortably but maintains his composure. "That's what we'll be investigating. For now, we need to secure the area to gather more evidence."

Rachael's eyes dart back and forth, her mind clearly racing. "This cannot be happening," she murmurs, her voice trembling with fear and disbelief.

I put a reassuring hand on her shoulder. "Take it easy. They'll get to the bottom of this. Just take a deep breath and breathe."

As we stand in the open doorway, the reality of the quiet house on the hill begins to crumble around us like a house of cards. It feels like we're standing on shifting ground, uncertain of what the next moment will bring.

"I must insist that you not leave Lost Creek Junction," Officer Ramos states firmly, his steady gaze fixed on Rachael. "This applies to everyone residing in this house until we receive the coroner's report."

Rachael's eyes widen, her disbelief clear. "Are you saying I am a suspect?" Her voice trembles with a mix of fear and indignation.

"At the moment, we don't have sufficient evidence to draw a definite conclusion," Ramos replies, his tone serious and his words heavy with the weight of the situation. "However, until we gather more information, you and everyone staying in this house are considered *persons of interest*." He pauses, allowing the seriousness of his words to sink in. "You will hear from me once I have more to report. Until then, I suggest none of you leave town."

Tapping the brim of his uniform cap, he turns away from the door, leaving Rachael enveloped in uncertainty. As she turns to face me, I notice tears glistening in her eyes, a whirlwind of emotions swirling within her.

Instinctively, I wrap my arms around her, creating a cocoon of safety amidst the chaos and fear.

"Oh, Taylor," she whispers, her voice trembling with vulnerability. "I am so frightened," she confesses, her fear echoing in the room.

DAY FIFTEEN

Monday, June 3, 2019

As the enticing aroma of freshly brewed coffee fills the air, Giles and I begin our morning jaunt downstairs. This particular morning feels special, filled with a unique anticipation, as Giles has surprisingly managed to wake up before noon. We walk toward the kitchen, but just as we approach, Giles diverts toward the parlor. "I'll let Beau out. You grab our coffees," he calls over his shoulder, his voice full of enthusiasm.

"Remember," I call back, "he needs to go out in the front lawn—we don't want him digging up the backyard. The cops have already done a fine job of that."

"Got it," Giles replies. "Front lawn it is."

With a chuckle, I shake my head at his eagerness to spend time with Beau as I head into the kitchen.

"Good morning!" I cheerfully greet Julie and Rachael, feeling irresistibly drawn to the coffee maker like a magnet to a refrigerator door.

"What's got you in such high spirits today, Taylor?" Julie asks, her eyebrows raised in curiosity. "You seem more cheerful than usual."

Rachael leans in close to Julie with a mischievous glint in her eyes. "I bet he got lucky last night," she teases, her words filled with playful mischief.

"I wish," I chuckle, shaking my head. "Honestly, I'm just in a good mood for no particular reason," I say, a genuine smile spreading across my face.

"Now that's a scary thought," Julie replies, eyeing me suspiciously.

Just then, Duncan strolls into the kitchen, his timing impeccable as always. "What's so scary?" he asks, eyeing each of us independently as if one of us is guilty of a secret.

"Why do you always seem to walk in at the most peculiar moments during our conversations?" Julie teases him, a mischievous glint in her eyes.

Duncan shrugs casually as he watches me pour two steaming mugs of coffee. "In this house," he says with a relaxed grin, "all conversations are peculiar."

He extends his arm expectantly toward me for one of the mugs. I pivot away and toward the table, cradling both mugs in my hands, a playful grin spreading across my face.

"Taylor?" Duncan archs an eyebrow, his tone playful. "When did you become a two-fisted coffee drinker?"

"What?" I chuckle, looking at the two mugs in my hands. "Did you think one of these mugs was for you? Sorry to disappoint, but this extra one is for Gill—he'll want it after walking Beau."

"Wow, surprises never cease," Duncan exclaims, his voice filled with genuine shock. "Gill is actually up and about before lunch?"

"Surprising, isn't it?" I nod, enjoying the moment. Just then, the tone shifts as Isadora shuffles into the kitchen like a ghoulish zombie. Her hair is tousled, and she's wrapped in an oversized hoodie that could probably shelter a small village. With her face free of makeup, I can't help but wish she had put some on before coming downstairs—she looks a bit frightening in her disheveled state.

"Dunkie," she calls out urgently, "where's my tea?"

"I didn't want to make it until you came downstairs," Duncan explains, a hint of concern creeping into his voice. "I know how much you dislike lukewarm tea." With a determined stride, he heads toward the kettle to prepare Isadora's favorite morning brew, his caring nature evident in every step.

Rachael glances at each of us at the kitchen table, her brow furrowing slightly. "We should probably move to the dining room," she suggests, gracefully standing up. Her elegance commands respect. "This kitchen table simply will not accommodate all of us."

"Oh, please don't move on my account," Isadora interjects, waving her hand dismissively. "I just came for my tea, and then I'll be going back upstairs. I need to get dressed—Dunkie is taking me on a tour of the house today."

"Watch your step in the attic," Julie warns, her voice filled with urgency. "There are bats up there, and believe me, they smell awful."

Isadora's eyes widen in disbelief. "Bats?" she gasps, shaking off a shiver. "Dunkie, you didn't say anything about bats."

Duncan, always the embodiment of calm reassurance, offers Isadora a warm smile as he extends a delicate cup and saucer of steaming tea toward her. "Don't worry, Izzy," he replies soothingly. "We're not going anywhere near the attic today, or any day." He flashes a quick side-eye at Julie.

"Oh, thank goodness!" Isadora sighs dramatically in relief, gently blowing on her cup to cool the inviting warmth of the tea. "I really should head back upstairs and get ready. I don't want to keep my Dunkie Wunkie waiting." With that, she turns and exits the room, leaving behind the lingering scent of English breakfast tea and a sour taste in everyone's mouth—a bitter reminder of the unspoken tension that seems to idle in the air when Isadora is present.

As the rest of us gather our coffee mugs and make our way into the dining room, Giles trails behind after taking Beau outside. When he joins us, I hand him a steaming mug, the rich aroma filling the air. "Did you have any trouble with Beau?" I ask, curious about whether my 'boy' had been on his best behavior.

"Nope," he replies with a smile. "He was a perfect gentleman."

I chuckle, recalling Beau's antics from last summer. "Guys, remember when Beau found that old stick last year? He became so possessive of it. He acted like it was made of gold or something. He'd stash it under the settee cushions whenever he went outside, and when he was indoors, he'd guard it as if it were his most prized possession."

"That doesn't sound like Beau," Giles says, his voice tinged with disbelief as he raises a skeptical eyebrow. "He's always willing to share his things."

"I know, right?" I nod in agreement. "There was just something about that stick that brought out a whole new side of him."

"Whatever happened to that stick?" Julie asks, interrupting the memory.

"I honestly don't know," I reply. "It's funny—I hadn't thought about that stick until just now. Isn't it strange how some memories fade away as if they never existed, and then something triggers them, causing them to pop up unexpectedly?"

"Not really," Duncan interjects with a knowing smile. "When we step away from familiar places, it's like our minds hit the pause button on the small details. They only resurface when something sparks them back to life."

I nod thoughtfully, taking a sip of my coffee as I reflect on his words.

A gentle stillness settles around us, each of us lost in our own thoughts. It's true—sometimes it takes a random comment or a shared laugh to awaken a memory. Our memories are not just our own; they are shared experiences that connect us in unexpected ways.

Suddenly, breaking the reflective silence, Rachael's voice cuts through, emerging from a fog of her own thoughts. "Not to change the subject, but I was wondering, how long does it take to get a coroner's report?"

"In Texas, it can take a month or even longer," Duncan replies, his tone steady yet weighed down with uncertainty.

"A month? That long?" Rachael exclaims, her eyes widening in disbelief.

"Keep in mind, in your case, they're working only with

bones, not a full corpse," Duncan explains gently to soften the blow.

"A whole month, you say?" Rachael's frustration is clear. "This waiting is going to drive me straight into the loony bin."

"There may be additional delays," Duncan says. "I doubt Lost Creek Junction has its own coroner. The bones were likely sent to Ballinger, Austin, or possibly even San Antonio for the autopsy."

"Why so far away?" Julie asks.

"Well," Duncan begins, leaning back in his chair as he considers her question, "those places have the resources and expertise needed for forensic analysis. Smaller towns like Lost Creek Junction don't have the facilities to handle something like this properly."

"Even so," Rachael murmurs, her anxiety evident as she twists her hands in front of her, "I cannot shake the feeling that we should have heard something by now."

"Patience, Rach," Duncan replies gently, his voice steady. "It's only been, what, eight or nine days? We have to trust the process."

Just then, a sharp, urgent knock at the door shatters our peaceful morning, demanding immediate attention.

"Who do you suppose that is?" Rachael asks curiously, her eyes darting at each of us. "Are any of you expecting someone?"

Beau—the ever-vigilant canine doorbell—barks fiercely, his sharp, staccato barks echoing through the parlor, before letting out a low growl that rumbles like distant thunder.

"If I had to guess," I chime in with a hint of humor, "I'd say it's Sergeant Ramos at the door. Beau has never liked him one bit."

With a shared glance of apprehension and intrigue, I follow Rachael into the parlor. As she approaches the front door, I usher Beau into an adjacent room to keep him from tearing the unexpected guest to shreds.

"Sergeant Ramos," Rachael exclaims, her voice filled with genuine surprise as she opens the door. "What brings you here?

I cannot imagine you have news for me, do you?"

Ramos stands stoically at the open door, his expression unreadable. The tension in the parlor thickens as we await his response, each second stretching longer than the last.

"Good morning, Miss Maguire," he replies smoothly. When his gaze shifts to me, standing beside Rachael, he adds with a hint of distaste, "Mr. Greene." The way he says my name is as if he just bit into a sour candy—sharp and uninviting. "The coroner's report has come back," Ramos states flatly.

"So soon?" I respond, a twinge of dread creeping in.

"I won't beat around the bush. The cause of death suggests possible decapitation," Ramos states matter-of-factly.

"Oh dear," Rachael gasps, her hands flying to her face as if to shield herself from the horror she has just encountered. The weight of the report hangs in the air like a thick cloud, suffocating and unsettling.

"I'm truly sorry about the blunt results of the report," Ramos replies, his voice steady but laced with concern. He removes his uniform cap and cradles it in the crook of his arm, a gesture that reflects the seriousness of the situation.

"But there's something else you should know..."

"Yes, Sergeant?" Rachael asks, her eyes wide with anticipation.

Ramos takes a deep breath, his expression becoming very official. "Neither you nor anyone staying in this house is now considered a *person of interest*," he states firmly, his gaze unwavering.

Rachael sighs, a heavy breath of relief escaping her as the tension of the investigation finally eases.

"What changed in the investigation?" I interject.

"Unless someone here is over two hundred years old," he adds with an almost wry smile, "none of you could possibly be suspects."

"Excuse me, I am not following," Rachael admits, her brow creasing in confusion as the mystery continues to linger in the air.

"During the coroner's examination of the bones, a chilling revelation emerged. To confirm his suspicions, he sent a few samples to the Radiocarbon Preparation Laboratory at Texas A&M University in College Station for further analysis. It turns out that no one currently living in this house could possibly be the murderer or have buried the victims in your yard," Detective Ramos states, his tone carrying the weight of certainty.

"Why do you say that?" I ask.

Ramos leans forward toward Rachael, his gaze intent. "The bones unearthed from your yard, Miss Maguire, belonged to two males who lived over two hundred years ago," he explains, a hint of astonishment in his voice.

"How do you know that?" Rachael interjects before I can voice the identical question.

"The carbon dating tests conducted at Texas A&M revealed a startling discovery—the bones found in your backyard are nearly two centuries old. What's particularly intriguing," he adds, "is that not a single skull was recovered during the entire excavation. How strange is that? Your yard was thoroughly searched, and every bone belonging to the two male victims is accounted for—except for their skulls."

"How is it possible that the bones haven't decayed?" I ask. "You would think that after two hundred years—"

"Human bones have remarkable resilience," he explains. "Unlike animal remains, they don't decompose as easily. When buried in the right soil composition and in a dry climate like ours, they could for all intents and purposes remain in excellent condition for thousands of years."

"So, let me get this straight," I say, turning to Ramos with a mix of disbelief and curiosity. "Are you saying that because the bones discovered in Rachael's yard are nearly two hundred years old, everyone in this house—including Rachael—is no longer considered a suspect in an alleged crime?"

Ramos shakes his head slightly, a hint of amusement playing at the corners of his mouth. "No one was ever considered a suspect. You and your friends were merely *persons of interest* until we gathered sufficient evidence to file charges."

Rachael leans forward, her brow knitted with concern. "So, there is absolutely no evidence against us now?" she asks, her voice teetering on relief.

"That is correct," Ramos replies with a wry smile. "Unless one of you happens to be two hundred years old. I appreciate your patience throughout this investigation. Someone from my office will return later to remove the yellow crime tape from your backyard."

"Thank you, Sergeant," Rachael says, her voice warm and appreciative.

"Ma'am," Ramos replies with a crisp salute as he adjusts his uniform cap back on his head and strides off the porch. I can't help but notice that he didn't glance in my direction or acknowledge me before leaving—just another reminder of the invisible walls that sometimes separate us.

As I watch him go, I feel a mix of relief and lingering questions. Where did those bones come from? How did they end up buried in Rachael's yard? These questions occupy my mind, fueling my curiosity. One thing's for sure: this isn't over yet. The legal aspect of this mystery may be resolved, but curiosity has a way of digging deeper than any shovel can.

Rachael and I head back to the dining room, where the comforting sounds of animated conversation fills the air. Ryan has joined Giles and Julie at the table, their laughter mingling with the clinking of mugs. The warmth of the room and the familiar faces make me feel at ease.

"Where's Duncan?" I ask, scanning the room.

"Remember? He's giving Izzy a tour of the house," Ryan replies with a grin.

"Hey, Taylor, who do I have to sleep with to get my personal tour?" Giles asks, his eyes sparkling with mischief.

"Whenever you want," I respond with a sly wink, settling into the chair beside him. The atmosphere buzzes with curiosity.

"So, who was at the door? If you don't mind me asking," Giles inquires.

"Actually, the person at the door brought news that involves all of us," I reply.

"What do you mean?" Julie interjects, her eyes wide with intrigue, her lacquered nails tapping against her mug.

"That was Sergeant Ramos—oh, wait!" I gasp, suddenly realizing I've forgotten something. "Beau is still locked in the other room. I have to let him out. Excuse me." With that, I dash out of the room, my heart racing and thoughts swarming like bees to a hive. The air feels heavy with anticipation, and the sound of my fast-paced footsteps echoes through the parlor. In my rushing, I can't shake the feeling that the news Sergeant Ramos brought with him is about to change everything. What had started as a relaxing morning filled with laughter and coffee now feels charged with unspoken tension and pending doom.

After releasing Beau from the adjacent room, he runs to the front door, sniffing at it, trying to track down the scent of a traitor who entered the house. Shaking my head in amusement, I return to the dining room, my heart racing with anticipation. Rachael is putting the finishing touches on the briefing that Ramos had just delivered, and the atmosphere is filled with relief.

"So, does this mean all the drama of the past week is finally over?" Ryan asks.

"Actually," Julie interjects, her voice tinged with concern, "this may just be the beginning."

"What makes you say that?" I ask, eager for answers.

Julie leans back, arms crossed, and gives me a knowing look. "Think about it for a moment. We're dealing with the remains of two two-hundred-year-old men—two male victims—and get this—no heads. Does anyone in particular come to mind?"

"Oh crap," Ryan exclaims, his eyes widening in realization. "Are you suggesting what I think you're suggesting?"

"Exactly! It's Ezekiel and Abrahim!" Julie declares, her voice a mix of excitement and dread that sends shivers down everyone's spines. "This could just be the beginning."

Rachael sits across the table, her brows furrowed and

confusion etched on her forehead. "But why do you say this is the beginning? The beginning of what?"

"Don't you see the bigger picture?" Julie insists, urgency gripping her voice. "Disturbing the bones of Ezekiel and Abrahim could have further riled up those two restless spirits, setting them on a path of vengeance for disturbing their resting places."

Ryan shakes his head, skepticism casting a heavy shadow. "It's been nearly two weeks since their bones were discovered. They've done nothing."

"Nothing that we are aware of," Julie counters, her tone resolute. "Just wait... one of these nights, when we least expect it, all hell might break loose."

The room falls silent, and tension crackles in the air like static electricity.

"Do you really believe that after two hundred years, those ghosts are going to care about their graves being disturbed?" I interject.

Julie leans in, her eyes burning with intensity. "Duh, just look how fiercely they guard that gold mine—even after two centuries, and it doesn't even belong to them." She pauses for dramatic effect. "And now we know—or at least suspect—that Mrs. Scruggs buried the bodies in a shallow grave right in her backyard."

"Hold on a second," I say, raising an eyebrow. "Do we have definitive proof that Mrs. Scruggs was the one who buried those bodies?"

Ryan jumps into the conversation in his usual top of the head manner. "Sure, why not? Their bones were discovered in what used to be her backyard."

"But that doesn't necessarily prove she did it," I counter.

Julie nods thoughtfully, acknowledging my point. "I understand where you're coming from. But think about it—no matter who buried those two men, disturbing their remains could ignite a powder keg of unrest among those two ghosts. We may not have witnessed the full extent of the havoc Ezekiel and Abrahim are capable of unleashing. We could be on the verge of a reign of terror like we've never imagined."

Dale Thele

DAY SIXTEEN

Tuesday, June 4, 2019

It's nighttime, and the Blackburn house is enveloped in a sleepy stillness—a tranquil sanctuary where dreams drift through the darkness. However, that peace shatters like glass when I wake up with an urgent need to use the bathroom. After a quick trip, I snuggle back under the sheets, ready to slip once more into dreamland. Just as I begin to surrender to sleep's embrace, a piercing scream slices through the silence, jolting me upright. My heart races as I leap from the bed, my mind convinced that something terrible has happened downstairs, and my body is already in motion before I fully comprehend the situation.

Wrapped in a bathrobe, my socked feet whisper against the soft fibers of the oriental runner rug as I scurry down the second-floor hallway and descend the stairs. In the kitchen, I find Julie—her face pale and her eyes wide with shock. Beside her sits Beau, my loyal dog, gazing up at her with concern etched across his furry face. His eyes reflect confusion as he whines softly.

"What's going on?" I ask as I step into the kitchen. "Julie, are you alright?"

"I'm fine," she replies, though her voice trembles like a fragile leaf in the wind. "It's just... I saw a shadow at the window."

"What kind of shadow?" I probe, trying to keep my tone light despite the tension in the air. "Was it a bird?"

"No," Julie gasps, her eyes wide with fear. "It was a person."

My heart races as I press for details. "Was it a man or a woman?"

"I don't know," she stammers, her breath hitching in her throat. "All I saw was the shadow, but it felt like they were staring right at me."

Just then, Duncan bursts into the kitchen. "What's going on? I thought I heard a scream."

"You did," I confirm, glancing back at Julie, who's still visibly shaken. "It was Julie—she saw someone outside the window."

Duncan's eyes dart to Julie and then back to me. "A person? Are you serious? Like... out there?" He gestures toward the backyard beyond the window, his voice rising slightly.

"Yeah," I reply, trying to remain calm. "Do you think we should check it out?"

Julie shakes her head vigorously. "No! Don't open the door—they might still be outside, and they could force themselves inside."

"Okay, okay," I say quickly, sensing her panic rising again. "Let's just stay calm and keep our heads. Maybe it was nothing."

As I huddle with Duncan and Julie in the kitchen, a sinking feeling settles in my thoughts, casting a darkness over my mind. The shadows outside stretch and twist in the moonlight, and suddenly, it feels as though we're being watched, as if we're no longer alone.

"Julie, what were you doing in the kitchen at this unearthly hour?" Duncan's voice, filled with concern, breaks through the eerie silence, heightening the suspense.

"I came downstairs for a glass of milk," Julie replies, her voice trembling with unease.

"Don't you girls ever sleep?" Duncan asks, his tone a mix of concern and frustration, likely recalling the night Rachael got up for cookies and milk in the middle of the night. "Never mind, just tell me what happened."

"Like I said, I came downstairs for a glass of milk," Julie reiterates.

Duncan's eyes widen, alarm flickering across his face as he takes a step closer to her. "Did they see you?"

"Probably not at first—just like I hadn't noticed them," Julie says, wringing her hands as she recalls the moment. "I hadn't turned on any lights yet. But when I opened the fridge door, the light inside illuminated the room, and that's when I saw the shadow and when they saw me. Then the shadow disappeared. The fridge light probably startled them."

"Well, under these unsettling circumstances," Duncan says firmly, his protective instincts kicking in, "we need to check that all doors and windows are secured and locked. It's better to be safe than sorry."

"Julie," I ask, glancing at the partially open back door, "did you open that door?" The air crackles with tension as we exchange worried glances.

"Oh my lord, no!" Julie gasps, shaking her head in disbelief. "I had no idea it was open."

Duncan steps forward, his brow furrowed with concern. "Taylor," he begins cautiously, "when you let Beau out before going to bed, did you close and lock this door when he came back inside?"

"I'm certain I did," I respond, absentmindedly petting Beau's head as he sits quietly beside me, watching us like a moderator overseeing a tense meeting.

With suspicion etched on his face, Duncan closes and latches the door firmly. The sound of the latch clicking echoes through the quiet room, amplifying the tension in the air and providing us with a false sense of security—a thin veil over our vulnerability.

Julie moves toward the window above the sink, the very spot where she saw that ominous shadow just moments earlier. Nervously, she scans the backyard for signs of movement. The moonlight casts eerie shadows across the lawn, and every rustle seems magnified, deepening the mystery.

"Do you think they're still out there?" she whispers, her voice barely audible.

"Doubtful," Duncan replies. "If someone was still out there, Beau would definitely let us know. Wouldn't you boy?"

Beau lets out a quick bark in acknowledgment.

Suddenly, Ryan strolls into the kitchen, yawning widely. His bare feet slap against the cool floor as he rubs the sleep from his eyes. "Hey, what's going on?" he asks, his voice groggy from sleep.

"Julie saw someone peeking through the kitchen window," I explain, my voice trembling slightly.

"Who was it?" Ryan asks, peering out the window into the dark, as if trying to identify whatever might be lurking outside.

"She only saw a shadow," Duncan interjects, cutting through the tension as he steps out of the room and heads toward the parlor.

"What are we doing about it?" Ryan inquires, his brow furrowed with deep concern, reflecting the worry in the room.

"We're making sure that every door and window is securely locked," I reply, testing the doorknob of the locked side door that leads to the detached garage. The darkness closes in around us, its heaviness intensified by the possible presence of lurking, indistinct shadows.

"Everything's secure in here," Duncan calls as he emerges from the parlor, his tone steady but tinged with urgency.

"The kitchen is locked up tight," I confirm, glancing at Ryan, who's surveying our surroundings with the intensity of a hawk. The air is thick with unease, and the hum of the fridge stands in jarring contrast to the silence around us. We exchange wary glances, each of us acutely aware of the unsettling atmosphere.

Just then, Isadora shuffles into the kitchen, her hair tousled and her puffy eyes still heavy with sleep. "Dunkie," she mumbles, rubbing her eyes. "Why is everyone out of bed?"

"Julie saw someone," Duncan replies, his voice grave and his eyes reflecting the seriousness of the situation. The weight of his words hangs in the air, amplifying the growing sense of alarm.

"In the house?" Isadora gasps, her wide eyes reflecting a mix of fear and disbelief, her shock echoing in the silence.

"No," Duncan says, his voice steady but laced with concern.

"Julie saw something—or someone—lurking outside the kitchen window."

"Who saw someone?" Giles asks as he steps into the room, skillfully tying the belt of his bathrobe, still half-asleep and bewildered.

"Julie caught a glimpse of a shadowy figure outside the window," I explain, my heart racing as the words spill from my mouth.

"Did someone try to break in?" Giles asks, frowning as he processes this unsettling news.

"Apparently not," Duncan replies, glancing toward the window as if expecting the shadow to reappear. "At least not that we know of. But it's still unnerving, isn't it?"

"Yeah, it is," I agree, my voice isn't as steady as I'd like.

The air is thick with tension as we exchange glances, half-expecting the figure to reappear. It's far too late in the night for this kind of drama.

"Shouldn't we call the cops?" Giles suggests, his voice rising slightly as urgency creeps into our conversation. The shadows outside seem to loom larger, and the tension in the room coils like a snake, alert and watchful. We're all on edge, our senses heightened.

"Without solid evidence, I'm not diving into that rabbit hole with Sergeant Ramos—what a jerk," Duncan declares, his frustration boiling over. He crosses his arms tightly over his chest, as if trying to shield himself from the very thought of the man.

"What's the deal with this Sergeant Ramos guy?" Giles asks, his curiosity evident as he tries to understand why Duncan dislikes the man.

"He's a complete idiot," Ryan interjects, shaking his head in annoyance at the mere mention of Ramos' name. "Last summer, we faced a similar situation, and Ramos dismissed us as having *overactive imaginations*." His disdain for Ramos is clear in every word he utters.

"I really don't want to go through that again," Duncan insists, his voice firm and resolute. "Not unless we have more than just Julie claiming she saw a shadow at the window."

"Hey!" Julie protests, her voice rising defensively. "I didn't *claim* I saw something—I actually *did* see someone." Her eyes widen with indignation, frustration bubbling inside her as she feels her experience is being dismissed.

"Alright, everyone, let's take a breath," Ryan suggests calmly. "It's late, and I doubt Duncan questions whatever Julie saw. I certainly don't. The issue is that we don't have proof to show Ramos." He offers Julie an encouraging smile, trying to ease the tension that hangs in the air, making each breath feel like a struggle against the weight of the situation.

I hadn't mentioned—and I assume Rachael hadn't either—that Ramos was the cop Rachael was working with regarding the bones found in her backyard. I see no reason to stir things up by bringing this up to the people currently in the room.

We all sit nervously around the kitchen table, weighed down by a heavy silence as we grapple with our circumstances. "You know," Ryan breaks the silence with a playful grin, "since we're already up, how about we make some grilled cheese sandwiches?"

Julie rolls her eyes, a playful smirk on her lips. "There you go again, Rye," she teases. "Thinking with your stomach instead of your brain."

I chuckle softly and add, "Actually, grilled cheese doesn't sound all that bad."

Duncan shifts his weight, his eyes sparkling with mischief. "What about scrambled egg sandwiches instead? That could be even better," he suggests.

Ryan's eyes light up at the suggestion. "You know what? I'm sold. Egg sandwiches it is."

"Hey, everyone," I call out, scanning the room with a concerned glance. "Where's Rach?"

"Seriously," Ryan chimes in, looking equally puzzled. "Where is she?" His brows wrinkle in concern, adding a worrisome tone to his voice.

"I'll go upstairs and see if she wants to join our midnight snack attack," Julie volunteers, rising from the table where she had been seated, her eyes sparkling with excitement at the thought of late-night treats. She pushes her chair back under the table with a loud screech that echoes in the room and walks toward the staircase, her long strides quickly closing the distance.

"No way," Ryan interjects, shaking his head like a determined bobblehead mounted in the rear window of a car on a pothole filled street. "Julie, you had a scare tonight. I'll go tell Rach. Besides, you always send me to check on people." His voice, filled with a mix of annoyance and amusement.

With that, Ryan marches up the stairs, his purposeful steps reflecting his determination. Meanwhile, Julie grabs a hefty cast-iron skillet from the cupboard. I dive into the fridge, gathering eggs and mustard—because who doesn't love a little zing? On the other hand, Duncan, the carb enthusiast, rummages through the pantry for bread.

At the kitchen table sits Isadora, slouched like a wilting flower, her eyelids heavy with sleep. She's about as useful as a bump on a log. What in the world does Duncan see in her? Sure, she's stunning—like one of those fashion models gracing the cover of those women's magazines—but when it comes to brains, let's be honest: she's as sharp as a polished marble.

A few moments later, a breathless Ryan appears at the top of the stairs, urgency gripping his voice as he yells down to us, "Rachael's not in her room!"

"Are you sure?" I ask, raising an eyebrow in surprise at Ryan's revelation.

"I'm absolutely certain," Ryan insists, practically bouncing on his feet.

"Oh no," Duncan groans, a heavy mix of dread flooding his tone. "It's happening again. Is everyone ready for a rousing game of hide-and-seek with our favorite ghoulish friends— Ezekiel and Abrahim?"

"What do you mean by *hide-and-seek*?" Giles asks, his

confusion deepening as he knits his brow.

"Let me explain," I say, fixing my gaze on Giles. "Last summer was a nightmare. Ezekiel and Abrahim abducted Duncan and Julie on two separate occasions. We searched the entire house for them—it felt like a twisted, sick game of hide-and-seek."

"Oh, I understand," Giles replies, shaking his head as if trying to rid himself of the absurdity of the situation.

"Duncan," Julie says thoughtfully, "do you really think Ezekiel and Abrahim are behind Rachael's disappearance?"

"Well, let's see," Duncan hesitates, rubbing the back of his neck. "Why would we suspect them? Those ghosts have no real reason to be angry with any of us—especially not Rachael. First, the cops dug up their buried skeletons from unmarked graves in the backyard, which isn't unusual. Then there's the gold mine they believe belongs to them, which was sold off, lock, stock, and barrel, against their will. Honestly, I don't see any reason for them to be upset about what's been going on around here."

"Okay," Julie replies, her voice steady but filled with urgency, the weight of the situation pressing down on her. "You don't need to get snippy about it. You've made your point."

"Dunkikins, I don't get it. Hide-and-seek?" Isadora twists her brow in confusion. "What does that even mean?"

"Sweetums, it means that the ghosts of Ezekiel and Abrahim have likely kidnapped and hidden Rachael, and it's up to us to find her," Duncan explains, his tone grave yet resolute.

"Can't we just call out *Olly olly oxen free?*" Isadora suggests hopefully, a hint of naive innocence in her voice.

"If only it were that simple," Ryan replies, shaking his head. "These ghosts don't follow any rules—at least none that we understand. They make them up as they go."

I look around the kitchen at my friends, feeling the weight of our predicament. Fear and determination mingle in the air. "It looks like we need to pair up in groups of two to search the house," I propose, trying to bring some semblance of strategy to our frantic situation.

"Wouldn't we cover more ground if we searched separately?" Giles counters, his skepticism hanging heavily in the room and casting doubt on my proposal.

"Yes, we would," I acknowledge. "But by teaming up, we reduce the chances of one of us disappearing at the hands of the ghosts—at least for tonight. Their previous strategy has been to snatch one of us when we were alone."

Giles nods slowly, beginning to see my point. The tension in the group is thick, with each member bracing themselves for the challenges ahead.

"Alright, everyone, listen up," I announce as I assign teams. "Duncan, you and Izzy—"

"I want to partner with Julie," Duncan declares, his confidence disrupting the team dynamics. "We made a great team last summer. Why wouldn't we be just as awesome this time around?"

I turn to Julie and raise an eyebrow. "Is that okay with you?" I ask, giving her a graceful way out of what could be an awkward situation.

"Sure, I guess I'm okay with it," she replies with a casual shrug, clearly not invested in the decision.

"Alright then," I concede reluctantly, sensing the shift in dynamics. Duncan's enthusiasm is contagious, but I can't shake the feeling that this might complicate our search and stir up potential conflict within the group. The tension is thickening, and the air crackles with the anticipation of what's to come.

"Rye, you're with me," I announce.

"Uh, if it's alright with you, can I partner up with Gill instead?" Ryan asks, his voice tinged with uncertainty, as if he's testing the limits of our group dynamics.

"If Gill's on board, then I don't see why not," I reply, making a conscious effort to keep the mood light and flexible, keeping my jealousy in check.

Giles responds with a casual shrug of indifference.

Ryan grins, but his acceptance of the change in plans worries me.

I squint at Ryan, intrigued by his behavior. His eagerness to partner with my Giles seems a bit excessive, and I can't help but wonder what's behind it.

"That leaves Izzy and me as the final team," I conclude. "Duncan, you and Julie search the garage and the garage apartment. Rye and Gill, you guys tackle the second and third floors, as well as the attic. Let's find Rachael and solve this mystery!"

"Gill, just a heads up—be careful in the attic—there are bats up there," Julie warns with a playful smirk.

"Got it," Giles chuckles, giving a thumbs-up. "I'll keep my eyes peeled for both Rachael and any flying mammals. Who knows, maybe I'll make a new friend up there."

Julie rolls her eyes playfully at Giles's joke but smiles nonetheless.

With our teams set, I finalize our assignments: "So that leaves Izzy and me to comb the first floor and the basement. Any questions?"

"Do I really have to go down into that dismal old basement?" Isadora whines, wrinkling her nose at the thought and crossing her arms defensively like a stubborn child. "It smells bad, and there are creepy crawlies down there."

"Don't worry, Izzy," I say, flashing her a reassuring smile. "I'll brave the darkness while you stay upstairs in the kitchen."

"That might not be the best idea," Julie interjects, her voice steady and serious. "We should stick together, no matter what. We don't want anyone else going missing—not tonight."

Duncan nods in agreement. "Julie's right. Izzy, it won't hurt you to join Taylor down there for just a little while. Besides, how unpleasant can it be for just a few minutes?"

Isadora scrunches her face like a pug dog, as if she can already smell something truly awful wafting up from below. The damp, musty air of the cellar seems to have reached her nostrils. The thought of going down into the basement makes her shiver.

"Come on, it won't be that bad," I say, trying to lighten the mood. "We'll only be down there for a short time, because the cellar isn't all that big."

Isadora lets out a dramatic, yet reluctant sigh. "Fine, but if we come across any creepy spiders or weird smells, I'm totally blaming you guys for making me do this."

"Deal," I reply with a grin. "Alright, everyone, let's spread out and search for Rachael. We'll reconvene back here in the kitchen in about half an hour." I check the time on my watch.

With determination, Isadora and I head into the parlor, despite her reluctance. As we enter, Beau, my ever-curious and eager companion, gives me a questioning look from the settee. "Beau," I ask with a smile, "do you want to help us search for Rachael?"

In response, he barks as if he fully understands the mission. Without missing a beat, he jumps down from the settee and starts sniffing the floor intently, as though searching for Rachael's scent. I don't have the heart to ruin his night by explaining the difference between a Great Dane and a Bloodhound. However, his heart is in the right place. Despite our best search efforts on the first floor they yield nothing, our little trio presses on to the cellar.

Isadora and I, united in our mission, cautiously descend the creaky wooden stairs, our hearts pounding with fear of what lies ahead. Meanwhile, Beau, our loyal sentry, positions himself at the kitchen doorway at the top of the stairs, his eyes wide with uncertainty about the dark, confined space below. It's understandable; who wouldn't feel uneasy about venturing into the darkness? He remains upstairs, in the light, guarding the door.

As Izzy and I reach the bottom of the stairs, the musty air envelops us, carrying the scent of decay and lost memories. The dim light from our flashlights casts eerie shadows on the damp, cracked walls. I glance at Isadora, who's covering her nose with a handkerchief. "Alright, let's split up," I suggest, trying my best to limit our time down here. "I'll take this side of the cellar while you check the shelves on that opposite wall."

"You know," I begin, sweeping my flashlight beam across the shadowy corners of the cellar, "last summer, when we first ventured down here, Julie discovered an old leather-bound cookbook. She was fascinated by it but utterly perplexed—it was written in a foreign language that made no sense to her."

"Really? How fascinating," Isadora replies coolly, her curiosity fully ignited as she examines the containers of herbs lining the shelves, their fading labels barely visible in the glow of her flashlight. "Do you recall what happened to that cookbook?"

"If I'm not mistaken, I seem to remember Julie putting it back on one of those shelves you're standing in front of," I say, casting my light around my half of the cellar one last time. The air is thick with the musty scent of forgotten things, and I can't shake the feeling that we're not alone down here. The damp walls seem to be closing in on us, the silence interrupted only by the occasional scurrying of unseen creatures. "Well, it seems Rach isn't down here after all." With a sigh, I turn towards the stairs leading back to the kitchen.

Isadora remains rooted, her fingers sifting through the jumble of shelves with the unwavering determination of a true treasure hunter. Her eyes shine with the thrill of discovery.

"What are you looking for?" I ask, my voice echoing in the dimly lit room. "Rachael isn't down here, so we can head back upstairs." Isadora doesn't respond immediately, her hands still busy among the bottles on the shelves.

She seems lost in her own world, focused on a task other than finding Rachael, as her flashlight dances over jars and containers filled with herbs and oddities. It feels as though she's on a separate mission. Suddenly, a burst of excitement lights up her face. "Aha! I found you!" she exclaims, her determination shining through. However, her thrill quickly shifts to a calculated indifference. "Is this the book you mentioned that Julie found?" she asks coolly, directing the beam of her flashlight at a leather-bound book lurking in the shadows, as if it's calling out to be discovered.

"Yeah," I nod. "That's the one."

Isadora eagerly flips through the pages, her eyes wide with wonder as she studies the strange symbols and illustrations illuminated by her flashlight. Her fascination is unwavering.

"You won't understand it," I caution, trying to keep her grounded. "The book isn't written in English. It might be in some ancient language—a mystery waiting to be unraveled."

"Do you think Rachael would mind if I borrowed this book?" Isadora asks, a spark of curiosity flashes in her eyes like lightning during a storm.

"I don't see why not," I reply, my fingers brushing against something familiar. I aim the light from my flashlight at the object. "My goodness, look at this—it's Beau's stick, the one he found last summer. It's just a simple piece of a tree branch, but it held a certain charm for him. How peculiar that it ended up on a shelf down here in the cellar. I remember how much Beau adored this stick—he treated it as if it were made of gold. What was it about this simple piece of wood that captured his heart so completely? It was his most cherished possession during our stay last summer."

"Perhaps I should take the stick with me and surprise Beau with it as a gift," Isadora suggests, her voice filled with excitement.

"Oh, he would absolutely love that," I say just as a joyful bark echoes from upstairs, where Beau is peering into the dimly lit cellar through the open door. "Looks like he heard us talking about him," I chuckle as I make my way toward the stairs.

"I won't let Beau in on our little plan," Isadora whispers, concealing both the book and Beau's stick in her robe as she climbs ahead of me. "This will be our secret," she adds, a hint of mischief in her voice.

As we ascend toward the light of the kitchen, I can't help but smile at the thought of Beau's delight when he is reunited with his beloved stick. His tail wagging furiously, his eyes sparkling with joy. Giving that stick to Beau will ensure that Isadora will be his friend for life.

Cautiously, we emerge from the oppressive darkness of the cellar, and the kitchen unfolds before us like a painting coming to life. It takes a moment for my eyes to adjust to the sudden burst of light. Duncan and Julie stand before me, their expectant expressions brightening their faces.

"Did you guys find anything?" I ask Duncan with hopeful anticipation.

"We've turned the place upside down, but found nothing," Duncan sighs, his frustration evident. "There's no sign of Rach in the garage or the apartment above it." His words hang heavily in the air, a collective sense of disappointment settling over us.

"We even searched the yard and perimeter of the house— nothing," Julie says. Worry lines appear across her forehead as concern etches her face. "What about you and Izzy? Any luck on your end?"

"We found nothing," I reply. "But maybe Rye and Gill will have better luck." The hope in my voice is clear—a glimmer amidst our disappointment, a beacon we cling to in this dark moment.

Just then, Ryan enters the kitchen with Giles, both looking equally defeated. Their shoulders are slumped, and their expressions are grim.

"We've come up empty-handed," Ryan admits, his voice weighed down by disappointment. The shared sense of letdown hangs in the air, creating a sense of frustration among us.

Julie glances at Giles, a teasing smile spreading across her lips. "So, Gill, I see you made it past the bats unscathed?"

"We didn't come across any," Giles replies, a puzzled expression on his face as he looks at Ryan, expecting him to support his statement.

"Strange, but the attic was spotless," Ryan adds, shaking his head. "It seems Rach must have taken care of the bat situation since last summer—there wasn't a trace that they had ever been there."

"Good for her," Julie responds, a hint of admiration in her

tone.

"Looks like we're back to square one," Ryan declares, urgency evident in his voice. "Where could Rach possibly be?"

"I don't know, but we have to find her," Giles replies, his worry undeniable.

"We will, Gill. We will," Julie reassures him, her voice steady despite the uncertainty.

In this moment of doubt, the atmosphere thickens with questions. Everyone's glances unite in our shared concern for Rach, as we search for answers that just aren't there.

"Wait, there's one place we haven't checked yet," Duncan interjects suddenly, his voice breaking through the tension like a gust of wind.

"The gold mine! Of course," Julie exclaims, her voice a mix of fear and excitement.

The thought of the mine sends a chill down my spine; that place gives me the creeps, especially after last summer when I was trapped inside during the cave-in. But this moment isn't about me; it's about finding Rachael. I turn to Giles, trying to keep my composure. "Gill, could you please grab the flashlights from the top drawer of the bureau in our bedroom?"

"Absolutely," Giles beams, his infectious energy lighting up the room as he bounds up the stairs, taking two steps at a time. Beau races after him, barking excitedly as if caught up in a spirited game of chase.

"Duncan," I continue, urgency creeping back into my voice, "would you mind driving us in your Land Rover? That way, we can all ride together in one vehicle—my Jeep can only hold four."

"I'm two steps ahead of you, bro," Duncan replies, holding his jingling keys in the air like a promise of action. "Ready to roll when you are."

Just as we're heading out the door, Giles bursts into the parlor with an armload of extra flashlights, and Beau trots closely beside him.

The atmosphere is charged with urgency as we make our way

into the crisp night air. Duncan jogs to the SUV and unlocks the doors; the overhead lights flicker on to illuminate the interior. That's when we see her—Rachael, bound by ropes and gagged in the back seat, her wide eyes filled with a mix of fear and relief. Panic kicks in, but we're fueled by one goal: to rescue Rachael. We scramble over one another in a flurry of movement. Duncan pulls out his pocket knife, slicing through the rope that binds her wrists with precision, while Julie loosens the bandanna gag that has stifled her voice.

"Hold on, Rach! We're here!" I call out, our hearts racing as we strive to rescue her from the nightmare she's been trapped in. The night is shrouded in darkness, but our determination shines like a beacon, guiding her back into the world of the living.

Duncan's concern is genuine as he asks, "Rach, are you okay?"

Rachael blinks in confusion, scanning her unfamiliar surroundings. "Where am I?" she replies, bewilderment etched on her face, appearing more confused than hurt.

"You're in the back seat of my Land Rover," Duncan reassures her, his voice a steady anchor amidst the storm of emotions swirling around us.

"How did I get here?" Rachael's brow furrows as she tries to piece together the fragments of her memory.

"You don't remember?" Ryan interjects, his tone blending curiosity with concern.

"The last thing I remember is switching off the lamp on my bedroom nightstand and sinking into my bed. Then—I woke up here," she exclaims, her bewilderment deepening.

"There's little doubt in my mind that Ezekiel and Abrahim are behind this," Julie declares, her tone a mix of annoyance and disbelief. Suspicion hangs heavy in the air. She glances around the brightly lit vehicle interior, half-expecting the ghostly duo to pop out and cackle with glee at the success of their latest prank.

"I agree with Julie," Ryan nods in agreement. "They pulled similar stunts last summer."

"Duncan and I were their targets last year." Julie adds,

shaking her head, recalling the chaos that unfolded, a true testament to the mischievous nature of the ghostly duo.

"What on earth have I done to provoke these spirits?" Rachael asks, her confusion creating a thick fog that wraps around her thoughts, making even simple ideas feel complex and unreachable. "The idea of angry ghosts was not something I signed up for when I moved into this old house."

Duncan rubs his chin in deep thought. "We were just discussing this very issue earlier," he says, his words carrying the weight of someone piecing together a puzzle.

"They might be upset because their graves were disturbed in your backyard," Ryan suggests, his voice low and serious. The weight of that statement hangs heavily in the night air.

"And let's not forget that selling the mine to that development company didn't exactly earn you any extra points with them," Julie adds with a knowing glance.

Rachael shakes her head in disbelief. "My gosh, I never imagined those ghosts would go to such extreme lengths for revenge. What have I gotten myself into?" Her eyes widen as she realizes just how deep this rabbit hole goes.

As we exchange glances filled with both fear and intense intrigue, one question lingers: How far will these restless spirits go to reclaim what was once theirs? The thought sends a shiver down my spine, but part of me can't help but feel a thrill at the prospect of confronting these mischievous apparitions.

Fighting ghosts may not be on my immediate summer bingo card, but I'm willing to stick it out to help Rachael. Buckle up, girls and boys; it looks like we're in for a wild and unpredictable ride.

Dale Thele

DAY SEVENTEEN

Wednesday, June 5, 2019

Each morning, as I stay in the big house on the hill, I eagerly anticipate the daily coffee klatch—it's a wonderful way to begin the day. In our cozy setting, Julie, Rachael, Duncan, and I gather around the kitchen table. The comforting aroma of freshly brewed coffee and warm cinnamon rolls fills the air, blending with our joyful laughter and engaging conversations. This creates a welcoming atmosphere, much like the first rays of sunlight breaking through a frosty dawn.

Just then, Ryan shuffles in. His tousled hair is a testament to last night's ghostly adventures, and his puffy eyes reveal a battle lost to sleep. "Morning," he mumbles groggily as he clumsily pours himself a mug of coffee, splashing some onto the counter. The comical mishap draws amused giggles from us, our shared humor adding a delightful twist to the morning.

"Hey, Rye," I chime in playfully, "watch what you're doing. You're making a mess."

"I'll clean it up," he grumbles, grabbing a wad of paper towels to mop up the spilled coffee, like a reluctant hero facing an epic quest.

"Sleep well, did we?" Duncan teases, a smirk on his face that rivals any mischievous woodland sprite.

Ryan responds with an exaggerated middle finger gesture that sends everyone into fits of laughter—everyone except him. His attempt at humor is sharply contrasted by his wide yawn, a clear sign that he's still struggling with the remnants of sleep. He grabs a chair and drags it over to the table, parking it between Duncan and me.

"So, Rach," Julie resumes the previous conversation, her voice filled with concern, "after last night's drama, how are you holding up?"

"I am fine," Rachael replies, her voice steady, but a hint of uncertainty trembles in her eyes, betraying her inner turmoil.

An awkward silence, thick and suffocating, hangs heavily between us, like flip-flops at a black-tie affair. This apparent contrast draws attention and sparks whispers with every move. No one seems eager to dive back into that chaos just yet.

Just then, Giles bursts into the kitchen, his smile as warm as the morning sun. "Good morning, everyone," he exclaims cheerfully as he makes his way to the counter to pour himself a steaming mug of coffee. His brisk and energetic movements create a stark contrast to the subdued atmosphere in the room.

"Someone's feeling chipper this morning," Duncan teases with a playful grin.

"Once my head hit the pillow, I was out like a light," Giles reflects as he stands beside the kitchen table, assessing the limited available space. He gently pushes aside a pan of cinnamon rolls to make room for himself and his freshly poured coffee.

Rachael scans the cramped kitchen, then suggests with a nod, "I propose we take this powwow to the more spacious dining room." Her words bring a sense of anticipation for a change of scenery and more elbow room.

As the sun filters gently through the kitchen window, warm beams of light dance through the cafe-style curtains, creating a peaceful atmosphere for our morning ritual. We rise in sync, like a harmonious choir. The comforting scent of freshly brewed coffee mingles with the sound of our chairs sliding against the floor, enveloping us in a sense of familiarity and comfort. With our steaming mugs in hand, we leave our usual spots around the kitchen table and move to the larger dining table, each of us choosing a new chair as we continue welcoming a day filled with the promise of new adventures.

Just as I settle comfortably into my chair, feeling that blissful moment of relaxation wash over me, Beau bounds over with an eager look in his eyes—the one that says *I wanna go outside.*

"Why is it that you always wait until I'm comfortable to come to me, begging to go out?" I ask him, half-laughing and half-exasperated. This routine has become familiar; Beau's timing is so predictable, always coinciding with my moments of relaxation. It's as if he's an essential part of my morning ritual—a quirky but beloved member of our little group.

He cocks his head at me, a picture of innocence, and adds a soft whine that tugs at my heartstrings. Guilt, like a heavy weight, washes over me. How can I resist that face and those soulful eyes?

"You stay here," Giles interjects with a grin. "I'll let Beau out."

"No," I reply, shaking my head, "Beau's my responsibility. I'll let him out." With that declaration, I rise from my chair, and Beau's excitement is obvious; he's practically vibrating with joy and anticipation, knowing what's coming next.

Together, we sprint through the kitchen to the back door. I swing it open, and he darts outside like a rocket, his sense of freedom evident as he eagerly chases fluttering bugs and explores every corner of the yard. His outdoor adventures showcase his natural behavior. Eventually, during his romp outside, he remembers to take care of business, which is why he wanted to go outside in the first place.

I leave the door slightly ajar for Beau's return and head back to the dining room. As I walk, I notice the cheerful chirping of birds in the backyard, creating a peaceful backdrop for the start of a new day. The sun is shining, and the world outside is buzzing with life.

Entering the dining room, Rachael is speaking. "After last night's events," her voice steady yet resolute, "I have made up my mind—I am moving back into the garage apartment."

Julie raises an eyebrow, concern etched on her face. "Do you really think that's a wise decision, given the circumstances?"

Duncan interjects, his tone serious and filled with worry. "If you stay in the house, we can keep a close watch on you. Moving to the garage apartment would make it harder for us to ensure your safety."

Rachael's eyes flash with defiance. "Oh? And how well did that work out last night? Just how closely were you watching over me then?"

"Touche," Duncan concedes with a wry smile.

Giles, maintaining a calm and measured tone despite the urgency of the situation, shares his perspective. "I understand that my opinion might not carry much weight as a newcomer to this group, but here's my two cents. Since you're being targeted by some ancient ghosts dating back two centuries, it's probably in your best interest to stay in the house under these unusual circumstances."

The air grows heavy with tension as we consider Giles's suggestion.

"I wholeheartedly agree with Giles," I say, pausing for a moment to let the weight of our situation sink in. "There's undeniable strength in unity, and now, more than ever, we need to stand together."

"Rach, I have an idea," Julie bursts out, her eyes shining with excitement. "Why don't you move in with me? My room is spacious enough for both of us."

"Really? You would do that for me?" Rachael asks, her voice softening with disbelief at Julie's generosity.

"Well, aren't we friends?" Julie replies with a warm smile. "And isn't that what friends do? We stick together through thick and thin."

"Rach, that sounds like the perfect solution," Duncan chimes in. "By rooming with Julie, you'll still be in the house, and you won't have to face the nights alone."

"Alright then," Rachael declares with a playful grin. "It is settled—I am bunking with Julie."

"It'll be a blast," Julie adds, her eyes sparkling with excitement. "Just like a slumber party."

Duncan leans in with a mischievous glint in his eye. "Now,

you'll keep me posted on any girl-on-girl pillow fights, right?"

"Duncan!" Julie scolds, her tone half-serious and half-amused. "Shame on you! You pervert."

"Hey, a guy can dream," Duncan retorts with a cheeky smile, glancing around for support from Giles, Ryan, and me. "Am I right, guys?"

There's a moment of silence, filled only by crickets and glassy-eyed stares. Giles scratches his head, while Ryan curiously searches Duncan with a raised eyebrow. I stifle a nervous laugh.

"Oh right," Duncan says with a smirk, "I forgot—you guys aren't into girls."

Before Duncan can finish his thought, Ryan jumps in. "But if it were oiled up guys wearing nothing but jockstraps and..." his voice drifts off, his eyes glaze over as he sinks further into the homoerotic fantasy playing like a sleazy adult bookstore movie inside his head.

"We know!" I laugh. "You'd be front and center."

"Most likely selling tickets," Duncan adds.

Laughter erupts throughout the room, filling it with a contagious sense of joy.

As the afternoon sun shines brightly overhead, casting a warm golden hue over Rachael's backyard, Duncan, Giles, and I find ourselves sweaty, dirty, and covered in grime, armed with shovels and rakes. The excavation crew left quite a mess behind, with holes scattered like craters across the lawn. Our mission is to transform this mess into a flourishing vegetable garden that Rachael can proudly cultivate. With a strong sense of shared purpose, we dive into the task at hand, our camaraderie strengthens with each shovelful of dirt we move. We envision the beauty of the garden, filled with rows of vibrant vegetables.

"Wow, this is tougher than I anticipated," I admit, but I refuse to let the challenge defeat me. Leaning against the hoe handle, I wipe beads of sweat from my brow, my determination unwavering as I commit to seeing this project through to the end.

"It's not so bad once you get the hang of it," Duncan replies cheerfully, his energy seemingly endless. He's digging with a rhythm that makes it look easy, and I can't help but feel a bit envious of his enthusiasm.

"Easy for you to say," Giles chimes in with a teasing grin. "You've got the physique for this kind of work. Seriously, though, how can someone as skinny as you pack on so much muscle?" The banter between Giles and Duncan adds a lighthearted touch to our laborious task.

Duncan chuckles and flashes a smug smile. "I guess I do have some muscle definition, don't I?" He pauses his digging to flex his biceps. "It helps to go to the gym a couple of times a week."

"I tried that once, but I didn't see any change," Giles admits, his tone a mixture of frustration and humor—a combination that easily manages to draw a chuckle.

"But did you actually work out while you were at the gym?" I ask, raising an eyebrow in the bright afternoon sun.

His laughter rings out as he replies, "No, I went to cruise the hot guys instead."

I smirk and tease him further, "You and Rye should have a heart-to-heart on that one. Sounds like a classic Rye move."

Duncan, always the serious one in our group, interjects, "I strictly go to work out. I'm not into guys. I'm straight."

"Oh really?" I tease, leaning closer. "There's an old saying— *straight men are like spaghetti—they're straight until they get wet.*"

Duncan's lips curl into a partial smirk, and he shakes his head. "I'm going to pretend you didn't just say that."

A playful thought crosses my mind as I add, "But let's be real—after a few beers, I bet Duncan would be singing a different tune. Just saying." It's all in good fun, besides, I think he gets off on the gay ribbing thing.

Duncan responds by driving his shovel hard into the ground

with a satisfying thud. His expression shifts to one of determination as he says, "I think we're done here." It's his subtle way of changing the subject, and he's keenly aware that he's outnumbered—two homos to his one straight self, a fact that adds a layer of tension to the conversation.

"Rach now has a vegetable garden," Giles exclaims, his eyes sparkling with satisfaction as he approvingly appraises the work we've done. His joy is infectious, and the three of us share in it.

"Yeah, but it's a garden without any vegetable plants," I reply, chuckling at the irony.

"Didn't Rach mention something about having some seeds she wanted to plant?" Giles asks, tilting his head as he recalls the conversation.

"I seem to remember her saying something along those lines," Duncan chimes in thoughtfully. "What are you getting at?"

"Well, it might be late in the season," Giles muses, tapping his chin, "but why don't we plant the seeds for her? It could be a fun little project. Besides, it would be a nice gesture since she's putting us up in her home."

"I see your point. It can't hurt to ask," Duncan agrees with a nod of enthusiasm, echoing the shared sentiment among us.

"I'll check with Rach and see if she's on board," I suggest. "If she gives the green light, we can get our hands dirty tomorrow morning when it's cooler."

"That sounds like a plan," Duncan replies eagerly. "But for now, I could really go for a refreshing glass of iced tea."

After an invigorating shower, I head downstairs, eager to find Rachel. I want to talk about the idea of Duncan, Giles, and me planting her vegetable seeds. As I enter the kitchen, I see her standing alone, gazing out the window, lost in thought, with an expression of deep contemplation.

"Rach, are you okay?" I ask gently, hoping to pull her back from whatever daydream has captured her attention.

Silence stretches between us—she seems miles away, as if

she's peering into another world.

"Excuse me, Rach," I say, adding a bit more urgency to my voice. "Did you hear me?"

Shaking off the cobwebs of her reverie, Rachel turns to me, a slight furrow in her brow. "Yes, Taylor? Did you say something?

I can't help but wonder what thoughts are swirling through her mind. Maybe she's daydreaming about her garden and the fresh veggies she could harvest before fall.

"Hey, Rach, I'd like to run something by you," I say, leaning casually against the kitchen counter. "Duncan, Gill, and I were wondering if it would be alright with you if we planted your vegetable seeds. I know it's getting late in the season, but there's still time to harvest some fresh veggies before fall."

"Yeah, sure," she replies, her voice distant and her glassy gaze fixed on a point beyond the kitchen window. The warm sunlight illuminates her face, yet her mind seems occupied with something far colder and darker, leaving me with a sense of unease.

"Rach?" I probe gently, with a concerned tone. "Are you okay? You seem a bit... off today." I can't help but notice the worry lines creasing her forehead, a stark contrast to her usual calm demeanor.

Her eyes snap back into focus with an intensity that startles me. "Taylor," she says urgently, her voice low and serious, urgency creeping into her tone. "We are in trouble—big trouble."

"Trouble?" I echo, my heart racing. "What do you mean?"

The air thickens with tension as I await her response, a mix of curiosity and concern swirling within me. The room, which moments ago was filled with the warm glow of the afternoon sun, now feels dim and foreboding, as if a dark cloud has rolled in overhead. What could be weighing so heavily on her mind? Is it about the garden, or is it something else entirely? I can't shake the feeling that whatever it is, it goes beyond just seeds and soil. Her silence is deafening.

"I am not sure if I should tell you this," she whispers, her eyes nervously darting about the room. "There is no one else in this house I can trust with this secret—except for you. If I do not confide in someone I will burst."

"What is it? You can trust me," I plead, leaning in with curiosity, eager to hear the secret she's keeping.

She steps closer, lowering her voice as if the walls themselves are listening. "It has to do with a leather-bound book I keep in the cellar. This particular book is not just any book—it is..."

"Wait a minute, are you talking about that old cookbook Julie found last summer?" I interject, trying to calm her nerves. "Trust me, it's not worth your time. It's written in a foreign language."

"You know about the book?" Relief washes over her face, and a smile breaks through her initial hesitation.

"Yeah, I remember Julie going through it last summer and getting frustrated. She thought it was some strange cookbook," I chuckle, recalling how Julie had given up on deciphering the recipes. "It won't do you any good since it's not written in English."

"Do you know where the book is now?" Rachael presses, her interest intensifying.

"Oh sure, I saw it in the cellar last night while we were searching for you, when you went missing," I reply, trying to keep the conversation casual.

"We?" Rachael raises an eyebrow, her tone skeptical. "Was there someone else with you?"

"Izzy," I respond, feeling a bit defensive. "And guess what? While we were down there, I also found Beau's favorite stick from last summer. He'll be thrilled to get it back."

"No!" Rachael's voice cuts through the air, sharp and urgent, and the tension is evident. Her sudden urgency sends a shiver down my spine. Then, as if realizing the weight of her response, her voice softens. "I mean... You can not give that stick to Beau."

I can't express how confused I feel. "What's going on with you?" I ask, sensing the abrupt change in her tone. Her demeanor shifted so suddenly that it's unsettling. Rachael bites her lip and looks down, as if the floor might provide the answers she's unable to give. The sudden change in her attitude leaves me feeling uneasy.

"I suppose I should come clean," she says, looking into my eyes with a steady and serious expression. The weight of her words hangs heavily in the air, like ripe, low-hanging fruit just waiting to be picked.

"What do you mean by, *come clean*? You're not making any sense," I snap, my frustration boiling over as she continues to speak in riddles.

"Just shut up and listen," Rachael commands, her tone stern. The order hangs in the air, thick with tension, and I can't shake the sense of unease creeping in.

Dread coils around me like a serpent, its cold scales slithering down my spine and leaving a trail of discomfort in their wake. This isn't the Rachael I know, and it's unsettling.

"That stick—as you call it—is not just any ordinary stick," she insists, leaning in closer as if she's revealing a closely guarded secret. "It is a magic wand." Her words hang in the air, shrouded in mystery, and I can't help but feel she's teasing me.

"A magic wand? You're joking, right?" I chuckle, unable to believe what I'm hearing.

But Rachael isn't laughing. Her expression is serious. The weight of her words hangs in the air, thick and ominous. I can't help but wonder: What if there's more to that stick than meets the eye?

"You're serious, aren't you?" I ask, my heart racing.

"I have never been more serious in my life," Rachael replies, urgency flashing in her eyes. "That stick, as you call it—if it falls into the wrong hands, it can be incredibly dangerous."

A chill of realization runs down my spine. "Uh-oh," I murmur, the gravity of the situation hitting me like a sledgehammer. "I might have told Izzy to take the stick and surprise Beau with it."

Rachael clutches the fabric of my shirt, her fingers balling it into a fist, and her voice trembles with desperation and disbelief. "Please tell me you didn't tell her that!" she pleads, her gaze intense and unnerving.

"I kind of did," I admit sheepishly, feeling the weight of my mistake settle in. "And I may have mentioned that Izzy could borrow the cookbook, too."

"You fool!" Rachael exclaims, twisting my shirt tighter in frustration, her anger evident in the air between us.

"I'm really sorry," I plead, guilt crashing over me like a tidal wave. "I had no idea how much those things meant to you."

"That book is no ordinary book," Rachael insists, her eyes wide with urgency.

"I know that," I reply. "It's written in some foreign language."

With a sigh of resignation, Rachael releases her grip on my shirt, frustration etched on her face. "You do not understand," she pleads, desperation seeping into her voice as she pats my shirt, as if trying to smooth out the creases she had created.

"No, I guess I don't," I admit. "What makes that book so important?"

"It is not just any book. It is a tome of enchantments—filled with spells, curses, and some truly dark magic," Rachael blurts out, her tone serious and urgent. "In the wrong hands, it can unleash unimaginable danger."

"Spells, curses, and magic? Are you serious?" I ask, disbelief ringing clear in my voice.

"The book contains all of that and more," Rachael responds, her eyes pleading for understanding.

"But what good is it to anyone if they can't read it?" I counter, my confusion evident and adding to the complexity of the book's mystery.

Rachael exclaims with bubbling excitement, "That is the catch! Anyone can unlock its secrets as long as they hold that stick—the one Beau found—in their hand. That stick is the key—it allows anyone to read the *Book of Enchantments*."

"Sure thing," I say with a nonchalant shrug, stepping back from the intense conversation. "No need to worry. I understand that these things are important to you. I'll just ask Izzy to return the book and the stick—easy peasy." I say this casually, trying to reassure Rachael, even though I don't fully understand her attachment to those items.

Rachael narrows her eyes at me. "You are not grasping the gravity of this. What if she knows the power she holds? You have no idea the havoc she could unleash."

"Alright, alright! Calm down," I respond, raising my hands in a sign of peace. "I'll talk to Izzy. But are you absolutely certain this isn't just a figment of your imagination? I mean, are we really living in a world of Harry Potter magic like at Hogwarts?"

"Trust me," Rachael asserts, her tone is serious. "This is no joke. Magic is real, and that book could alter everything."

"Fine! I'll get the stick and the book back from her," I say with a smirk, my tone a mix of resignation and amusement. "But in the meantime, if she conjures up a three-headed dragon or something just as scary, you owe me a pizza."

Rachael rolls her eyes but can't suppress a small smile breaking through her serious facade. "You got yourself a deal," she says, her voice a blend of exasperation and amusement.

DAY EIGHTEEN

Thursday, June 6, 2019

As the first light of dawn filters into the dining room, a beautiful transformation occurs. The room, once cloaked in darkness, is now illuminated by a warm, golden glow from the morning sun. This radiant light streams through the east-facing windows, dancing on the sheer drapes and casting a soft warmth over the dining table, where a light breakfast awaits. The space, now a blend of light and shadow, exudes a sense of joy and comfort, perfectly setting the tone for the day ahead. We're gathered around the large table, though Isadora is absent. The air is filled with laughter and cheerful chatter as we enjoy our breakfast of crunchy dry cereal swimming in cold milk and slices of warm toast generously spread with butter and jam. Between bites, we share amusing anecdotes about each other, with every story more entertaining than the last.

"There was one morning last summer when Rye was eating his breakfast cereal," I begin, but I'm quickly interrupted.

"No way," Ryan chimes in, shaking his head. "You don't have any breakfast stories about me. You're just making stuff up to embarrass me."

"Shh! I want to hear the story," Rachael insists with a grin, her eyes sparkling with anticipation.

Undeterred, I continue, "Well, there was Rye, shoveling spoonful after spoonful of his beloved Captain Krinkle cereal as if he were preparing for an Olympic event. Seriously, you'd think he was training for a world record in breakfast cereal consumption."

Duncan and Julie giggle, exchanging knowing glances at

Ryan's now crimson face.

"And just a few feet away," I say, "there was Beau, crunching on his kibble with all the finesse of a dog food critic. It was uncanny how both of them attacked their food, as if they were both in a breakfast-eating competition."

"I couldn't help but notice the striking resemblance," Duncan chuckles, his eyes twinkling mischievously. "It was just too irresistible not to point out the family resemblance," he adds, unable to contain his amusement.

Rachael furrows her brow, not fully understanding the *family resemblance* reference.

"You see, Rach," I chime in, a grin spreading across my face, "Rye and I were still together as a couple at the time. Beau was like our 'child' ..."

"*Family resemblance*? I get it," Rachael bursts into a fit of contagious laughter, her joy spreading like wildfire and lifting everyone's spirits with her infectious giggles.

Like a detective uncovering clues, Duncan leans in closer, his voice filled with playfulness. "We were left wondering who was imitating whom—was Rye copying Beau's habits, or was it the other way around?" His laughter fills the room with warm, lighthearted energy, drawing everyone into the playful banter.

Ryan crosses his arms, a frown creasing his forehead. "I don't see how that's funny at all," he huffs indignantly. "Not even a little."

"Maybe it pales in comparison to that time you ran out of Captain Krinkle cereal," Duncan teases, barely able to contain his laughter.

"No way!" Ryan squeals in protest. "You're not bringing that up!"

"What's this Captain Krinkle story?" Giles asks, his curiosity piqued and his eyes dancing with eagerness to learn more about Ryan's quirks.

Duncan can barely hold back his chuckles as he starts to explain. "Picture this—it was a lazy Saturday morning, and Rye had been looking forward to his favorite cereal all week. You know how obsessed he gets with those sugary little shapes—like a kid in a candy store."

Despite his initial resistance, Ryan rolls his eyes. "Alright, fine!" he concedes, a smirk playing on his lips. "But you owe me one," he adds with a determined glint in his eye.

"Well," I begin, eager to share the memory, "last summer, Ryan plopped down at the kitchen table for breakfast. His empty cereal bowl sat before him, waiting like an old friend. He reached for the box of Captain Krinkle—his beloved breakfast staple—"

"The very same cereal he has devoured since childhood, mind you," Duncan interjects with a wink.

"Anyway, Rye eagerly tipped the cereal box," I continue, "anticipating a delightful cascade of sugary goodness to tumble into his bowl. But instead—"

"Nothing came out," Duncan interjects with a mischievous grin.

"Right! Just a sad little puff of air," I chuckle, recalling the utterly surprised look on Ryan's face. "He shook the box like it was a maraca, hoping to coax out even a single morsel. But nope, it was as empty as his hopes at that moment."

"Classic Rye," Duncan laughs. "You'd think he'd check before pouring."

"Exactly! But that's Rye for you—always diving headfirst into things without checking the details first," I say, shaking my head fondly. "So there he was, staring into that empty bowl like it was some kind of cruel joke."

Julie covers her mouth with her hand, suppressing a giggle.

"Rye tilted the box even further," I continue, "as desperation crept into his expression while he shook it vigorously."

"Still nothing," Duncan chuckles, barely able to contain himself. "The sight of Rye, determined yet defeated, was too much for us, and we burst into laughter."

"With determined scowl," I continue, "Rye examined the box closely, nearly burying his head inside as if hoping to uncover some hidden treasure. But alas! The box was completely empty—no crumbs, no morsels. Just empty disappointment."

"Rye nearly cried when he realized he was out of his favorite cereal," Duncan explains.

"I did not!" Ryan protests indignantly, his cheeks turning a shade redder as he vehemently denies the accusation.

"Rye," Julie chimes in with a playful grin, "I was there, and trust me, you cried like a baby."

"Oh great, here we go again. Let's pick on poor defenseless Ryan," he sighs and rolls his eyes in exasperation.

"Come on, Rye. We're not picking on you," Julie reassures him with a warm smile. "We're just sharing some hilarious stories about each other."

Ryan raises an eyebrow, clearly not convinced. "Why don't you share stories about someone else? So far the stories have been only about me," he challenges, crossing his arms as if daring any of us to respond.

Duncan chuckles and shakes his head in amusement. "Rye, no one else's stories are as entertaining nor can they compare to yours."

A comfortable lull surrounds the group as we return to our breakfast. The unmistakable sound of spoons scraping against Corelle bowls of cereal fills the air.

Suddenly, between spoonfuls of cereal, Giles breaks the tranquility. "Hey, where's Izzy?"

Duncan doesn't lift his gaze from his cereal. "She mentioned something about not feeling well," he replies quietly.

Rachael leans back in her chair, a thoughtful frown creasing her brow. "Is it just me, or does anyone else find it strange that we haven't seen or heard from her since the night I went missing?" Her concern resonates with everyone at the table, adding a layer of tension to the otherwise casual atmosphere.

There's an edge of accusation in her voice that makes all of us pause.

"Rach, are you suggesting something?" Duncan asks, furrowing his brow as he looks up from his bowl of cereal. The question hangs in the air, creating a growing tension over our breakfast. We exchange uneasy glances, and a knot of unspoken worries replaces the previously lighthearted mood.

"Not to change the subject or anything," I interject, eager to steer the conversation toward something lighter. "The guys and I are planning to plant Rachael's garden today."

"Oh, really?" Giles responds, surprise evident in his tone. "So, you're just now telling us this?"

"Did you have something else planned?" I ask Giles.

"No," Giles shakes his head. "Some advance warning would've been nice."

"Surprise!" I exclaim, feeling a bit squeamish as I hope Giles won't remain upset with me.

"Isn't it a bit late in the season to be planting seeds?" Julie asks, raising a skeptical eyebrow.

"The seeds will go to waste if they are not planted this year," Rachael explains, her determination clear in her voice. "If I wait until next year, there is a real risk they will go stale and will not germinate as well."

"I suppose I see your point," Julie concedes with a nod. "Will you be helping the guys?"

"Oh, heavens no," Rachael replies firmly, a playful glint in her eye. "However, I will supervise."

"That's probably a wise choice," Julie chuckles. "You know how boys can be when left to their own devices." She and Rachael burst into laughter at their inside joke, while we guys chuckle nervously.

The late morning sun bathes Rachael's backyard in a golden glow, transforming every mundane object into a glistening jewel that brims with potential. The air is filled with the earthy fragrance of freshly turned soil and the melodious chirping of birds. Duncan, Ryan, Giles, Rachael, Julie, and I are outside. While us guys' hands are covered in dirt planting seeds, Rachael and Julie supervise from a short distance away. The soil, cool and moist, feels pleasant against my fingers. After a while, I decide to take a break and quench my thirst with a cool drink of water from the kitchen tap.

As I fill my glass with tap water, the tranquility of the outdoor scene through the kitchen window is abruptly shattered. Isadora suddenly appears in the room, her presence starkly contrasting with the peaceful setting outside.

"Where is everyone?" she asks, scanning the empty kitchen.

"We're out back planting Rach's garden," I reply between gulps of water.

"Is *everyone* outside?" she inquires, peering curiously through the back door's window curtains.

"Yes," I confirm. "You must be feeling better." I wipe my mouth with the back of my hand.

"Feeling better?" Isadora repeats, her brow furrowing in confusion. "Whatever are you talking about?"

"Duncan mentioned you weren't feeling well," I explain gently.

"Oh, that," she says, then lets out an unexpected cough that seems a bit too exaggerated. "Yes, it's true—I'm not feeling at all well." Her posture suddenly changes, appearing weak and frail.

Her sudden change in demeanor makes me raise an eyebrow. I can't help but wonder if she's putting on an act. I shift my weight from one foot to the other, trying to read her expression.

"Perhaps you shouldn't be up and about then," I suggest, feigning concern. "Especially if you're not feeling well."

"You're probably right," Isadora admits between faked coughs, her voice dripping with theatricality. "I had best get back to bed."

"I'll walk you to your room," I offer, trying to keep my tone light. "While we're at it, I can grab that book you borrowed from the cellar and Beau's stick. It's only right to return them to where we found them."

Isadora tilts her head, a flicker of confusion crossing her face. "What book are you talking about? What stick?"

Before I can respond, Rachael's accusation pierces the air from behind me like a sudden thunderclap. "The book and stick you took from my cellar," she states, her tone clear and unwavering.

I wasn't aware that Rachael entered the house; I thought she was still outside with the others.

"I have no idea what you're talking about," Isadora insists, her eyes darting away as if searching for an escape route; her discomfort is evident.

"Don't you remember? You took that leather-covered cookbook and Beau's stick when we were down in the cellar looking for Rachael," I say, trying to jog her memory.

"I don't know what you're talking about," Isadora replies, her blatant lie hanging heavy in the air between the three of us.

"You took them both," I assert firmly. "I saw you. You even asked if I thought Rach would mind if you borrowed the book."

"What do you want with that book?" Rachael demands from Isadora, her eyes narrowing.

"Like I said, I don't have your damn book," Isadora spits, the tension crackling around us.

"I know you have it," Rachael says, crossing her arms defiantly.

"And I know it too," I agree with Rachael, feeling the heat of our shared conviction.

"Without tangible evidence to prove your accusations," Isadora smirks, "it's your word against mine." She turns her back to return up the stairs.

"Not so fast, sister," Rachael snaps, stepping into Isadora's path. "This is my house, and you're a guest here. I have every right to search your room. Do you really want to go down that road?"

"You wouldn't dare," Isadora shoots back, her eyes ablaze with fury, her glare fierce enough to cut diamonds.

"Try me," Rachael counters, her defiance filling the room as she stands her ground like a warrior ready for battle.

"I refuse to tolerate this kind of disrespect from someone like you," Isadora declares, her indignation adding fuel to the fire.

"Someone like what?" Rachael shoots back, her eyebrows

raised in challenge, her voice dripping with sarcasm. The air crackles with hostility as both women stand their ground.

In the charged atmosphere of their confrontation, Isadora's voice slices through the tension with the precision of a surgeon's scalpel, precise and unyielding. "A deceitful, accusing bitch like you," she responds with disdain. "I'm returning to my room now. You know where to find me when you're ready to come crawling back, begging for my forgiveness." With that said, Isadora turns and heads up the stairs.

Seething with anger, Rachael mutters through clenched teeth, "I am going to rip that woman's hair out." Her frustration is clear as she prepares to confront Isadora. Before Rachael can act on her impulse, I grasp her arm firmly, holding her back.

"Hold on a second," I say, making a conscious effort to diffuse the situation before it spirals out of control. "Is this really worth it? A hair-pulling match? Come on, let's think this through rationally."

Rachael glares at me for a moment. I know her anger isn't directed at me. Then her expression softens. "I can not let her walk away after talking to me like that."

"I understand," I reply, keeping my grip steady but gentle. "But if you go after her now, it will only make things worse. Let's take a moment to cool off and figure out a better way to handle this."

With a frustrated sigh, Rachael relents and takes a step back. "Fine. But I am not done with her," she declares with steely resolve.

"Fair enough," I say, nodding. "Let's try to settle this without turning it into World War III. Shall we?"

As we stand at the bottom of the stairs, the air feels tense, like a balloon stretched to its limit—one small prick away from bursting. This growing tension is clear evidence of a potentially escalating feud between Rachael and Isadora.

DAY NINETEEN

Friday, June 7, 2019

As the sun sets below the horizon, painting the sky in hues of orange and pink, a deeply tranquil evening unfolds around us. The birds have nestled into their cozy roosts among the gnarled branches of the majestic Live Oak trees, creating a serene backdrop for our outdoor gathering. The rhythmic chirping of crickets serenades us, their music acting as a soothing balm for our souls.

Giles and I find comfort in the gentle sway of the patio swing—a delightful addition to the porch since last summer. It's the perfect spot to unwind and soak in the peaceful evening ambiance. Nearby, Beau sprawls on the cool stone patio floor, lost in peaceful dreams and utterly unfazed by the world around him. His gentle snores blend with the evening sounds, enhancing the tranquil atmosphere.

Meanwhile, Duncan and Ryan lounge in separate wicker chairs at the center of the porch, engaging in lighthearted banter that mingles effortlessly with the warm evening air, wrapping us in a comforting embrace. Their laughter is infectious, creating a sense of camaraderie that makes it feel as though we're all part of an inside joke shared only among friends.

Julie and Rachael fan themselves with handheld cardstock paper fans featuring teak handles, advertising the local mortuary, their laughter filling the air like a refreshing breeze as they sit closest to the driveway, while enjoying the serene ambiance of the front porch. The soft rustle of leaves dances around us, blending perfectly with our conversations to create a beautiful, gentle soundtrack for this tranquil evening. It's one of those moments where time seems to stand still, filled with good friends, laughter, and a sky that looks like a commissioned masterpiece painted just for us.

The conversation fades like the last notes of a lullaby, just as the cheerful chirping birds in the trees fall asleep. Here we are, basking in the tranquil charm of Lost Creek Junction, a quintessential small-town gem in America. A gentle breeze carries the distant melodies of carnival music, mingling with the exhilarating screams of roller coaster riders and the joyful laughter from the bustling downtown street carnival. These delightful sounds drift effortlessly across the patio—soft and inviting, bringing smiles rather than annoyance.

"Will you look at that?" Rachael says, staring intently at something in the distance.

"Look at what?" Julie replies, squinting as she searches beyond the porch and over the driveway.

"Just look at that," Rachael exclaims, rising from her chair. Her curiosity grows as she focuses on the garage apartment at the end of the driveway. "There is a light on over there," she adds, her eyes widening with intrigue.

"It's probably nothing," Duncan replies nonchalantly, his focus glued to the magazine in his hands. "Maybe it's a faulty switch or something like that."

Rachael isn't so easily convinced. She narrows her eyes, drawn in by the oddity, which sharply contrasts with Duncan's indifference. "Has anyone been in the apartment recently?"

A unison chorus of "no's" and shaking heads from Julie and the rest of us confirms none of us have been in the garage apartment.

"Excuse me, I am going over there to check it out," Rachael declares, her determination evident in her stride as she heads toward the edge of the patio with unwavering confidence. The sound of her flats clicking on the stone floor echoes in the quiet evening, adding to the sense of purpose in her step.

"I'll go with you," Julie chimes in, eager to tag along.

"No," Rachael replies firmly. "You stay here. Besides, I will not be long."

With that, she strides toward the garage, leaving Julie looking a bit deflated, her excitement now replaced with a hint of disappointment. Beau, my ever-curious pup with his wagging tail and a nose for adventure, springs up from the porch floor to trot alongside Rachael, as if he shares her curiosity.

"You know," I remark to Giles, who's sitting beside me and watching the scene unfold, "it must drive Beau crazy not knowing what's going on every minute of the day. He follows everyone around like he's afraid of missing out on something. What a nosy dog I have."

My comment hangs in the air for a moment, a heavy silence, pregnant with unspoken thoughts, envelopes us. Everyone returns to their reading, while Julia gently fans herself, seemingly unbothered by my musings.

"Have you guys noticed how loud those crickets are this evening?" Julie suddenly interrupts the calm, her voice cutting through the crickets' chatter. "I swear, I've never heard them quite this noisy before."

"I suppose they do seem a bit more boisterous tonight," I agree, straining to hear over their relentless chorus. It feels almost as if they are cheering Rachael on as she walks to the garage apartment. As I sit here, I can't shake the feeling that this night might turn out to be one for the books—filled with peaceful contentment, a rarity at the Blackburn House.

"I've had enough of these darn crickets," Julie exclaims, her frustration clear. It's hard to tell if she's annoyed by the crickets or upset because Rachael wouldn't let her join. "I'm going inside," Julie declares firmly. "I can't even hear myself think over their racket. Besides, I have an Agatha Christie novel waiting for me that won't read itself."

"Which one are you reading?" Duncan asks, curiosity lighting up his face.

"*Death on the Nile*," Julie replies, her enthusiasm shining through. "I finished *Dumb Witness* before leaving Austin, I'm tackling the novels in the order they were published—you could say I'm embarking on a literary journey." Her eyes sparkle as she speaks about her reading adventure, and her passion for books is evident in every word.

Duncan raises an eyebrow, intrigued. "So, once you finish *Death on the Nile*, I suppose your next read will be *Murder in the Mews*?"

Julie chuckles softly and shakes her head. "Actually, that was published before *Dumb Witness*, and I've already read it. The next book in chronological order is *Appointment with Death*," she corrects him with a gentle smile, sharing her literary knowledge while her patience is evident in her tone.

Ryan's eyes widened in skepticism. "Wait a minute! The great know-it-all, Duncan Campbell, made a mistake?" he exclaims, his voice filled with stunned disbelief and a not-so-subtle hint of gloating.

With a smirk, Duncan rises from his chair, rolling the magazine in his hand. The sun is setting, casting a warm glow over the porch. "I can't claim to be perfect all the time, but I agree with Julie about going inside. I have my own book waiting for me," he says, expressing his agreement with her.

"What? Are you referring to the *Encyclopedia Britannica*?" Ryan asks teasingly.

"No, smartypants," Duncan retorts with a playful sneer. "If you must know, it's *War and Peace*."

"Ew." Ryan shudders. "That's way too high-brow for me."

"I suppose so," Duncan chuckles. "It doesn't have pictures like your comics do."

"Very funny," Ryan replies, rising from his chair with an exaggerated sigh. As he heads inside, he turns the comic book cover toward himself, likely to avoid unsolicited comments about his reading choice.

As everyone prepares to go indoors, Giles and I slip off the porch swing just as Beau approaches to rejoin our group. Once we're in the parlor, we settle into our favorite spots—Julie, Duncan, Ryan, Giles, and I—each engrossed in our books. The familiar comfort of our chosen seats envelops us like a warm blanket, enhancing our reading enjoyment in this peaceful setting.

As we all get comfortable with our reading materials, Beau lets out a dramatic sigh and curls up on the floor beside the settee where Giles and I are sitting. I hadn't even considered that we had unceremoniously commandeered his favorite piece of furniture. Beau, always the easygoing one, doesn't seem to mind, as long as we don't make it a habit.

In this peaceful retreat on the hill, where laughter and lighthearted teasing create a sense of camaraderie and humor, we gather to share stories, enjoy each other's company, and even poke fun at one another's reading choices. Whether it's *War and Peace*, an Agatha Christie novel, a Louise Penny detective series, or a dollar-store comic book, we can all appreciate each other's company without judgment.

The parlor is as quiet as a long-forgotten tomb, with only the gentle rustle of turning pages and the occasional sip of a drink breaking the silence, punctuated by Beau's erratic soft yelps as he dreams of whatever dogs dream about. Each of us is lost in our reading while the end table lamps cast long shadows that seem to reach across the room, grasping at the desolate darkened corners. Even the crickets have grown quieter.

Then, like a sudden thunderclap on a clear day, Julie's voice cuts through the stillness, jolting us from our reading and causing Beau to spring up in cautious alarm.

"I wonder what's keeping Rach," Julie asks the room, glancing up from her book. "She's been gone for what feels like an eternity. It's been ages since she went to the garage apartment."

Ryan furrows his brow, concern etched on his face. "Yeah, even Beau managed to come back before Rach did." His words hang in the air, causing a wave of unease to wash over us and making the room feel ominously heavier.

Beau tilts his head, looking at Ryan quizzically with his soulful eyes.

"Do you think something might be wrong?" Julie inquires.

"What could possibly be wrong?" Giles interjects, his voice laced with dismissiveness as he waves his hand. "She just went to the garage apartment. It's not like she went on an African safari."

"She's probably cleaning or tidying things up," Duncan adds. "She's always busy doing something."

"Still," Ryan counters, his tone more serious now, "doesn't it strike you as odd that Beau returned but Rach hasn't?"

Beau cocks his head to study Ryan curiously. The wheels inside that head of his are turning a hundred miles an hour.

As we sit in contemplative silence, an uneasy feeling settles over me. The mystery of Rachel looms large; what could be keeping her? It's not like her to disappear like this. The thought lingers in the air like a thick fog, wrapping around us as we exchange curious glances filled with deepening concern for our host.

"Maybe I should check on her?" Julie suggests, breaking the silence once again.

"Yeah, I'll join you," I agree, feeling a surge of urgency. "It wouldn't hurt to check in on her."

With a collective nod, we set our books aside, preparing to unravel the mystery that has captured our attention. Whatever is going on with Rachel, it's time to find out.

"You guys are just working yourselves up over nothing," Duncan says, furrowing his brow in skepticism.

"Maybe so," I reply, unable to shake the feeling that something might be off. "I think we should check the apartment—just to be safe."

"I'm coming with you," Giles declares, his resolve unwavering and his eyes filled with determination.

"Me too," Ryan echoes.

Duncan hesitates for a moment before conceding, "Alright, I might as well come along."

As we step out of the house in single file, curious Beau brings up the rear. A question hangs in the air: What if our fears are more than mere figments of our imagination? The heavy weight of uncertainty, like a dense fog that blinds our vision and chills our bones, envelops us as we make our way to the garage.

As we enter the garage, the air feels warm and stagnant, and an eerie silence surrounds us, intensifying the tension that has been building since we decided to come here. Climbing the stairs to the apartment, a sense of unease settles over us. When we reach the apartment, we find the door is firmly locked, which only heightens our growing apprehension.

"It seems Rachel has locked up and left," Ryan notes, his tone carrying a sense of finality that deepens our unease. He turns to leave.

"Wait, guys—there's a light on inside," Julie points out, her voice filled with curiosity that we all share.

"You're right," Duncan agrees, glancing at the light shining from under the door, as if it might reveal its secrets. "Wasn't that the reason she came out here in the first place?"

"Can someone just knock on the door already?" I suggest, my heart racing. I can't shake the feeling that something is off. "Let's see if she's in there."

Duncan, being closest to the door, raps on it. We hold our breath, waiting for any sign of life from within. Suddenly, a muffled, desperate voice pierces the silence.

"Help! I'm locked in here!"

"That's Rachael's voice," Julie gasps, a mix of panic and urgency sending chills down my spine. There's an immediate need to help. The sound of her voice, muffled and desperate, echoes through the narrow landing outside the door, intensifying our urgency. "Rach?" Julie calls out, her voice trembling as she squeezes by Duncan on the narrow landing. "Is that you?"

"Yes," comes Rachael's muted response, tinged with frustration. "Help me, please. The door is locked."

The weight of the moment hangs heavily in the air as we exchange glances, our expressions reflecting both concern and a fierce determination to help Rachael. Julie moves closer to the door, her brow furrowing. "What happened? How did you get locked in there?" she asks, her voice a mix of concern and confusion.

"I don't know," Rachael replies. "I unlocked and opened the door, and then I must have been shoved inside. Immediately, the door slammed shut behind me." Her voice trembles slightly, and I can picture her pacing back and forth in the space beyond the door.

"Can't you unlock the door from the inside?" Duncan asks, his concern growing evident.

"The door has two locks: a newer one on the inside and the original deadbolt that requires a key from the outside," Rachael explains, sounding exasperated. "Someone locked the outer deadbolt with a key."

Duncan rubs his chin in thought. "Okay, it's clear that we need the key to unlock this door."

"I left the key in the door lock," Rachael replies. "It should still be there."

"There's no key here," Duncan states firmly. "There's no doubt this was a deliberate act."

"There is a spare key hanging on the keyboard in the kitchen," Rachael suggests.

Without missing a beat, Ryan says, "I'll go get the key," and dashes down the stairs, determination etched on his face, showing his commitment to the task at hand.

Julie furrows her brow, her confusion mirroring ours as she gazes at the locked door. "Rach, how did this happen? Who would pull such a prank?" she wonders aloud.

"None of us could have done it. We were all together inside the house, and before that, we were outside on the porch," Duncan chimes in, his tone serious. "All of us have been together the entire evening."

"All of us... except for Izzy," Julie shakes her head vigorously.

"She wouldn't do something like this... would she?" Giles asks, his voice tinged with uncertainty, reflecting the confusion gripping all of us.

Just then, Ryan returns, breathless but triumphant. "Here's the spare key," he exclaims as he rushes up the stairs and hands it to Julie.

With a swift turn of the lock, Julie opens the door to reveal Rachael standing just beyond it, relief washing over her features like sunlight breaking through clouds.

"Thank goodness!" Rachael exclaims as she steps into freedom. As we gather around her, the air is thick with curiosity and concern. Who could have done such a thing? And why? The questions hangs heavy in the air as we exchange glances, each of us wondering if Izzy had anything to do with this or if there might be a deeper mystery lurking just out of sight.

"Thank you so much, everyone," Rachael says, wrapping her arms around us in a warm embrace. "I can not believe she would stoop so low as to do something like this. What was she thinking?"

"Hold on a second," Duncan interjects, raising an eyebrow. "How can you be so sure Izzy is behind this? It seems a bit premature to jump to conclusions."

"Oh, I wouldn't put it past her," Rachael replies, frustration bubbling beneath the surface. "She is not fond of me, and honestly, I can't say I feel warmly toward her either."

"You've got Izzy all wrong," Duncan adds, shaking his head. "I'm sure she likes you. Why wouldn't she?"

"Wait, everyone," I exclaim, shaking my head in disbelief. "Yesterday, I witnessed Rach and Izzy having a heated argument. I have to side with Rach on this. I wouldn't be surprised in the least if Izzy wasn't behind what happened here this evening."

As the tension thickens in the air, it's clear that this is no ordinary disagreement. With accusations flying and friendships at stake, we all sense one thing: the situation is spiraling into a complex web of conflict, each of us with our own personal stakes and hopes for resolution.

"This is the first I'm hearing of a disagreement," Duncan replies, his eyebrows rising in surprise. "What exactly did Izzy say to you, Rach?"

"She called Rach the *B* word right to her face," I interject, the weight of the revelation hanging heavily in the air and casting a somber tone over all of us.

Julie gasps audibly, her eyes widening in shock as the gravity of the situation sinks in.

"No way," Duncan protests, disbelief evident in his voice. "Izzy wouldn't use that kind of language. She's not like that."

"Duncan," Rachael begins slowly, "you really do not know your girlfriend. She has a dark side. Trust me when I say she is evil to the core."

"Isn't that a bit extreme?" Duncan counters, frowning. "Evil?"

"Duncan, hear me out," I urge him earnestly. "You weren't there for the confrontation between Izzy and Rach. It escalated quickly. Rachael was trying to be civil, but how can you remain nice when someone like Izzy is throwing around insults?"

The tension thickens as Duncan grapples with this new information. He's torn between defending Isadora and accepting that she might not be the person he thinks she is, leaving an unresolved conflict hanging in the air.

Rachael looks at him with a mix of frustration and pity; she understands how difficult it is to see someone you care about in a different light, and I can tell her heart aches for Duncan's predicament.

"I don't know what to say," Duncan stammers, his voice filled with uncertainty. "I'm truly sorry for whatever you think Izzy may have intended. I'm sure it was just a simple misunderstanding." His words reflect the turmoil inside him, caught between his feelings for Isadora and the unsettling truth about her, a truth that could shatter their relationship.

"Duncan," I reply firmly, my heart racing, "I was there. I saw it unfold. There was no misunderstanding." My voice is resolute, determined to make Duncan understand the gravity of the situation.

Julie steps in, her calm demeanor a stark contrast to the

tension in the air. "Let's take a breath and approach this from a different perspective," she suggests, her eyes darting between us like a referee trying to restore order in a heated sports match.

"What different perspective?" Duncan retorts, frustration bubbling beneath the surface as anger ignites in his gaze.

"Maybe what happened this evening was the doing of Ezekiel and Abrahim," Julie proposes thoughtfully, her brow furrowed with concern. "This could have been their strategy all along—to divide us into opposing camps."

The idea hangs in the air, laden with implications. It's a wild notion, but it resonates with a strange logic. Suddenly, the argument feels less like a personal attack and more like a game we didn't sign up to play. The uncertainty of our roles in this situation adds an intriguing layer to the tension, making the air in the garage crackle with suspense.

"I still say it was Izzy who locked me inside the apartment," Rachael shoots a fierce glare at Duncan, her frustration evident, and the intensity of the confrontation rises.

It feels like a scene straight out of one of my favorite detective novels—I love reading detective stories. The air in the garage is a taut wire, stretched and ready to snap at the slightest touch.

"Rach," Julie chimes in, her voice smooth and calming, a soothing balm in the midst of the storm, "let's take a moment to step back and think this through. What evidence do you have? It's easy to point fingers without concrete proof."

Rachael hesitates, her resolve starting to crumble under Julie's logical approach. She shifts her weight from one foot to the other, arms crossed defensively. "Alright, I see your point," she concedes, her voice softer now, less accusatory.

"So, can we all agree that without solid evidence, we can't blame Izzy, Ezekiel, or Abrahim?" Julie asks, her tone steady but firm. "Until we have definitive proof, the identity of the person or persons responsible for locking Rachael in the garage apartment remains a mystery. From what I've gathered tonight, Izzy, Ezekiel, and Abrahim all had motive and opportunity. But remember, no one should be presumed guilty until we have solid evidence."

Leaning into my ear, Ryan whispers, "Has Julie been watching law shows on TV?"

I snicker.

As the air grows heavy with unspoken accusations and lingering doubts, it's clear that this isn't just about a locked door; it's a complex puzzle waiting to be pieced together. Who really had the most to gain from Rachael's confinement? The night is still young, and with every second that ticks by, the mystery deepens. So here we are, left wondering: who's really behind this evening's shenanigans?

DAY TWENTY

Saturday, June 8, 2019

As the morning sun fills the dining room with its warm glow, a sense of peace settles over us. We're gathered around the dinning room table, sharing laughter and lighthearted conversation over a breakfast that is truly a feast for the senses. The crunch of the bacon, the buttery aroma of the toast, the burst of flavor from the locally sourced eggs and strawberry jam, the tangy sweetness of the orange juice, and the rich aroma of the coffee all come together to create a delightful spread that feels like a comforting slice of the past.

Despite the lingering tension from last night's episode in the garage apartment, where a heated argument had broken out, we choose to savor this tranquil moment together. The conversation flows easily as we enjoy our meal, each bite grounding us in the present. It's funny how food brings people together.

Suddenly, without saying a word, Duncan rises from his chair with a clear purpose. He begins to prepare a breakfast tray for Isadora, carefully assembling a cup of tea, a saucer, and a plate of toast.

"Uh, Duncan," Rachael interrupts, her brow furrowing in genuine curiosity and a hint of disapproval in her voice. "Dear, what exactly are you doing?"

Duncan replies with a mischievous glint in his eye, "I'm making a breakfast tray for Izzy." He continues to spread jam generously on a slice of toast, the sweet scent of strawberries filling the air and creating a cozy, comforting homey atmosphere in the room.

Rachael, with her arms crossed in defiance, asserts her

position with unwavering determination. "I do not think so. If Isadora wants breakfast, she can come downstairs and join the rest of us. Otherwise, she can go without." Her tone is resolute, leaving no room for negotiation.

"But she's not feeling well," Duncan argues gently, concern etched on his face as he turns to face Rachael.

"Oh, I beg to differ," Rachael retorts sharply. "I believe she feels well enough to make the trek downstairs. This is my house, and I set the rules here." Her voice carries an air of authority that brooks no dissent.

Duncan sighs heavily, his shoulders slumping as he mutters, "Izzy's not going to like this." His tone reflects resignation, a sense of helplessness in the face of Rachael's authority.

"Too bad," Rachael shoots back, her eyes glinting with determination. "We have all endured Izzy's antics for far too long." Her words reveal deep frustration and weariness from dealing with Isadora's questionable behavior, which seems to weigh her down.

With that bold statement hanging in the air like a challenge, Duncan reluctantly steps away from the tray he had been assembling and sinks back into his chair at the table.

The atmosphere in the room crackles with anticipation, putting all of us on the edge of our seats, waiting for a storm to break. The spat between Rachael and Isadora has escalated to a point that demands resolution before it spirals into utter chaos. I, for one, am not eager to witness what could easily be the beginning of World War III.

The dining table has transformed into a tense battleground, with silence so thick it would take an axe to break through it. It feels as if we're all tiptoeing through a minefield, where each step could trigger an explosion of emotions. The tension hangs in the air like a storm cloud ready to burst, and I feel the weight of our unspoken fears pressing down on us. What's about to unfold? A heated confrontation? An awkward silence? The suspense is killing me.

Then, in a moment that could have been lifted from a

dramatic play, Isadora makes her grand entrance. She stands in the archway of the dining room, her figure a striking silhouette against the light, clad in a flowing nightgown. Her presence is commanding, instantly capturing our attention and shifting the dynamics of the room.

"Dunkie darling," she calls out, impatience creeping into her voice. "Where's my breakfast? I've been waiting."

All eyes dart toward Duncan, and the tension in the room is heavy. Everyone seems to hold their breath, exchanging glances as if silently debating who should speak first. Meanwhile, Duncan remains fixated on his breakfast, lost in thought—or perhaps wishing he could vanish altogether. His hands tremble slightly, revealing the internal struggle he's facing.

"*Dunkie darling*," Rachael mocks Isadora, a smirk dancing on her lips. Her confidence sharply contrasts with Isadora's innocence. "Duncan will no longer be providing you with room service." The underlying tension between the two women is undeniable, adding yet another layer to the already charged atmosphere.

Isadora blinks innocently, her voice filled with childlike wonder. "What's she talking about, Dunkie Poo?"

"Well, it's like this—" Duncan begins, but his words are abruptly cut off.

"Because I made it abundantly clear to him that he can no longer provide you with room service," Rachael interjects firmly, her tone leaving no room for argument. "As a guest in my home, you are expected to respect the other guests—and me—by joining us in the dining room for meals at the designated times. If you choose not to show up on time, that is your decision, but you will forfeit that meal. It is as simple as that." The tension in the air builds like dark storm clouds on the horizon, signaling an impending thunderstorm.

Isadora pouts, clearly unaccustomed to being called out like this. The rest of us at the table exchange knowing glances; it's not every day that Rachael stands her ground against Isadora's whims, showcasing the complex dynamics at play.

"Dunkie, what's going on?" Isadora's voice is not only high-pitched but also dripping with petulance, reminiscent of a spoiled child who has just been reprimanded.

The room remains silent, an uncomfortable silence that heightens the tension; each passing second feels heavier than the last. Duncan remains silent, his gaze fixed on his breakfast, as though he's searching his plate of eggs and bacon for the right words.

Rachael, however, is not one to let the moment pass without comment. "I, for one," she declares, her tone firm and resolute, "have had enough of your feigned illness and childish antics. You are an adult—so start acting like one!"

Isadora's eyes widen as she turns to Duncan for support. "Dunkie, why is she being so mean to me?" Her voice oozes with the kind of entitlement only a spoiled child can muster, and her words hang in the air with audacious confidence.

"Izzy," Duncan replies coolly without even looking at her, "it's probably best if you join us for breakfast. After all, Rachael is our host, and we are guests in her home."

"But she invited us," Isadora protests, crossing her arms defiantly, as if that somehow absolves her of responsibility. She attempts to shift the blame onto Rachael, like a child trying to dodge a timeout.

"Yes, I did invite Duncan," Rachael interjects, her eyes narrowing into a glare that could shatter glass. Her voice is laced with a simmering anger. "But you showed up with him uninvited and have taken advantage of my gracious hospitality."

The atmosphere thickens as Rachael's words hang in the air. It's clear that this conversation is no longer just about breakfast; it's about boundaries and respect.

Duncan lifts his head, glancing between the two women and finding himself caught in the middle of this escalating tension. "Let's just eat our breakfast," he suggests quietly, his voice laden with discomfort. His attempt at a peaceful resolution is evident, but the strain in his voice reveals his true feelings. He knows that this breakfast is bound to be anything but calm from this point on.

"Duncan," Isadora retorts, clenching her fists at her sides. "Are you really going to let her talk to me like that?" In an instant, Isadora's facade of innocence crumbles, and anger simmers just beneath the surface. Red-faced, she turns to face Rachael, her eyes blazing with fury. "I'll have you know I have just as much right to be here as any of these bozos!" She extends her arm in a sweeping gesture, indicating that she's referring to all of us.

The tension in the room escalates, a mix of indignation and defiance hanging in the air as each woman refuses to back down. Isadora's hands tremble slightly, and Rachael's jaw tightens as their eyes lock, intensifying their silent battle.

"Izzy," Duncan pleads, his gaze fixed on his barely touched breakfast, "can you please, for my sake, dial it down a notch? Rach is right—you weren't invited. I assumed bringing you along would be fine without first checking with Rachael." Apparently, he's regretting his assumption, feeling torn between his loyalty to Isadora and his desire to keep the peace.

"Well," Isadora huffs, her voice tinged with a mix of hurt and indignation, "I never—" Her words trail off into a wounded silence as she storms out of the room, likely retreating to sulk in her bedroom. The atmosphere shifts, leaving Duncan caught between Isadora and Rachael, along with the awkwardness of the tense situation. The discomfort is undeniable, making the rest of us feel uneasy.

The air is thick and heavy, much like molasses. Our breakfast remains unfinished—actually, it has barely begun—but the tension in the room is discernible, creating a wave of discomfort. We sit frozen around the table, each of us acutely aware of our surroundings, waiting for someone to break the stifling silence.

Finally, the tension shatters like icicles falling to the ground. "Excuse me," Rachael says, her voice cutting through the oppressive quiet. In a sudden, unexpected move that shocks us all, she rises from the table, tosses her twisted linen napkin down onto the table, and storms out of the room.

An awkward stillness envelops us, stretching like a taut rubber band ready to snap, with the tension lingering in the air like a heavy fog over a marsh.

In an unexpected move, Duncan rises from his seat, disrupting the calm with his abrupt declaration: "Excuse me." He strides toward the parlor, and before we can fully comprehend his actions, the front door slams shut, the sound reverberating through the house and dramatically altering the atmosphere. This is soon followed by the roar of Duncan's SUV engine and the squeal of tires as he drives away.

We're all in shock, exchanging bewildered glances with raised eyebrows and half-eaten toast still in our hands. His sudden departure has thrown us off balance, and we're bracing ourselves for the next unexpected twist in the story, like the moment just before a TV commercial begins.

"Well," Julie finally speaks up, her tone a mix of relief and disbelief, "that was certainly intense." Without another word, we gingerly return to our breakfasts, chewing in silence, our shared hope for normalcy binding us together. But deep down, we know this start of the day is anything but ordinary.

"Am I the only one getting the impression that Izzy and Rach have some serious issues?" Giles observes, his brow furrowed with concern as his eyes dart between us.

"Issues?" Ryan scoffs, a grin spreading across his face. "Gurrrl, they're like two feral cats in heat fighting over the same tomcat." His humor lightens the mood, and we can't help but chuckle at his comparison.

Snickers erupt around the table, lifting the heaviness that had settled over us. Just like that, normalcy begins to return for Julie, Ryan, Giles, and me—even if only for the moment.

Reflecting on what happened earlier this morning, Isadora and Rachael's exchanges resembled a scene from a reality show about complicated friendships. Their snide remarks, eye rolls, and sharp comments created a spectacle similar to a live-action soap opera, with two frustrated divas reading each other.

However, beneath the drama lies the potential for a deeper conflict. What's the untold story here? Is there a jealousy-fueled issue brewing beneath the surface that we are unaware of? Or could it be something entirely different? Regardless of the cause, it's clear that the breakfast incident was more than just a simple disagreement.

As I finish washing and putting away the last of the breakfast dishes, a heavy silence settles over the house. Where is Duncan? He hasn't returned since he stormed out during breakfast, and there hasn't been a word from Isadora or Rachael. The air crackles with tension, as if I'm standing on the edge of a volcano, waiting for it to erupt. A knot of worry tightens in my chest.

I head upstairs to my bedroom to grab my favorite UT baseball cap and sunglasses, eager for a distraction. Julie convinced us guys that a vigorous walk outdoors would do us good—she promised that fresh air would clear our minds. After the intense drama of the morning, the four of us are feeling the weight of what we had witnessed. Even though none of us were directly involved in the confrontation, it left a lingering impression that I doubt any of us can shake off—at least not right away.

As I walk the upstairs hallway toward my room, I'm surprised to find Rachael kneeling outside Isadora and Duncan's bedroom door. The door is firmly closed, but what I'm seeing is anything but ordinary. Rachael is meticulously shredding a handful of herbs into a small bowl on the floor. I stop beside her, feeling a surge of both curiosity and unease, intrigued by this strange scene.

"What's up, Rach?" I ask, genuinely puzzled by her unusual behavior. She's hunched over, clutching a handful of weeds as if they're treasures. Surprisingly, she doesn't even look up. Instead, she seems deeply absorbed in her own world, muttering a phrase over and over that sounds like gibberish—totally incomprehensible but oddly captivating. It's as if she's unraveling a secret code, a mystery that only she can decipher. Whatever she's doing has aroused my curiosity. Usually, I'd stick around to see what Rachael is up to, but not today; I'm on my way to retrieve my cap and sunglasses.

I dismiss whatever Rachael is doing. This is her house; she can do as she pleases. As I make my way to my bedroom, I concentrate on finding one thing: my cap. I know it must be in my room since I wore it while digging up Rachael's garden and again when we planted the vegetable seeds. Isn't it funny how the things we search for seem to turn up in the last place we look? Running out of places to check, I finally decide to look beneath the bed. Aha! Here it is, hiding in the most unexpected spot. I can't help but chuckle at the cap's clever hiding place as I pull it out and triumphantly place it on my head, feeling a wave of relief wash over me. How it got there, I'll probably never know.

Next, I grab my sunglasses from atop the bedroom bureau, sliding one arm of the frames down the top opening of my shirt so they dangle effortlessly against my chest. I'm set, and it's time to join the others downstairs for our late morning walk.

As I exit the bedroom and step into the stillness of the hall, I notice that Rachael has left her post outside Isadora and Duncan's closed bedroom door. Even the bowl of shredded weeds is gone. I rush down the hall toward the stairs, my mind focused solely on rejoining my friends. Suddenly, an alarming scent pierces the air: smoke. It's not the lingering smell of a lit joint, but the unmistakable odor of something burning—like a fire. My heart races as I pause in the hallway, glancing back at the corridor I just came from. Pale gray smoke curls ominously from beneath Isadora and Duncan's bedroom door. Duncan hasn't returned yet, but I'm fairly certain Isadora is inside. Without thinking, I shift into auto-drive and sprint back to their door, adrenaline coursing through my veins. The smoke thickens, swirling like a dark cloud determined to keep me away, but I push forward; my determination to reach Isadora overpowers both my fear and my mixed feelings for her.

"Izzy!" I shout, pounding on the door as my voice echoes against the walls. There's no answer. Panic grips me tighter than ever as I continue to beat the door, feeling its heat radiate through the wood. What if she's asleep? What if I'm too late?

"Izzy!" I call out again, striking the door with all my strength. "Are you in there?"

"Yes! I'm in here! I can't get out!" Her voice trembles with fear.

I twist the doorknob frantically, but it won't budge—it's locked. And it's hot to the touch. "Izzy, please, unlock the door!" I plead, my voice thick with desperation as time slips through our fingers.

"The door isn't locked!" she cries back, her words filled with panic.

Just then, Giles appears beside me, his brow furrowing with concern. "What's going on?" he asks, glancing at the thickening smoke seeping from under Isadora's bedroom door. "I thought I smelled something burning…"

"Oh my gosh!" Julie exclaims as she and Ryan join us, her eyes wide with alarm. "Rye! Go grab the fire extinguisher from the kitchen—and hurry!"

Without a moment's hesitation, Ryan bolts downstairs like a shot. My heart races. Every second is crucial. I turn back to the door, my mind racing for a solution to rescue Izzy before it's too late.

"Hang tight, Izzy! We're not giving up on you!" I shout, my voice a beacon of unwavering determination amidst the chaos. Panicking, Giles bangs on the door, his fear echoing mine. This is not just a scare; it's a terrifying ordeal we're facing.

"Come on, Rye, come on!" I mutter under my breath as we wait for Ryan to return with the extinguisher. The smoke grows thicker, and every second feels like an eternity. My lungs burn from inhaling the thickening smoke.

"Izzy! Listen carefully. Wrap yourself in a blanket and move away from the fire!" Giles's voice booms through the chaos, urgency lacing every word. It feels like a scene straight out of a horror movie, and I fear we're running out of time.

"Why isn't this door opening?" he shouts, desperation filling his voice as he attacks the doorknob with increasing force.

"I don't know! It must be jammed or something," I yell back, my voice tinged with panic. "Izzy claims it's not locked!"

"What do we do?" Julie frets, her hands twisting together as if wringing her hands like a wet dish towel. "We can't let her die in there!"

Ryan bursts into the hallway, clutching the fire extinguisher as if it's the Holy Grail. Smoke wraps around us, swirling like a dark cloud of despair. We're all coughing now—each breath is a painful struggle, our eyes watering and throats raw. If it's this suffocating out here in the hall, imagine the horrors Isadora is facing on the other side of the closed door—and she's all alone. Time is running out—every second counts. We must act quickly before it's too late.

Rachael suddenly appears in the smoke-filled hallway, her presence a beacon of calm amidst the craziness of the situation. Relief washes over me at her arrival, a stark contrast to the panic that has gripped us. "Good, Rach! You're here," I exclaim, the relief evident in my voice. "We can't get the door to open, and Izzy's trapped inside!"

"Rye, do you have your cell on you? Call the fire department!" Julie commands urgently, her eyes wide with panic, the urgency of the situation clear.

"Rye, stop. There is no need for that," Rachael interjects smoothly, her voice steady like a cool breeze on a sweltering day. "There is no fire."

"What's wrong with you? Izzy's room is engulfed in flames!" Julie insists desperately. "We have to do something to help save her!"

With a calm air of confidence, Rachael raises her hands over her head and claps twice. The bedroom door swings open with a bang.

Ryan rushes into the bedroom, fire extinguisher raised like a knight wielding a sword, ready to battle the flames. He halts abruptly, his eyes darting around the pristine room—no smoke, no fire, no singed curtains—just an oddly serene atmosphere. His surprise is evident; his readiness to fight the fire is replaced with confusion.

As we stand in the hallway, the once oppressive smoke and acrid scent of burning wood have inexplicably vanished, leaving behind a strangely calm and clean environment, as if a fire had never occurred.

"What in the world just happened?" Ryan asks, his voice reflecting the bewilderment that all of us are feeling.

Julie stands frozen, her brow knitted in confusion. "I... I don't know what just happened," she stammers, glancing at Rachael.

Rachael chuckles lightly, her eyes sparkling with mischief as they meet Isadora's wide-eyed gaze. "Consider yourself warned," she says, a heavy note of challenge in her tone. "Do not mess with me, Isdadora. There might be real flames next time."

With that cryptic remark lingering in the air, Rachael turns on her heels and struts down the hall toward the stairs.

Ryan scratches his head, trying to piece together this bizarre puzzle. "Seriously, can someone tell me what on earth just happened?" he mutters, glancing at Julie, Isadora, Giles, and then at me as we all struggle to understand the inexplicable events we just witnessed.

Dale Thele

DAY TWENTY-ONE

Sunday, June 9, 2019

Breakfast is an awkward affair, to say the least. Picture this: Isadora and Rachael are seated at opposite ends of the dining table, engaged in a silent duel, their eyes locked in suspicion. The unresolved conflict between them, stemming from Isadora's recent rebellious actions and Rachael's retaliation, hangs in the air like an impending storm, dark and ready to unleash chaos. Neither of them dares to touch their meals. The rest of us, caught in the crossfire, remain silent, too afraid to break the ice while feeling the weight of the situation. It's a standoff reminiscent of an old Western movie; instead of guns, we have toast, bacon, and scrambled eggs. The tension is unmistakable, like high noon at the O.K. Corral.

"Rye, could you pass the sugar, please?" Julie's soft, nervous voice slices through the silence like lightning splitting a tree. It's a brave move—one that could either diffuse the situation or escalate it further.

Ryan reaches for the sugar bowl, but just before he touches it, something extraordinary happens. The bowl, seemingly possessed by a mischievous spirit, gracefully lifts off the table and hovers in the air, guided by an unseen force. It then moves smoothly through the air toward Julie. Everyone, except for Rachael, stops breathing, and our eyes widen in shock and disbelief. Rachael's smugness morphs into a leer, a sinister glint in her eyes. Isadora's defiance shifts to anger, while Julie's nervousness transforms into a mix of awe and curiosity. The tension in the room gives way to confusion and unasked questions.

Just for reference, Julie, Ryan, Duncan, and I experienced similar phenomena last summer, but those were caused by the benevolent ghosts that inhabited this house. However, this time is different because Ezekiel and Abrahim have frightened all the ghosts away. What we just witnessed wasn't due to ghosts; it was something altogether different.

We all sit frozen, our jaws hanging in disbelief, as if a bolt of lightning has just struck us. Rachael's long, slender finger points like an accusing arrow at the levitating bowl, a sight that defies all logic and reason.

"What in the world?" Julie gasps, her reaction mirroring our collective astonishment. The air crackles with the sheer intensity of the moment.

With a mix of awe and disbelief, we watch the sugar bowl glide into Julie's waiting hand just as Rachael lowers her finger. The tension, once thick with hostility, now crackles with pure astonishment, a testament to the inexplicable event we have just witnessed.

Let's take a brief pause from the narrative to ensure everyone's up to speed. Yesterday, following the incident where Isadora's bedroom was engulfed in flames, Julie turned to me, her eyes wide with shock. "Rach is a witch, right?" she suddenly asked.

I nodded in response.

"And exactly when were you going to let us in on this little bombshell?" Julie demanded, her frustration evident. It's no secret that Julie hates being kept in the dark, even though she's not above keeping her own secrets.

I sighed and ran a hand through my hair. "Well," I replied slowly, "I suppose I always knew deep down, but I hadn't connected the dots until now."

"What dots?" Julie asked, her curiosity bubbling like a pot of water about to spill over.

"Hold on," Giles interjected, his hands raised like a referee stopping a match. His calm and diplomatic nature helped balance the situation. "Taylor, why don't you take a step back and explain what you know?"

"You'd better start explaining," Julie insisted, her tone firm and unwavering. "From the beginning, buster."

With a playful grin on my face, I acted as if I were preparing to give a presentation to my classmates in elementary school. "Okay, I was born on a Tuesday afternoon at—"

"Not *that* beginning," Julie exclaimed, rolling her eyes dramatically. "I meant the part where you realized Rach is a witch."

"Alright, it was last summer," I said, my voice filled with warmth as I recalled the past. "You, Duncan, and Rye had all left town, leaving just Beau and me in this big, old, quiet house. Then the phone rang. It was my attorney inviting me to his office because he had something urgent to discuss."

"So, you drove downtown to meet with him?" Ryan asked, trying to encourage me to hurry up with my story.

"Yes," I replied, recalling the unease that settled in my stomach like a heavy stone as I drove there. That feeling only deepened when I arrived at his office and saw Mr. Andrews speaking with a woman dressed in all black. He introduced her as Mrs. Blackburn—"

"Wait a minute! Not the *widow* Blackburn?" Julie gasped, her eyes wide with disbelief, echoing the shock I felt at that moment.

"Believe it or not," I said with a wry smile, "she turned out to be very much alive."

"How was that possible?" Julie asked.

"That's a whole other story for another time," I said.

"Please continue," Ryan urged eagerly. "You were in the attorney's office with Mrs. Blackburn…"

"That's when everything changed. I discovered that Mrs. Blackburn was actually my aunt—an aunt I never knew existed. The weight of this revelation was so heavy that it shook me to my core," I concluded, my voice trembling with the emotional impact of the discovery.

The revelation hung in the air like a dark storm cloud filled with unanswered questions and hidden family secrets. Standing on the brink of this newfound connection, one thing became clear: life has a way of revealing surprises when you least expect them.

"How could you not know about your aunt?" Ryan asked, his voice full of disbelief and curiosity, his brow furrowed.

I took a deep breath, before untangling the threads of my past. "It's a long story," I began, my words heavy with the weight of unspoken history, and my throat felt dry. "I was adopted, and my biological mother was Mrs. Blackburn's sister."

"Adopted?" Ryan's eyes nearly bulged. "Did you say you were adopted? I've known you for almost all my life and there's no way you were adopted."

"Yes," I confirmed. "I was adopted."

Ryan's expression showed surprise. "But why didn't your real mom ever try to contact you?"

"Rye, you goof," Julie interjected. "Don't you know anything? His real mom gave Taylor up—she didn't want anything to do with him."

The weight of my revelation hung heavily in the air as I continued, "Actually, she never tried to contact me because she died giving birth to me."

"Why didn't Mrs. Blackburn attempt to contact you?" Duncan asked.

"According to the adoption agreement, Mrs. Blackburn couldn't legally reach out to me until after my twentieth birthday."

Ryan ran his fingers through his hair, absorbing the impact of my words. "Wow, that's intense."

"Wait just a moment, let me get this straight," Julie said, her eyes widening in disbelief. "So, you're saying that Mrs. Blackburn, the woman we thought was dead, is actually alive? And she's your aunt—your biological mother's sister?"

"Exactly," I confirmed, feeling a mix of relief and apprehension wash over me. It felt as if a huge weight had been lifted from my shoulders as I began to unravel the threads of my past. However, with each revelation came a new wave of uncertainty. It was similar to the relief I felt when I first came out to Ryan about being gay. The burden of my past and the fear of an unknown future felt like heavy chains around my heart, while the honesty of finally sharing my truth was like a breath of fresh air.

Giles interjected with a puzzled expression, "All of this is very interesting, but what does any of this have to do with Rachael being a witch?"

"I'm getting to that," I replied, my voice steady but filled with anticipation. "It turns out my aunt—Mrs. Blackburn—is a direct descendant of Mrs. Scruggs, the person for whom this house was originally built. And as we all know from reading the old journal, Scruggs was a witch. It seems that the legacy of old Mrs. Scruggs runs deep—her descendants were also witches."

"Are you saying what I think you're saying?" Julie's eyes widened in disbelief, her excitement barely contained.

"Yes, my aunt is indeed a witch," I confirmed, embracing the weight of the revelation. The air seemed to crackle with the energy of the news, and I could almost smell the faint hint of magic potions lingering around us. It felt as if a spell had been cast over our conversation, transforming an ordinary day into one filled with the extraordinary.

"So if your aunt—Widow Blackburn—is a witch, what does that make you? A wizard?" Julie asked, raising an eyebrow. I could see the gears turning in her head, waiting for my response.

"Julie, don't you know anything?" Ryan interjected with a smirk. "Male witches are called warlocks."

"Sorry to disappoint," I said with a playful shrug. "But the witch bloodline flows only through the female descendants, bypassing the male gene."

"Who says?" Ryan challenged, raising an eyebrow.

"According to my aunt," I said, relishing the thrill of sharing my family's secret.

"You still haven't explained how you came to suspect

Rachael of being a witch," Giles pressed, curiosity dancing in his eyes as he eagerly anticipated juicy details.

"Rachael is my aunt's distant niece," I explained, allowing the weight of my words to hang in the air like a spell, making the gravity of the situation evident. "She comes from a long line that traces back to Mrs. Scruggs—though she's a very distant descendant."

Julie furrowed her brow in thought. "I understand how those connections might lead you to that suspicion. However, this brings me to another point: I don't understand how Rachael ended up with your house. Your aunt entrusted it to you for a reason, didn't she?"

I took a deep breath, the memory still vivid in my mind. "My aunt returned to Lost Creek Junction with an urgent warning about a curse on the house."

"A curse?" Julie repeated, disbelief coloring her voice, her eyes widening as if I had just revealed a shocking secret. "What kind of curse are we talking about here?"

"This house is under a very peculiar curse," I revealed, each word heavy with significance, almost as if they were laced with magic themselves. "The house can never be owned by a *male* descendant of the old Lady Scruggs."

"Why is that?" Julie asked, her curiosity growing.

"There's a centuries old curse, a deadly legacy that claims any male heir of the Scruggs bloodline who owns this house will meet an unimaginably horrific fate," I said, urgency thick in my voice. "My aunt, driven by this dark secret, returned to town to save me from its deadly grasp."

"How did she save you?" Giles asked.

"I sold the house back to her for one dollar," I replied, the sheer absurdity of it all still lingering in my mind, casting a veil of mystery over the situation.

"A dollar?" Ryan echoed, incredulous. "The land alone is worth a fortune. How could you sell your house for just a measly dollar?"

"I know," I said, shaking my head. "But I couldn't take

advantage of her kindness. Giving back the house wouldn't necessarily ensure my escape from the curse. Besides, I was running out of time. I needed to dump the house before the curse took hold of me. I had to sell it—fast."

Julie's eyes widened with intrigue as she sought clarification. "Let me get this straight—your aunt repurchased the very house she left you in her will, and she wasn't actually dead after all?"

"That's right," I confirmed, the weight of the revelation settling around us like a heavy shroud, casting a solemn air over our conversation.

"You still haven't explained how Rachael ended up with the house," Giles pressed, his voice tinged with curiosity that hung in the air.

"After my aunt repurchased the house from me, she gifted it to Rachael," I explained, recalling how that twist had unfolded. It was one of those quirks that seemed perfectly normal at the time but now felt like a plot twist from a Gothic novel.

"Now we've come full circle," Giles mused thoughtfully, his words carrying the weight of his contemplation. "You haven't answered how you came to suspect Rachael is a witch."

"Simple," I replied, a hint of mischief in my voice. "She's a descendant of that infamous widow Scruggs. You know, the one who was rumored in the journals to have dabbled in all sorts of mystical nonsense back in the day."

"Why did you wait until now to tell us all of this?" Julie asked, her curiosity piqued like a cat spotting a laser pointer.

"Because, until a few days ago, I hadn't had the chance to see all of you to convey this information," I replied, acknowledging the validity of her question. After all, it's not every day you reveal dark family secrets over morning coffee and honey buns.

"I guess in a convoluted way, that makes sense," Julie nodded, her brow furrowing as she processed the implications.

Now that I've shared the intriguing backstory of how I came to know Rachael and my aunt, the enigmatic widow Blackburn, let's return to our peculiar breakfast—a meal that's about to take an extraordinary turn.

"Duncan, could you please pass the butter?" Giles inquires politely, his tone casual as if he were discussing the weather. But as Duncan reaches for the butter dish, something astonishing happens: it floats effortlessly from the table and glides gracefully through the air toward Giles.

Rachael points at the levitating dish with a triumphant air, casting a sly glance at Isadora, as if to say, *La-di-da, see what I can do?*

However, Isadora is not one to be outdone. Her fury simmers just beneath the surface, and her face turns a fiery crimson as anger bubbles up with each passing moment. With a sudden burst of determination, she rises from her chair, producing Beau's stick and points it over the table. The tension in the room mounts, thickening the air.

"*Altr phira spectumas*," she intones dramatically, sweeping the stick across the table like a conductor leading an orchestra. In response to her incantation, the salt and pepper shakers, sugar bowl, and an assortment of small dishes begin to shake and shudder as if awakened by an earthquake. Slowly, the dishes levitate precariously above the table, the air thick with tension. Each second stretches into an eternity as everyone holds their breath. Isadora smiles smugly.

"Isadora," Rachael warns, her voice low and menacing, "if I were you, I would think twice before making your next move."

The room feels like a battlefield of wills, with everyone acutely aware that this situation has escalated beyond a simple dispute over butter—it's a clash of power. The tension is overwhelmingly thick in the air.

We sit at the grand table frozen in shock, grappling with the startling revelation: Isadora is also a witch? The disbelief hangs heavy in the air, and it's clear she possesses some magical abilities. This revelation sends ripples of surprise through the group. However, let's be honest—her skills, while impressive, pale in comparison to Rachael's formidable talent. The stark contrast only heightens the tension in the room.

As if the atmosphere weren't tense enough, the items hovering around us start to tremble and sway, as though they are experiencing a mini panic attack. It seems the invisible force keeping them aloft is losing its grip.

Then, with a grand flourish, Isadora waves Beau's stick and declares, "*Zynara kata volushin.*" Instantly, all the struggling objects gently descend to their original places on the table, and Isadora settles back into her chair.

"Isadora," Rachael warns, her voice steady yet laced with anger. She jabs the air with an accusatory finger toward Isadora. "You shouldn't meddle in matters you know very little about."

Just when I thought things couldn't get any more bizarre, Isadora's chair defies all laws of gravity and lifts off the floor. Her eyes widen in disbelief as she nervously glances down at the floor, now several feet below her. Frightened, she clutches the edges of the chair to keep from falling. An eerie silence fills the room, heightening the tension as we stare at her, half-expecting her to float away like a rogue cartoon balloon character in the Macy's Thanksgiving Day Parade.

"Do not mess with me," Rachael declares, her voice sharp as a knife. With a flick of her wrist, her fingers move in small, deliberate circles, and suddenly, Isadora and her chair become a spectacle—spinning mid-air like an out-of-control carnival ride. The chair spins faster and faster while Isadora's face turns a sickly green, as if she might hurl at any moment. It's a display of Rachael's absolute control over the situation.

The air crackles with energy as Rachael halts Isadora's fast spinning chair by raising her open palm toward her. In an instant, the chair stops its dizzying motion, landing on the floor with a loud thud, releasing the tension that had filled the room.

Flushed with anger, a dazed Isadora rises from her chair, indignation clear on her face. She staggers out of the room, leaving an unsettling silence that envelops us all.

"I truly apologize for that display of power you just witnessed," Rachael says, her tone shifting from triumph to calm reflection. "But as a guest in my home, Isadora must learn her place." With that, Rachael gracefully stands and exits the dining room, leaving a lingering tension in her wake.

"Wow," Ryan mutters, his eyes wide with surprise. "I didn't see that coming at all." His astonishment adds to the intrigue of the situation.

The atmosphere is heavy with unspoken words as we all try to process what just happened. Who knew breakfast would turn into such a wild showdown?

"Duncan," Julie interjects with a scornful frown, "why on earth didn't you tell us Izzy was a witch?"

"I had no idea—until now," Duncan admits, his voice barely above a whisper as he tries to digest the revelation. Obviously, his mind is racing, trying to make sense of everything he thought he knew about Isadora.

"Are you telling us you didn't know Izzy was a witch?" Ryan's voice is laced with disbelief, his raised eyebrow clearly showing his shock.

"Honestly, I'm just as shocked as you are," Duncan replies, rubbing his temples as if trying to fend off an impending migraine.

Just then, Rachael breezes back into the dining room, her bright smile lighting up the space. "Anyone for cinnamon rolls? They're fresh out of the oven!" She circles the table, offering the warm, sticky buns as if nothing extraordinary had happened moments earlier. The scent of cinnamon fills the air, and the golden crust of the buns glistens in the morning light.

Rachael pauses beside Duncan, her expression suddenly turning serious. "You need to get that leather-bound book away from Isadora," she warns urgently. "She does not understand its true power—and besides, it belongs to me. It is not just a book—it is a key to something much bigger."

"Are you referring to that old leather-covered cookbook I found in the cellar last summer?" Julie interjects.

"Julie, it's not a cookbook," I quietly clarify. Now that I've said it, I wish I could take my words back, but I can't, I have to continue. "It's a book of spells, curses, and enchantments."

The room falls silent for a moment as everyone processes this new twist in our already chaotic morning. The scent of cinnamon rolls lingers in the air, but it feels like we've stepped into a different kind of recipe—one filled with secrets and magic rather than sugar and spice. Suddenly, Duncan's brow furrows, Julie's eyes widen, and I sense a new tension building in the room; the atmosphere shifts abruptly.

"Moments ago," Rachael adds with an intensity that sends shivers down my spine, "Isadora recited two incantations from that very book."

I sit in stunned silence, questions swirling in my mind like leaves caught in a whirlwind. What secrets does that book hold? And what will happen if Isadora continues to wield its power, unaware of the danger she's inviting? The book is not merely a collection of recipes; it's a powerful tool that, in the wrong hands, could unleash chaos and destruction. And a power hungry Isadora is now in possession of it.

"Rach, I'm curious. Why was Izzy waving Beau's stick around while reciting those incantations?" Ryan asks, his brow furrowed with interest as he eagerly tries to unravel the mystery. His curiosity mirrors that of Julie, Duncan and Giles, drawing them deeper into the enigma of the book's power.

"Rach," I say, mindful of our hostess, "do you mind if I answer Rye's question?"

"Please," Rachael replies. "Be my guest."

I can't help but grin, excitement bubbling up inside me. "The stick that Beau found last summer is actually a magic wand," I reveal, my voice barely containing my enthusiasm. "It's also the key to unlocking the secrets of that ancient book Julie discovered." I see the anticipation in my friends' eyes as they eagerly await more details about this magical discovery.

Rachael speaks up, her eyes sparkling with intrigue. "When someone holds the wand—what you refer to as *Beau's stick*—in one hand, they can read the text within the *Book of Enchantments*. This so-called *cookbook* is a tome filled with spells and mysteries waiting to be uncovered. In Isadora's case, she recited memorized incantations from the book."

Julie nods slowly, her face a mix of awe and frustration. "So that's why I couldn't read the writing inside that cookbook, I wasn't holding Beau's stick," she exclaims, her voice filled with wonder. It's as if a light bulb has flickered to life above her head, illuminating the mysteries that had been swirling around us. Her eyes widen, and her breath catches in her throat as she grasps the implications of this revelation, her wonder mirroring our own fascination with this magical world.

"And it gets even better," Rachael continues, her enthusiasm infectious. "Magic can be channeled from the book through that very stick. Mrs. Scruggs harnessed her magic through it, just as generations of women before her have done."

The room buzzes with excitement as the implications of Rachael's words sink in—this is no ordinary cookbook; it's a gateway to something extraordinary.

Julie turns to me, a question burning on her lips. "Yet another secret. Why didn't you tell us this sooner?"

"I asked him not to share the secret," Rachael interjects gently, her tone soothing. "If he had revealed it earlier, would you have believed him?"

Julie pauses, weighing Rachael's words thoughtfully. "I suppose you've got a point," she concedes, a smile creeping onto her face as the tension begins to dissolve.

"Alright then," Duncan declares, rising from his chair with a sense of purpose that commands attention. "It looks like Izzy and I are long overdue for a heart-to-heart." He strides confidently toward the staircase, each step echoing his determination as if he's embarking on an epic quest, inspiring those around him.

"Duncan?" Rachael calls out, her voice soft yet steady.

"Yes, Rach," he replies, pausing to meet her gaze.

"While you're up there, could you please retrieve my *Book of Enchantments* from Isadora?"

Her request hangs in the air like a spell waiting to be cast.

"I'll see what I can do," Duncan assures her with a nod before resuming his journey up the stairs.

As the afternoon sun, a golden orb, approaches the horizon, it casts a warm, honeyed glow through the dining room windows. We are gathered around the large table, laughter mingling with the sound of shuffling cards. It's a delightful scene, but two members of our group are missing—Duncan and Isadora—who haven't been seen since breakfast. What's going on in their upstairs bedroom?

Just as the tension in the room reaches its peak, in walks Duncan, his face a mask of panic. But he's alone, leaving us to wonder about Isadora's whereabouts.

"Rachael," he gasps, "you were right—Izzy has your—" His voice breaks, and the urgency in his tone is evident. Yet, his voice falters, caught in his throat like a trapped bird.

"Duncan?" Julie's voice is laced with worry. "Are you okay?"

In a sudden, alarming twist, Duncan's body convulses as if struck by a bolt of lightning. His hands instinctively fly to his neck, fingers clawing at an invisible force. His lips move frantically, as if trying to shout out a warning that never escapes. Fear flickers in his wide eyes—a silent scream for help.

"Calm down, Duncan," Rachael urges gently. "Isadora must have cast a spell on you. She's preventing you from revealing something crucial... perhaps about the *Book of Enchantments*? Just the mention of the book sends shivers down my spine, for its power is both alluring and dangerous."

With a resigned nod, Duncan confirms her suspicion without uttering a word; a sense of betrayal lingers in the air.

"I knew it," Rachael declares, her voice filled with unwavering certainty. "It's a straightforward spell, and I can reverse its effects. Just hold still for a moment." With a flick of her fingers, she intones, "*Dalas showrei urnathar.*"

The air around us crackles with energy as Rachael's words resonate. Duncan's eyes widen, a mix of hope and anxiety swirling within him. We watch closely, our hearts racing as we wonder what secrets Duncan holds that Isadora wants to keep hidden. As Rachael's magic begins to take effect, she focuses intently on Duncan, her brow furrowing in concentration. "Come on, come on," she mutters under her breath, willing the magic to break through Isadora's hold. The atmosphere is thick with anticipation, and each of us hold our breath.

Suddenly, Duncan gasps as a wave of relief washes over him. The tension in his shoulders eases, and he begins to breathe normally. "I... I can speak again," he exclaims, his voice shaky but filled with urgency and determination. "Rach, I know where your book is—"

"Shh," Rachael interrupts gently, placing her fingertips on Duncan's lips to silence him. "You must not divulge any more information— otherwise, you will fall mute once again."

"But you just reversed the spell," Duncan protests, confusion etched across his face.

Rachael nods knowingly, her confidence in her understanding of the spell evident. "Yes, but only for a short time. The moment you try to reveal the location of the *Book of Enchantments*, the spell will once again trap you in silence. You are free to discuss anything else you like, but not the whereabouts of that book."

DAY TWENTY-TWO

Monday, June 10, 2019

As I carefully dry—washed and rinsed dishes, the rhythmic sound of splashing water fills the air, creating a soothing backdrop to our washing of the breakfast dishes. Rachael stands before the kitchen sink, her brow furrowed in concentration as she absently scrubs the dishes while peering out the window.

"I am convinced Isadora has the *Book of Enchantments*," she suddenly says, glancing over her shoulder at me with a hint of urgency. "You told me so yourself that she borrowed it, and we have seen her use the book's incantations."

A wave of guilt washes over me. "I deeply regret telling Izzy she could borrow your book," I confess, my voice barely audible as the weight of my mistake bears down on my heart. "I never imagined that book was so valuable."

Rachael hands me a freshly scrubbed plate, her tone softening as she reassures me. "Do not beat yourself up about it. You were being your wonderful, generous self. Honestly, if I were in your shoes and did not realize its significance, I might have done the same thing."

She pauses for a moment and adds with a wry smile, "I keep telling myself it is just a book. If I repeat that enough times, maybe I will start to believe it."

"But Rach," I gently interject, "it's not just *any* book—you know that."

She gazes out of the kitchen window, as if searching for answers among the fluffy, drifting fair-weather clouds. Her hands move in a repetitive, almost mechanical motion, scrubbing a plate repeatedly as if trying to erase the delicate rose pattern glazed on it. The atmosphere hums with unspoken thoughts, vibrating like the strings of a plucked guitar.

"Hey, Taylor," Julie calls as she strides into the kitchen. "Aren't you two finished with those dishes yet?"

"Sorry," I reply sheepishly, adding a sparkling clean plate to the stack of dried dishes. "We got caught up in conversation and—"

Before I can finish my thought, Rachael snaps back to reality, her expression suddenly fierce. "I have had enough of Isadora's lies and scheming." She hands me the last plate and wipes her soapy wet hands on a dish towel, flinging it onto the counter with a dramatic flourish. The atmosphere hums with unspoken words, like a live wire waiting to spark.

Sensing that Rachael is on a mission fueled by a potent mix of frustration and determination, Julie and I step aside to give her a wide berth. The anger etched on her face serves as a clear warning; she's on the verge of an explosive confrontation. She reminds me of a festering boil—eventually, the pressure builds until it bursts. Without saying another word, she storms up the stairs toward the bedrooms.

Julie and I follow her to the bottom of the staircase, where the two of us huddle together, exchanging worried glances as our curiosity intensifies. What will happen next? We wait with bated breath, eager to eavesdrop on what promises to be a drama filled confrontation. The air is thick with tension, like the charged atmosphere before a violent storm, and I can't help but wonder: how far will Rachael go to confront Isadora?

The sharp, thunderous sound of a fist pounding against a closed door shatters the quiet of the house. The reverberations echo through the walls, making my heart race even faster. I can only assume it's Duncan and Isadora's bedroom under siege. My heart races as I imagine what's about to unfold.

"I know you are in there," Rachael calls out, her voice slicing through the air like a sword in battle, bold and unwavering. "Open this door this instant!"

There's a moment of silence before I hear a door slowly

creak open.

"Yes, Rach?" Duncan replies, his tone surprisingly polite and soft despite the brewing storm. "What can I do for you?"

"For starters, you can tell that girlfriend of yours to get out of my house right now," Rachael demands, urgency flowing from her words like a torrent, creating an immediate sense of pressure. Julie and I exchange bewildered glances, our mouths drop open at this sudden and unexpected turn of events. I don't think either of us saw this coming.

"Tell her to pack her things and be out of my house within the hour," Rachael insists, her voice unwavering and firm, adding to the building tension in the house.

"We'll be out as soon as we're packed," Duncan replies calmly, trying to diffuse the tension.

"Duncan," Rachael interjects, her tone less sharp, "you are welcome to stay. It is your girlfriend that I do not want in my house."

Julie leans into my ear and whispers, "Things just got real." Her voice is barely above a breath, but the weight of her words hangs heavily in the air. I nod in agreement, my heart racing. Curiosity gnaws at me, yet fear keeps me rooted in place.

"What if Rachael catches us eavesdropping?" I whisper, my voice barely audible, filled with the fear of being discovered.

"Don't worry, she won't catch us," Julie whispers back.

"And while we are on the subject," Rachael interjects, her words flowing effortlessly like water bursting through a dam, eager to fill the emptiness. "Tell that inconsiderate girlfriend of yours that I want my book back. It belongs to me, and I will not allow anyone to treat it like a toy."

A heavy silence blankets the house, thick with tension. My mind races, wondering what chaos is unfolding upstairs. I can almost hear echoes of past arguments mixed with whispers of long-buried secrets.

"What, may I ask, are the two of you up to?" Rachael demands, her sudden appearance at the upper landing catching Julie and me off guard, my heart pounds in my chest. Her gaze pierces down at us like a hawk eyeing its prey, adding a sense of urgency to the situation.

"We were—" Julie stammers, her cheeks turning a bright shade of crimson. The embarrassment of being caught is evident in her voice, and her eyes dart around nervously, searching for an escape route.

"I know exactly what you two are up to," Rachael replies confidently as she descends the stairs, each step echoing like a drumbeat in the stillness. "Thank you for looking out for me," she says. Her gratitude feels sweet yet sincere, like honey. Just as we begin to move away from the staircase, a heated argument erupts between Duncan and Isadora. Their voices are loud and clear, even behind the closed bedroom door one floor above us.

The intensity of their voices is too tempting to ignore, drawing us in like moths to a flame.

"You've done nothing but lie to me and my friends since we arrived in Lost Creek Junction," Duncan's voice reverberates beyond the closed door, his frustration evident. "It's like I don't even know who you are anymore."

Isadora's voice is barely audible beyond the closed door, a whisper filled with deep hurt. We strain to hear her words but can't make them out. The air is thick with tension, and the sound of their voices echoes in the hall and down the stairs.

"I don't give a flip," Duncan snaps back, his voice sharp and filled with anger. "You've become obsessed with Rachael and that damned book of spells, as if nothing else exists anymore."

"Rachael has been rude to me ever since we arrived," Isadora retorts, her tone revealing the deep sting of betrayal.

"Things would have been different if you hadn't barged in uninvited on this trip," Duncan begins, frustration bubbling to the surface.

"I specifically asked if I could come with you," Isadora interjects, her voice trembling with rising emotion.

"You didn't ask—you declared that you were coming along whether I liked it or not." His tone is razor-sharp.

"Why do you always take Rachael's side?" Isadora's voice

quivers, and it sounds like she might start crying at any moment.

"I'm not taking sides," he insists, though his tone suggests otherwise. "But if I had to choose right now... it wouldn't be yours."

The weight of his statement hangs heavily in the air. Just then, Ryan joins Julie, Rachael, and me at the bottom of the stairs.

"Hey, guys, what's going on?" he asks, scanning our faces.

"Shhh!" Julie hisses urgently, her eyes wide with excitement. "We can't hear what they're saying."

Ryan curiously asks, "Who are you...?" His question trails off as he catches a snippet of the heated conversation coming from upstairs. He's as eager to eavesdrop as any of us.

"I'm fed up with your bullshit," Duncan declares, his voice filled with frustration.

There's a momentary pause in the conversation.

"Are you breaking up with me?" Isadora's voice quivers, sounding as if she's on the brink of tears. I suddenly feel a pang of sympathy for her, even if she doesn't deserve it.

"What do you think, Izzy? Of course I am. I've had it up to here with your crap." Duncan's words, sharp as a blade, cut through the air, leaving no room for misunderstanding. The tension is evident, hanging heavy like a dark storm cloud.

"Well, fine! Besides, you're not who I thought you were," she retorts defiantly, her voice cracking under the weight of her words.

"So, you're figuring out I'm not the blank check you thought I'd be, am I?" Duncan shoots back with a bitterness that cuts through the air. "Well, honey, from now on, you're paying your own frickin' way."

The finality in his tone leaves no doubt that this isn't just a spat; it's the end of something that once felt solid.

Without warning, a door slams shut with a force that reverberates through the house like a clap of thunder. We scatter like startled cockroaches, desperate to avoid being caught eavesdropping on the drama that is Duncan and Isadora.

"I don't know what I ever saw in her," Duncan mutters under his breath as he stomps down the stairs, his voice heavy with regret. "She and her whole friggin' family are nothing but damn gold diggers—" He stops abruptly when Beau approaches him, whining softly. "I'm sorry, Beau," Duncan says, settling onto a stair step and gently stroking my dog's fur. "Did Uncle Duncan upset you?" His tone carries an unfamiliar weight of remorse. For the first time since I've known him, I see tears glistening in his eyes. This unexpected vulnerability catches me off guard. It's clear he had a soft spot for Isadora, but now her true colors have shown themselves, like a stormy sky breaking through a sunny day.

Quietly, I inch further behind the doorframe where I'm trying to stay out of Duncan's line of sight. The tension in the air is undeniable; it feels as though I'm underwater, holding my breath. Just when I think I'm completely out of his view, Duncan looks up and catches my eye.

"I see you, Taylor," he calls out softly. "You can come out now." I'm caught between wanting to comfort him and feeling like an unwelcome intruder in this personal moment.

Crap! How could he possibly know I'm here? With a heavy heart and a hint of embarrassment, I step into his view. The air feels thick with unspoken words, and I can almost taste the tension. My heart pounds in my chest, and I feel the heat rising in my cheeks. "Sorry," I mumble, feeling like a frightened deer caught in the headlights.

Duncan looks at me with sincere eyes, and I can't help but feel a little comforted. His shoulders are slumped, and he looks emotionally drained. "You have nothing to apologize for," he reassures me, his voice steady but tinged with regret. "If anyone should be apologizing, it's me—for bringing Isadora into this house." His voice shakes as though he's carrying the weight of the world on his shoulders.

I shake my head, trying to dispel the tension in the air. "No," I respond gently but firmly. "Izzy's behavior is not your fault." It's true; she has her issues, and Duncan doesn't deserve to carry that blame. I hope my deep empathy for him is evident in my voice, making him feel truly understood.

"In a way, I suppose it's my fault," Duncan admits, his voice heavy with regret. "I brought her here, not entirely of my own accord—it was all her doing. I should have stood firm when she insisted on coming along. Now, I've ruined what was supposed to be our homecoming reunion. Remember the laughs and good times we shared last summer? Those memories feel so distant now."

As if summoned by his words, Isadora silently appears at the top of the stairs, her disheveled hair framing her red, puffy eyes as she struggles with her matching designer luggage. Each step is a battle, like a clumsy clown juggling in a circus act.

My instinct is to rush up and help her, but Duncan grips my wrist, halting my progress. Confusion flickers across my face—*what's the big deal?,* I think to myself.

"Let her learn to fend for herself," Duncan insists, his tone unwavering. "This is how she will learn to become independent."

"But—" I begin to protest. However, he cuts me off.

"I've ended things with her," he states plainly. "We're no longer dating. She's on her own now, and I'm a free agent."

Tension fills the air, thick with shock and deep uncertainty about what the future holds for the three of us. I can't help but wonder if destiny played a role in this and whether this is how our summer reunion was meant to unfold.

Isadora, her eyes filled with determination, struggles with her luggage. A large tote slips from her grasp and thunders down the stairs, shattering the silence in the house until it lands unceremoniously on the first floor. When she reaches the bottom step, she turns to us with a fierce and unyielding gaze, as if challenging either of us to question her resolve. Her eyes, like smoldering embers, flicker between Duncan and me, as if she is trying to interpret the unspoken words hanging heavily in the air.

I desperately want to help her with her struggles, sensing her frustration. However, I'm immobilized by Duncan's vise grip on my wrist. She rolls her eyes, clearly directing her irritation at Duncan and his unyielding hold on me.

"Don't mind me. I've got everything under control," she snaps, brushing past us with an exasperated huff. It's clear that she has nothing under control. As we watch her struggle through the parlor, dragging her numerous bags of luggage, the sound of the wheels on her larger bag rolling against the hardwood floor echoes through the silence.

"I can tell you right now, things are about to get messy," Duncan mutters under his breath.

"No kidding, Sherlock," I reply, sensing the weight of the situation. The laughter from last summer feels like a distant memory, overshadowed by the uncomfortable reality we are now facing. We used to be so carefree, but something has shifted in our story. Is it a secret? A betrayal? The uncertainty of it all leaves me feeling uneasy, like a storm cloud gathering on the horizon.

"Let's try to keep things civil," I suggest, though I'm not entirely sure if that's even possible at this point.

Duncan nods slowly, lost in thought as he glares at Isadora's retreating figure. "Civility might be asking too much," he replies quietly.

Our homecoming reunion, which once seemed like a familiar script, has taken an unforeseen turn. It has become an uncharted chapter, brimming with tension and uncertainty—an unexpected twist none of us anticipated. This sudden shift has left us all on edge, our senses heightened by the surprise.

Moments later, Duncan, ever the calm in the storm, stands beside his SUV, seemingly oblivious to the dark cloud hanging over Isadora. Meanwhile, Isadora struggles with her many bags of matching luggage as if she's wrestling with wild crocodiles— flipping and tugging, her face flushed with a mix of determination and panic. Her eyes dart around, searching for an easy solution, while her hands move with frenetic energy. After a tremendous amount of effort and a broken nail or two, she finally manages to shove all her bags into Duncan's Land Rover.

There are no lingering goodbyes or heartfelt farewells. Not a single tear is shed for Isadora. The air feels thick with an urgent need to escape and salvage whatever minuscule shred of dignity Isadora may still possess.

As the rest of us peek from between the parlor curtains, I can't help but feel like a nosy neighbor, eager to catch a glimpse of a thrilling neighborhood scandal. What is Isadora thinking? Is she feeling regret, excitement, or simply confusion? As she disappears into Duncan's Land Rover, a cloud of disgrace and uncertainty envelops her, leaving us to ponder what truly happened. Did she lose her composure, or is there a deeper truth we're overlooking? One thing is for certain—her thoughts are likely as chaotic as the crazy scene we just witnessed with the luggage. The mystery surrounding her actions puts us all on edge, leaving us hungry for answers—answers we'll never be privy to.

Duncan drove Isadora to the Lost Creek Junction bus station, marking the bittersweet end of her time at the house on the hill. What happened during that ride remains a mystery. Did their silence convey deep, intense feelings, or were there unspoken words hanging in the air like a charged storm, just waiting to break? I can only imagine the tension; it would have been fascinating to be a fly buzzing around in Duncan's SUV, witnessing the sparks fly between them. However, perhaps they exchanged nothing more than fleeting glances and polite nods, each lost in their own thoughts as they face an uncertain future—a future without each other.

Dale Thele

DAY TWENTY-THREE

Tuesday, June 11, 2019

As the early summer sun slowly sinks into the southwestern horizon, it bathes the sky in a breathtaking palette of orange and pink—a sight that never fails to inspire awe. I'm relaxing on the spacious porch of the grand house perched on the hill, surrounded by friends: Duncan, Julie, Rachael, Ryan, and Giles. The warm evening breeze dances through the twisted Live Oak trees, creating a serene backdrop for our impromptu gathering. Meanwhile, Beau is nowhere in sight; perhaps he's sprawled out on the settee in the parlor, dreaming of chasing squirrels or embarking on whimsical adventures—whatever dogs dream about. This idyllic moment captures not just the end of the day, but also the beauty of friendship and nature intertwined, all under the spell of a magnificent unfolding sunset.

"Has anyone else noticed how much more relaxed and easygoing everything has become since Isadora left?" Ryan muses aloud. "She really had a talent for stirring the pot, didn't she?" Surprisingly, the mention of Isadora's absence doesn't seem to affect anyone. I guess we're all just glad she's gone.

Julie's brow furrows with curiosity. "Rach," she begins tentatively, "I have a question for you—no pressure to answer if it's none of my business."

"What is on your mind?" Rachael prompts gently, her voice a soothing balm amidst Julie's curiosity.

Julie hesitates, her words lingering in the air as she struggles to phrase her question. "I'm not quite sure how to put this... please bear with me."

"Just ask it already," Rachael encourages with a smile. "We

are all friends here. Am I right?"

Taking a deep breath, Julie finally asks, "Okay! Here goes—was Izzy a real witch?"

The question hangs in the balance like the last rays of sunlight before twilight. We exchange glances, half-laughing, half-serious. It's one of those moments where curiosity dances with disbelief. The atmosphere thickens with anticipation, and each of us is on the edge of our seats, eager to hear Rachael's response.

Rachael's eyes twinkle mischievously as she chuckles. "That is a very good question. In some circles, Isadora might not be considered a 'real' witch," she says, using air quotation marks. "Unlike me, who has natural witch blood, Isadora's journey was quite different."

"So how does someone like Izzy become a witch?" Julie asks.

"Well," Rachael explains, her voice animated with enthusiasm, "she most likely learned through training and spent countless hours immersed in studying books. Her magic relies heavily on incantations and spells meticulously gathered from ancient tomes. In contrast, I possess an innate ability that allows me to perform basic magic without needing to recite elaborate spells."

"What's the difference between incantations and spells?" Ryan asks, his eyes sparkling with curiosity. "Aren't they basically the same?"

Rachael smiles, her enthusiasm evident. "Not quite! Incantations involve the rhythmic chanting or uttering of words that summon magical effects. Remember when Isadora made the dishes float during breakfast? That was pure incantation magic. Without those spoken words, she would not have been able to make those inanimate objects dance through the air."

She pauses for dramatic effect, clearly enjoying the moment. "On the other hand, a spell is more complex. It is a carefully crafted combination of magical words, actions, and sometimes even ingredients, designed to achieve specific outcomes. Just a couple of days ago, I cast a spell to make Isadora believe her room was engulfed in flames. I mixed some enchanted ingredients in a bowl and recited an incantation. Unfortunately, it did not actually scare her out of my house."

Ryan raises an eyebrow, intrigued. "So, if that spell was meant to create an *illusion* of fire for Isadora, how is it that we saw smoke and smelled wood burning?"

"Ah," Rachael replies with a knowing smile, "that is where the spell gets interesting. What you experienced—the fire and smoke—was the residual effects of the spell. For the spell to work, it was necessary for you to perceive an imminent danger so that Isadora would also sense it as real and urgent."

"Oh, I see how that works now," Ryan nods slowly, processing this newfound understanding.

"I have another question," Julie interrupts, a mischievous glint in her eye. "I guess I'm just brimming with curiosity this evening, aren't I?" Her eyes sparkle with interest, infusing the conversation with a sense of adventure.

Rachael chuckles warmly, her laughter filling the space between us with comfort. "Not a problem. What is on your mind?" she invites, her tone warm and reassuring.

Julie's eyes light up with curiosity. "At breakfast that morning, when you and Izzy made the dishes float effortlessly through the air, I noticed something intriguing. Izzy recited some words and waved Beau's stick to make the dishes hover, while you simply pointed your finger. Why is that?"

Rachael nods thoughtfully, her expression transitioning from casual to serious, yet animated. "Ah, that is a great observation," she responds, her eyes sparkling with excitement. "You see, Isadora's magic relied on incantations, spells, and a fancy talisman like a wand. It is almost like cooking—every word and gesture adds its own flavor to the magical stew."

She takes a brief pause, letting the imagery sink in before continuing, "But me? My abilities are an integral part of who I am. I can tap into higher powers and create magic without needing all those props or lengthy chants." Rachael leans in closer, as if sharing a juicy secret. "However," she adds with a mischievous twinkle in her eye, "when it comes to performing those bigger, intricate spells, I also have to use ancient words and rituals. It is all about knowing when to keep it simple and when to bring out the big guns." Her confidence in her abilities is unwavering, providing a reassuring presence in the room.

"Honestly, all this talk of magic and spells is starting to wear me out," Duncan admits wearily, his voice heavy with exhaustion as he rises from his wicker chair with a sigh.

"I am truly sorry," Rachael responds, her voice filled with genuine concern. "I did not mean to burden you—especially not so soon after everything with you and Isadora."

"No, really, I'm fine," Duncan insists, waving his hand dismissively as if to brush away the weight of the conversation. "However Rach, I found something of yours after Isadora left." He hands Rachael a peculiar stick that seems to shimmer faintly in the light.

"My wand! Thank you, Duncan," Rachael replies, her eyes lighting up. "With Isadora leaving this wand behind, I have a strong feeling that the *Book of Enchantments* is still somewhere on the property. Without the wand, that book is useless to her."

"Why do you say that?" Ryan interjects.

"This wand and the *Book of Enchantments* are like a matching set," Rachael explains passionately. "One cannot function without the other. Just as this wand holds no power without its counterpart—the *Book of Enchantments*—it too is of no value without the wand."

I lean in closer, captivated by her enthusiasm. "Last summer, when Beau found that stick—no, wait, that *wand*—he instinctively knew it was something extraordinary. Is that why he guarded it so fiercely?"

Rachael nods, her eyes sparkling with insight. "Absolutely. Animals have an acute sense of awareness—far beyond our own. They can detect when something holds great significance, even if they do not fully understand its value. Their instincts drive them to protect items without a second thought. It is astonishing to consider how much we underestimate our furry friends. They seem to know when something is off or special, even if we do not always recognize it."

Duncan settles back into the wicker chair, frustration evident in his voice. "I just wish I knew where Isadora hid your book of magic."

"I truly hope she did not take it with her," Rachael replies, her voice filled with determination. "Without this wand, the book is worthless to her. It will turn up someday, I am sure of it."

"Rach, how exactly does the wand work in conjunction with the book?" Ryan asks, his curiosity ablaze.

"*Conjunction*?" Duncan raises an eyebrow at Ryan, a playful smirk spreading across his face. "And you even used the word correctly in a sentence. That's quite a complex word for you. I'm impressed."

"Oh, just zip it, will you, Duncan," Ryan shoots back, glaring at him like a classic villain.

Duncan chuckles softly, enjoying the banter that often characterizes their interactions, as Ryan continues with his question.

"Anyway," Ryan presses on, brushing off Duncan's teasing with the determination of a seasoned warrior. "Seriously, though—how does the wand interact with the book?" He casts a smug glance at Duncan, his eagerness to learn shining through.

Rachael's eyes sparkle with excitement as she prepares to share her knowledge. "The wand channels the magic from the *Book of Enchantments*," she explains, barely containing her enthusiasm. "When the bearer holds the wand in their left hand, they can unlock and read the contents of the *Book of Enchantments*. Without that connection, it is just an indecipherable jumble of shapes and symbols—gibberish, if you will."

Julie's face lights up, her eyes wide with newfound understanding. "That makes so much sense," she exclaims, her voice filled with the joy of enlightenment. "No wonder I couldn't make heads or tails of that book. After struggling to decode its text and getting nowhere, I assumed it was written in some ancient foreign language."

"I have faith that one day," Rachael adds with a hopeful smile, her eyes shimmering with optimism, "the *Book of Enchantments* will turn up. It is more than just a book to me—it is a part of my history, my identity."

As dusk gracefully surrenders its light to the night, the sun gently dips below the horizon, casting a warm golden glow that will gradually fade into the cool embrace of twilight. The world around us is bathed in a warm hue, softly transitioning into the calm of the evening. Lively birds find their nests, surrendering to the tranquil stillness that envelops the air. In this moment of peace, crickets begin their melodic serenade, filling the evening air with a symphony of unique sounds. One by one, stars twinkle into existence alongside a delicate crescent moon in an indigo sky that deepens with every passing minute. A cool breeze carries the scent of freshly cut grass across the expansive porch, inviting us to pause and soak in this fleeting beauty for just a moment longer, instilling a sense of calm in our hearts.

Suddenly, Beau bounds up onto the porch with an air of mischief. Something is in his mouth—what could it be? In this dimming light, my curiosity is piqued, and a wave of concern washes over me. I'm not fond of him picking up strange objects from who knows where. The mystery of his find adds an intriguing element to the evening.

"Beau," I call out firmly but gently, "What do you have in your mouth?"

He pauses and looks at me with his big brown eyes, as if I'm the one with the strange question. He then trots over to Rachael, dropping his curious find at her feet.

"Oh. My. Gosh!" Rachael squeals, her eyes lighting up as if it's Christmas morning. "It is my *Book of Enchantments*!" Her voice, filled with such joy, is like a warm blanket on a cold day, spreading happiness to everyone around.

My heart races as I ask, "Beau! Where did you find that

book?" But before I can delve deeper into the mystery of his heroic gesture, Rachael bends down to hug my big furry friend, her joy radiating like sunshine.

"Look, everyone! I have my book back!" she exclaims, holding it high for all to see—an actual triumphant reunion. Her victory is evident, filling the air with a sense of achievement.

What better way to end the day than witnessing Rachael glow, practically doing a happy dance as she's reunited with her beloved book once more?

As night falls, thick as velvet, it envelops the house on the hill. Long shadows, like ghostly dancers, pirouette through the streets and around the modest dwellings of Lost Creek Junction, creating a scene ripe with suspense. Inside the big house, tranquility reigns as we drift into a deep slumber. The sweet and intoxicating scent of lavender lingers in the air, blissfully allowing us to remain unaware of the storm brewing beneath our dreams.

But then—shattered silence! Two simultaneous screams pierce through the stillness like shards of glass. I jolt upright in bed, my heart thundering in my chest and my pulse pounding in my ears.

"Gill! Did you hear that?" I turn to him, my voice filled with confusion and fear, the uncertainty in my voice mirroring the confusion in my mind.

"I did," he replies, springing to attention like a jack in the box. "What was it?"

"That sounded like Julie and Rachael," I exclaim groggily, my eyes wide with alarm and my voice trembling with fear.

Without a moment's hesitation, we leap from our bed and sprint toward the girls' bedroom. Duncan arrived before us, standing in the hall outside the girls' room, he pounds against the door with frantic urgency.

"Girls?" Duncan calls out anxiously. "Are you okay?" He attempts to twist the doorknob, but it stubbornly resists his efforts—a familiar scene in this house, where screams often coincide with locked doors.

"Unlock the door!" he demands, his voice rising with concern.

"It's not locked," Julie replies shakily from inside, her voice trembles with obvious fear.

"What's all the commotion?" Ryan asks through a yawn as he joins us in the dimly lit hallway outside the girls' room. His hair is a mess, and he looks like a disheveled zombie.

"The girls are in trouble, and the door won't budge," Duncan exclaims, urgency thick in his voice, each word heavy with the weight of the situation. The air feels charged with a sense of impending crisis, and every second seems to stretch into eternity.

"Why don't you just knock the door down?" Ryan suggests, still groggy and clearly unbothered by the gravity of the situation.

Duncan shoots him a look that says, *Seriously*?

"Hold on a second. I have an idea," Giles interjects, his voice cutting through the tension as he urgently rummages through his bathrobe pockets to produce a hairpin. Seriously, who carries a hairpin in their robe? Yet, that's not the most pressing issue at hand; we have more urgent matters than to question Giles about the hairpin. The clock is ticking, and Rachael and Julie are trapped on the other side of the closed door.

"What good is a hair pen on the door lock?" Duncan questions. "The girl's have already said the door isn't locked."

With determination etched on his face, Giles ignores Duncan's pessimism and holds the hairpin up like a makeshift sword. "Let's do this!" He kneels in front of the door, inserts the hairpin into the keyhole, and gives it a little wiggle. A soft click echoes in the otherwise silent hallway. Victory is sweet! With a swift motion, he swings open the door—and what lies beyond is a twist that none of us saw coming.

Julie and Rachael stand on top of the bed mattress, their bodies trembling with fear as they cling to each other like two shipwrecked sailors adrift on a makeshift raft at sea, surrounded by circling, hungry sharks. With wide eyes filled with intense terror, they focus their gazes and point toward something in the corner of the room.

I squint in the direction they are indicating, bracing myself for whatever horrors I might encounter—a looming shadow? A lurking monster? But when I look, nothing is there. Just the bedroom furniture arranged tastefully against the wall. Everything seems normal and in its place.

"What are you two pointing at?" I ask, trying to keep my tone light despite the tension in the air.

"They were—over there," Julie gasps, her voice quivering with fear as she continues to point with a trembling finger, referring to something they claim to have seen.

"Yeah! Right there!" Rachael adds, her shaking finger jabbing the air at an empty space across the room.

"They were right there," Julie exclaims, urgency in her voice as she emphatically points toward the empty shadow. "Rach saw them too!"

"I did," Rachael confirms, her voice trembling. "But when the door swung open, they vanished as if they had never existed."

"Who are *they*? Who are you talking about?" Duncan inquires, furrowing his brow in confusion.

"Ezekiel and Abrahim, of course," Julie replies with an exasperated roll of her eyes.

"Are you absolutely sure?" Duncan presses, skepticism lacing his tone.

"Duh! Don't you think we'd recognize them if we saw them?" Julie shoots back, her frustration boiling over.

"They are no longer just floating heads," Rachael chimes in. "They have bodies now!"

Duncan's eyes widen as he processes this revelation. "Uncovering their bones in the yard must have triggered something... supernatural," he says to himself as if trying to solidify a fragmented thought in his head.

Julie shivers involuntarily, her eyes darting around the dimly lit room. "They're even scarier now that they have bodies," she exclaims, her voice a mix of terror and disbelief.

Ryan clears his throat, trying to lighten the mood. "Well, it looks like they've decided to take a hike. So-o-o, we can head back to bed now," he says, but his attempt at humor is met with skeptical glances.

"I am NOT spending another minute in this room!" Julie declares defiantly, her arms crossed as if to ward off any lingering doubts. "No way! Not happening! I'd rather face the unknown than stay in this room and risk seeing those two ghosts again!"

"I am with Julie on this," Rachael agrees, her determined eyes speak volumes. "I would rather face whatever is out there than stay in here!"

Silence prevails while we assess the situation.

"Why don't we have a slumber party?" Ryan suggests, his enthusiasm bubbling over. "Just imagine it—everyone cozying up in the same room for the rest of the night. We can tell stories and eat snacks."

"Sounds good to me," Julie nods in agreement, a wave of relief washing over her as the excitement of the plan takes hold.

"What do you think, Rach? Are you in?" Julie asks, her eyes sparkling with anticipation.

Rachael grins widely, clearly on board with the idea. "Count me in," she replies enthusiastically. "Anything is better than spending another minute in this room."

Duncan raises an eyebrow, glancing at Giles, Ryan, and me. "Guys? Any objections?"

"No objections here," Ryan, Giles, and I declare in unison.

"Then it's settled," Duncan proclaims triumphantly. "Everyone to my bedroom. It's the largest and it can accommodate all of us. Bring blankets and pillows—we'll be roughing it on the floor."

Carefree laughter replaces the earlier tension as a new plan takes shape, transforming a scary night into one big outrageous slumber party.

DAY TWENTY-FOUR

Wednesday, June 12, 2019

"Julie," I say, leaning in with curiosity, "just moments ago, you took coffee to Rachael in the bedroom you share. You must know what's going on with her."

"I wish I knew," Julie replies, shrugging her shoulders, her brow furrowed with concern. She takes a seat on the edge of a kitchen chair, the wood creaks beneath her petite frame. Her fingertips nervously tap on the table, the sound echoing in the quiet room. "She let me into the room to drop off a breakfast tray. I saw her completely engrossed in that book of incantations, as if she were cramming for a final exam."

Duncan takes a deep gulp of his coffee, his brow knitted in confusion. "I wish I had some clue about what's going on with her."

"All this secrecy is driving me nuts," Ryan exclaims, throwing his hands up in exasperation.

"Rye," Duncan retorts with a teasing grin, "most days you're completely clueless as to what's going on around here. What makes today any different?" His tone is light, a stark contrast to Ryan's frustration.

Ryan shoots him a glare sharp enough to cut glass.

Duncan chuckles softly, adjusting his ever-present fedora as if it's armor against Ryan's irritation. His nonchalant demeanor contrasts sharply with Ryan's tension, adding to the emotional strain of the moment.

"Alright, boys, that's enough from both of you," Julie interjects firmly but gently. "This isn't the time or place for bickering. We need to come together and support Rach through whatever she's experiencing right now."

"Support her?" Giles questions, his brow furrowing in concern. "But we don't even know what she's up to."

Ryan leans forward, as if he has all the answers. "If you ask me," he says, "I bet what Rachael is dealing with has something to do with those ghostly visitors from last night."

"Whatever it is," Julie responds, her tone respectful, "we should respect her privacy and give her the space to do what she feels she needs to do."

A heavy silence envelops the room as Julie, Duncan, Ryan, Giles, and I sip our morning coffee, each lost in our own thoughts. The air is thick with unspoken worries, and the eerie events of last night still linger in our minds. What could Rachael possibly be hiding?

As morning turns into noon, a heavy silence, like a thick fog, overtakes the house, and the air feels dense with unspoken words. Rachael is still tucked away in the bedroom like a treasure waiting to be discovered. Julie, ever the concerned friend, can't shake the feeling that something is off. She checks in on Rachael from time to time, hoping that one of the visits will be the moment Rachael finally opens up.

"Rach, do you need anything?" Julie asks softly, her voice barely breaking the stillness. "I'm leaving a lunch tray for you. It's just outside the door."

I don't know Rachael all that well, but I've known her long enough to sense that something is brewing beneath the surface. Every time Julie offers to help, Rachael responds only with silence—no hints, no clues about what's happening behind that closed door. What could be so important in that book to demand such secrecy? It's a mystery that lingers in the air like an unfinished puzzle, gnawing at our curiosity. It's clear that Julie wants to help, to be there for our friend, but all she can do is knock softly on the door and hope for a response.

"I can't help but wonder if Rach is dealing with something heavy, or if she's simply enjoying some solitude," Julie says to me as she paces the hallway. As a compassionate and persistent friend, Julie is always there for those she cares about. "Whatever it is, I know one thing for sure—I'll keep checking in on her until that door swings open and Rach lets me in on whatever secret she's guarding so tightly." Rach's guarded nature adds a layer of mystery and complexity to the situation. Julie's determination is evident as she takes a deep breath and wraps on the door once again, refusing to give up.

The grandfather clock strikes once as we finish our light lunch of bologna sandwiches, and Rachael is notably absent. Suddenly, the kitchen is filled with her presence as she bursts in, her eyes sparkling with excitement.

"I've got it!" she declares, her voice ringing with triumph, her excitement contagious and drawing us all in.

"What have you got?" a baffled Julie asks.

"I have figured out how to banish Ezekiel and Abrahim for good," Rachael exclaims. "We can send them packing back to the original ceramic container from which they came."

"After everything we've been through, she now decides to share her brilliant plan," Ryan quips, raising an eyebrow skeptically at Rachael's revelation.

Undeterred by Ryan's sarcasm, Rachael continues, "It wasn't until Isadora took the *Book of Enchantments* that I realized there might be a spell in the book capable of permanently ridding us of those two angry ghosts. That is why getting the book back was so important to me."

Ryan crosses his arms in skepticism. "So what's the deal? Do you recite some magic words and—poof—they're back in their little ceramic prison forever?"

The air buzzes with anticipation as everyone leans in closer, our hope rising at the possibility of a daring solution. Could the answer to our ghostly problems really be that simple? The prospect fills us with a sense of optimism.

"No, not quite," Rachael says, her voice urgent yet steady. "It's much more complicated than that. First, I need to summon them, and that's where all of you come in. The five of you will contain the spirits while I perform the banishing incantation."

"What?" Ryan exclaims, his eyebrows shooting up in disbelief. "Why do we have to be involved?"

"Because someone must hold the ghosts in place while I conduct the ceremony to send them back to the ceramic container," Rachael explains, her eyes filled with determination, emphasizing the crucial role of the team.

"How on earth are we supposed to hold a ghost?" Julie interjects, her voice trembling with fear.

Rachael chuckles lightly, her eyes sparkling with mischief. "You won't be holding them in your hands. We will trap and contain them within a magic circle."

"Absolutely not," Julie snaps, crossing her arms defensively, her fear evident. "Count me out. I've encountered those ghosts up close and personal by accident—I have no desire to relive that experience, especially not on purpose."

"It is not as scary as it sounds," Rachael reassures her, her voice calm and steady. "Each of you will wear a protective charm—a pendant crafted from special herbs, suspended by a string around your neck. These herbs will shield you from any ghostly encounters."

"But why do you need all of us?" Giles asks, furrowing his brow with concern. "Couldn't this ritual be done with two or three people?"

"To ensure its success, everyone must participate," Rachael explains, her voice still calm. "Once the ghosts are summoned, you must join hands, creating an unbroken circle around them."

Duncan leans forward, curiosity evident on his face. "But what stops them from just flying away?"

"The herb pendants serve a dual purpose," Rachael replies, her eyes sparkling with determination. "They not only protect you from the ghosts, but also neutralize the ghosts' powers. As long as the circle remains intact, they will not be able to escape."

All of us, except for Rachael, exchange glances, our initial fears slowly giving way to intrigue. This may not be as bad as we thought. We're beginning to trust in Rachael's plan.

Sensing the urgency in the air, I ask, "How long do we have to hold them before the magic of the amulets fades?"

Rachael's expression turns serious. "Not long, I'm afraid— just enough time for me to complete a brief ritual. Then we will finally be free from Ezekiel and Abrahim forever."

"When do we do this?" Duncan's voice cuts through the tension in the room.

"We have no choice but to perform the ceremony tonight," Rachael replies urgently, her eyes ablaze with determination.

"Tonight?" Ryan exclaims in disbelief, his eyes widening.

"Yes, tonight," Rachael confirms. "The timing is crucial. The ritual must align with the peak of the Waxing Moon, when its magic is most potent. The moon rises in the East at 4:03 p.m. this afternoon and will reach its zenith in the night sky by 10 p.m. That is when I can tap into its power."

We exchange silent glances, each of us grappling with the gravity of the task at hand. We all feel the weight of our responsibility, the duty we have to see this through. I have my reservations, a million reasons why I'd rather not be part of this. But this isn't about me. It's about Rachael.

"Here is a list of the herbs you will need to create the protective pendants," Rachael announces, handing a neatly handwritten piece of paper to Julie. "You will find all the herbs in the cellar. Gather the containers and bring them back up here to the kitchen table, where everyone can help assemble the satchels with gauze fabric, tied securely with string."

Duncan raises an eyebrow, curiosity sparkling in his eyes. "What about the string? Do we need something special to tie the satchels?"

Rachael smiles at his question. "That's a good point! Yes, the herbs need to be placed inside circles made of soft, 100% unbleached cotton gauze and secured with 100% hemp twine. You should be able to find some twine and gauze in one of the kitchen drawers."

"I think I saw a ball of twine in this drawer," Julie exclaims as she rummages through a kitchen drawer. With a triumphant flourish, she holds up both the twine and gauze for everyone to see.

"Perfect," Rachael beams. "While you are crafting those herb pendants, I have some preparations of my own to take care of."

With that, she gracefully ascends the stairs to the upstairs bedrooms.

As the grand old grandfather clock in the hall tolls nine, a chill runs down my spine. The witching hour is creeping closer, and I sense the tension thickening in the air. The anticipation of what is to come is evident, like the charged atmosphere before a violent storm. I glance around at my friends, none of whom seem to be handling the situation well. Julie sits at the kitchen table, her foot tapping a frantic rhythm against the tile floor as she nervously bites what little remains of her thumbnail. Can you blame her? The atmosphere is electric with anticipation, and every hair on my arm stands on end.

Meanwhile, Duncan pretends to be engrossed in a book, but I see right through his facade; any moment now, his calm demeanor might shatter like glass. Across from him, Giles and Ryan are engaged in a lackluster game of cards. However, their glazed expressions reveal that their thoughts are clearly elsewhere. It's as if they're merely going through the motions—shuffling cards about while shadows loom large around us. The clock on the kitchen wall continues to tick, each second dragging on longer than the last. We're caught in this strange limbo between fear and dread, trying to ignore the whispers of our imaginations. The night has only just begun, and we are about to discover what happens when the witching hour arrives and the true nature of the danger lurking in the shadows is revealed.

Rachael descends the stairs with an air of mystery, holding the legendary *Book of Enchantments* in one hand and, yes, Beau's stick—I really should start referring to it as a *wand*—in the other. Dressed in a flowing black robe that sweeps the floor, she looks less like a magical witch and more like a solemn judge ready to deliver a scathing verdict. However, if she added a classic black pointy hat with a wide brim, I could then better envision her as a sorcerer.

As she enters the kitchen, we snap to attention like soldiers responding to a commanding officer. The anticipation in the air is apparent, each breath heavy with eagerness about what will unfold next.

"Have you finished making the herb pendants?" Rachael asks, her voice steady and authoritative, each word resonating with the weight of her command.

"Yes, we have," Julie exclaims, her eyes sparkling with excitement as she gestures toward the array of enchanting pendants laid out on the table. They look interesting—like individual satchels of weed, waiting to be rolled and smoked.

"When do we get to wear them?" Ryan asks.

"In a few moments," Rachael replies with a knowing smile that hints at secrets yet to be revealed. "But first, I must infuse them with the proper magic."

"What do you mean by *infuse them*? Like charging crystals?" Julie inquires.

"Something along those lines," Rachael nods.

We exchange eager glances, our hearts racing with the thrill of what's about to happen. The anticipation is almost unbearable. Magic is about to unfold, and we're about to embark on the most thrilling experience, if not the scariest of our lives.

With a graceful flourish, Rachael stands beside the table, her excitement practically bubbling over. She takes a deep breath, allowing the anticipation to wash over her as she prepares to work her magic. With a flick of her wrist, she waves her wand in a gentle clockwise motion above the herb pendants lying before her, each one glinting with potential. The air seems to shimmer and crackle with energy as she weaves her spell.

"By the powers that be, let these charms come alive," she exclaims, her voice rising in an incantation that dances through the air like a playful breeze. The words flow effortlessly from her lips:

> *"By starlit whispers and shadows entwined,*
> *With winds of the ancients, let power unwind.*
> *From dusk till dawn, as the moonlight weaves,*
> *Grant now my plea, as twilight breathes.*
> *With the flick of my wrist and the strength of my heart,*
> *Awaken the magic—let the journey start."*

As she lowers the wand, an energy fills the room. "Alright, everyone. It is showtime!" Rachael announces, uniting us all in this magical, yet frightening journey. The anticipation is evident as we glance at our herb pendant necklaces, their vibrant colors glowing bright under the overhead fluorescent lights.

"Now, slip the string loop over your head, letting the string rest around your neck, and allow the magic satchels to hang freely over your chest, near your heart."

"Are you absolutely certain these herbs will protect us?" Ryan's voice trembles with anxiety, and his eyes dart around the room like a deer caught in headlights.

"Without a doubt," Rachael replies, her tone unwavering. She's the rock in our stormy sea of insecurities and nerves. "But remember, you must keep the circle intact once the ghosts are confined. Do not break the circle—no matter what may happen."

Duncan checks his watch—his expression conveys everything. "It's ten minutes to ten."

"Thank you, Duncan, for the heads-up," Rachael acknowledges, her gaze becoming steady and serious. "Listen closely—when Ezekiel and Abrahim manifest, it is crucial that all five of you immediately join hands to form an unbroken circle around them. Do you understand?"

"Yep, got it," Giles chimes in, putting on a brave face and nodding along with the rest of us as we share a collective breath of determination. The anticipation for the upcoming ritual is building, the atmosphere buzzes with a mix of excitement and dread. There's no doubt in my mind that tonight's going to be one for the books.

"Is everyone ready?" Rachael asks, her voice barely above a whisper. The tension in the air is thick as we all nod in unison. "I am about to summon the spirits of Ezekiel and Abrahim."

After releasing a deep breath as if doing yoga exercises, she begins to recite the incantation, her words flowing through the air like a gentle breeze:

"Spirits of the ancient, hear my call!
Come forth from the shadows, answer my thrall!"

The candles on the table flicker to life as if dancing to her rhythm, and the atmosphere thickens with an electric charge. She continues the incantation:

"Whispers of the astral winds,
come forth, ye lost and forsaken.
Ink of shadows, entwine my will in twilight's embrace.
Arise from the depths, spirits bound in echoes,
grant my heart the fervor to ignite the flame of truth.
By the stars' shimmering tongues,
I summon you, Ezekiel and Abrahim, forthwith!"

Almost instantly, Ezekiel and Abrahim materialize before our eyes—just as Rachael had predicted. The air thickens with a crackling, electric energy that sends shivers down my spine. The five of us—Julie, Duncan, Ryan, Giles, and I—quickly join hands, forming an unbroken circle around these ethereal beings before they can comprehend what is happening.

"Who dares summon us through witch's sorcery?" snarls the ugliest of the two ancient ghosts, its voice echoing ominously off the walls. I feel the chill of its presence wrapping around me like a blustery winter wind.

"It is I, Rachael," she replies without missing a beat, her

voice steady and bold, a beacon of courage in the face of danger. "I am a direct descendant of the late Mrs. Scruggs, who nearly two centuries ago imprisoned you within this ceramic vessel for eternity."

The tension in the room is almost unbearable as we hold our breath, waiting to see how these angry, vengeful spirits will react to Rachael's audacious claim. This is not your average Wednesday night Bible study; it feels more like an episode of a supernatural reality TV show gone awry.

"What is it that you inquire from us?" the second ghost asks, its tone a mix of curiosity and trepidation.

The air crackles with tension as Rachael, unwavering in her bravery, stands her ground.

"Silence! Both of you!" Rachael commands, her eyes blazing with determination. "I want nothing from you except to banish you from this place. I am sending you back to the dark shadows from which you came."

"Release us at once from this witchery that binds us! I command you!" the first ghost orders, his voice resonating with undeniable authority.

"You have no power here," she asserts confidently. "The circle holds you captive, and your magic powers are but whispers in the wind."

"You shall suffer greatly for this transgression," the first ghost threatens, its malevolent gaze fixed on her like a dagger.

With a determined glint in her eye, she raises her wand high and waves it in the air. The sparkling silvery light of the Waxing Gibbous moon, a time when magic is at its peak, bathes her in an ethereal glow, illuminating her fierce resolve. With a voice that resonates like a gentle breeze whispering secrets through the trees, she begins to recite from the ancient *Book of Enchantments*:

"By the light of the moon and the power of this night,
I command you to return from whence you came,
to fade into the shadows and relinquish your claim!"

As her words flow from her lips, the air becomes thick with magic, crackling like static electricity. Each syllable she utters carries the weight of the entire world, resonating with power.

The ghosts moan and wail in protest, their forms flickering like lightening during a storm as the banishing spell begins to takes hold. Their struggle is real, adding a tense energy to the atmosphere.

Rachael stands tall, her determination a formidable force that radiates from her, a testament to her strength and resilience. She is prepared to face whatever comes next. After all, when it comes to battling spirits, it's all about who possesses the stronger will—and tonight, that's definitely—six of us against two ghosts. She continues to recite:

"*By the shimmering glow of the Waxing Gibbous moon,*
Spirits of shadows, I summon you to depart.
With soft-spoken winds, I cleanse this night,
Release your grasp—take your flight!
From this sacred space where you linger and dwell,
Return to the realm where forgotten souls swell.
By my will and this hallowed rite,
I cast you away—away from the light.
Begone now, Ezekiel and Abrahim,
To the pottery vessel from whence you came."

Both spectral forms begin to spin as if caught in a whirling tornado. They merge into a single wisp of grayish smoke, their ethereal bodies intertwined as one in a desperate dance from which they cannot break free.

"Please, we beg of you, set us free!" Their voices echo—a haunting plea that resonates through the stillness, tugging at our hearts with an urgency that feels like an approaching storm we can scarcely ignore.

The column of twirling smoke grows thinner and thinner as it disappears into the ceramic container. As the last tendrils of their essence vanish into the open vessel, Rachael acts with lightning speed, slamming the lid shut and trapping the ghosts inside. Her eyes blaze with determination as she lights a black candle; its flame flickers to life, casting dancing shadows across our awestruck faces.

In awe, we watch intently as dark molten wax drips onto the lid and down the sides of the container, each drop forming a protective seal that encases the spirits within.

"This act is not merely one of containment—it is a sacred duty to ensure that their restless souls cannot and will not escape to wreak havoc upon the living," Rachael reveals.

Once the container is sealed, Rachael takes her wand firmly in hand, and traces repetitive circles around the sealed container. Each movement serves as a powerful invocation of ancient magic. The air shimmers with energy as she infuses the container with her will, binding the spirits within with a spell designed for protection and restraint.

"This potent magic, a tradition of power, safeguards both myself and future souls from the duo's torment—a responsibility I carry with solemn determination," Rachael shares.

As Rachael, feeling exhausted, slips into a heavy silence, the only sounds in the kitchen are the hum of the refrigerator, the soft ticking of the wall clock, and the gentle crackling of the candle flames on the table. The flickering flames, though they dance, never goes out, symbolizing Rachael's unwavering resolve. They serve as a poignant reminder that even in the depths of darkness, a glimmer of hope remains.

DAY TWENTY-FIVE

Thursday, June 13, 2018

As a new dawn breaks over the big house on the hill, my friends remain blissfully lost in their dreams—everyone except for me. I stand at the top of the stairs, enjoying an unobstructed view of the spacious ground floor below. I'm captivated by the mischievous spirits flitting above my head; their playful dancing and acrobatic antics are quite amusing. With Ezekiel and Abrahim gone for good, the ghosts of this old house have come out to play and celebrate their newfound freedom. It's an incredible feeling to see the friendly ghosts back in the house where they belong.

I'm startled from my thoughts by the clatter of dishes coming from the kitchen; I suppose Rachael is already busy preparing coffee. I thought I was the only one awake. As part of my usual morning routine, I head down the staircase toward the parlor to check on Beau. He's awake, perched on his settee like a guardian, growling at the whimsical apparitions shimmering like moonlight and swirling like mist around him. This is a new experience for him.

"Beau, you silly pup," I chuckle softly, my voice filled with reassurance. "Those ghosts aren't being mean. They're just playing with you, like your butterfly friends in the backyard."

He pauses his growling and tilts his head, as if trying to process what I just said. His intelligent eyes seem to be asking, *What are you talking about?* He takes a moment to assess the situation, and I'm impressed by the way his sharp mind works.

With a deep sigh of relief, Beau relaxes into the cushions. It's as if he's finally grasping the idea that not all things that go bump in the night are bad. His body language exudes a sense of calm and understanding. For a brief moment, it seems like he's smiling back at me, as if he understands and his eyes curiously follow the ghost's eradicate movements.

This is just one of many peaceful mornings to come in the haunted house on the hill, where laughter will echo and spirits will roam free once again, promising a future of tranquility and joy.

"Do you wanna go potty?" I ask, and in an instant, Beau is filled with unbridled joy, forgetting completely about the flitting ghosts. With a burst of energy that rivals a rocket launch, he leaps off the settee and bounds toward the back door, his happiness clear as if he were propelled by an invisible spring.

I catch up to him at the back door—his tail wagging furiously and his whole body quivering with anticipation as he eagerly waits to go outside. The fresh morning air fills my lungs as I swing the door open, and he dashes out like a cannonball into the crisp, dewy air. I leave the door ajar just enough so that when he's ready to come back inside, he can slip in without interrupting my morning coffee.

It's these simple, uncomplicated moments that make mornings with Beau so special. His excitement is contagious, and I can't help but smile as I watch him run and play without a care in the world.

"Morning, Taylor," Rachael greets me with a warm smile.

"Good morning to you too," I respond as I settle at the kitchen table, perhaps for the last time. "How did you sleep last night, now that you're back in the comfort of your own bedroom?"

"You want to know something? I haven't slept that peacefully in a very long time," Rachael replies, her voice filled with a deep sense of relief. "I can breathe again, not having to be constantly on guard and worrying about what Ezekiel or Abrahim might do next."

"I can only imagine," I say just as Giles strolls into the kitchen, his expression slightly bemused.

"Have you let Beau out yet?" he asks, swatting at an annoying hovering ghost that seems to be drawn to him like a curious gnat.

Rachael chuckles at Giles situation. "Looks like you have got yourself an admirer," she says with a twinkle in her eye, adding a touch of humor to the morning.

I grin at Giles and add, "To answer your question—yes, Beau is outside as we speak."

"By the way, Taylor," Rachael begins, her eyes sparkling with curiosity, "I've been meaning to ask you, how long have you had Beau?"

"I got him as a gift when he was a puppy, and I was sixteen at the time," I reply, a fond smile creeping across my face. The memories of his big eyes and clumsy paws flood back, making my heart swell a little.

Rachael tilts her head back as she silently calculates. "So, that makes him what—six years old?"

"Pretty much," I nod, feeling a wave of nostalgia wash over me. It's hard to believe how time flies when we've spent so many good times together.

Just then, Duncan strides into the kitchen, tipping his fedora with flair and adopting an exaggerated Irish brogue. His playful entrance immediately captures our attention. "Top of the mornin' to you all!"

Rachael giggles, her eyes sparkling with amusement. "Well, someone is certainly in a good mood. What do we owe this occasion?" she asks, her laughter adding a delightful note to the morning.

Duncan shrugs nonchalantly as he takes a seat at the table. "Does one need an occasion to feel great? Life is too short for that," he replies. His carefree attitude brings a soothing lightness to our morning. It's good to have my old friend Duncan back again. I was afraid that Isadora had truly broken him.

"I suppose you are right," Rachael agrees, handing him a steaming mug of coffee. The rich aroma fills the air—it's a perfect start to a perfect day.

Meanwhile, Beau, his impatience reaching a crescendo, barks from outside the partially open back door.

"Why can't he just nudge the door open and come in on his own?" I grumble under my breath.

"Get with the program, Taylor. He's not just any ordinary dog—he's a prince who demands royal treatment," Duncan chuckles, his amusement turning into a full-blown grin.

I shoot him a playful side-eye as I swing open the door, allowing his *royal highness* to enter. Beau, with a regal air that would make any monarch proud, struts into the kitchen and heads straight for his food and water bowls, where his morning feast awaits him.

"Taylor," Rachael asks with genuine curiosity, "how did you know Beau wanted inside when he barked?"

"Oh, that's easy," I reply, a grin spreading across my face, "he has different barks for different situations."

"Really? Is that so?" Rachael leans in closer, intrigued.

"Absolutely," Giles responds enthusiastically. "It took me a couple of weeks to learn each of Beau's unique barks."

"Interesting," Rachael muses thoughtfully. "I have never had a dog myself, so I did not realize they could communicate so distinctly."

"Like I said before, Beau isn't just any dog," Duncan smirks, a playful glint in his eye. "He thinks he's a person. Right, Beau?" he teases, as if expecting a response from the regal canine.

On cue, Beau pauses his enthusiastic kibble crunching and turns to look at Duncan, his big brown eyes sparkling with an almost human-like understanding.

"You know, dogs really have life all figured out," Giles chimes in with a grin.

"Oh, really? How so?" Duncan raises an eyebrow, intrigued.

"Well, they eat, sleep, get showered with love—then they poop. And not necessarily in that order," Giles chuckles, a twinkle in his eye. "What more could one possibly want from life?"

Laughter erupts in the kitchen like confetti at a party, filling the air with warmth and camaraderie. Rachael wipes away tears of laughter, Duncan's smirk widens, and Giles's grin becomes irresistibly infectious, spreading joy to everyone present.

Just then, a drowsy Ryan shuffles in, curiosity etched on his face. The sound of our hearty laughter fills the room, bouncing off the walls. "What's so funny?" he asks, his voice a mix of confusion and anticipation.

"Nothing," Duncan replies with a sly grin, mischief glinting in his eyes. He clearly enjoys moments like this. The joke, a playful jab at Ryans expense, is a testament to their ongoing banter.

"There you go again," Ryan huffs. "You guys never let me in on the joke. I enjoy a good laugh too, you know."

Duncan mutters under his breath, "You *are* the joke."

Ryan's face falls, a mix of hurt and resignation crossing his features. He's used to Duncan's barbs, but they still sting.

Ryan shoots Duncan a piercing glare, his expression a mix of irritation and intrigue, which adds an extra layer of tension to the moment and intensifies their ongoing banter.

"Care for some coffee?" Rachael chimes in, breaking the tension as she hands Ryan a steaming mug. He settles into a chair, eyeing everyone with an air of suspicion—like a detective trying to decipher a cryptic case. You can practically see the wheels turning in his head as he takes cautious sips, weighing his options.

Just then, Julie bounces into the kitchen like a burst of sunshine. "You won't believe who visited me last night," she exclaims, her excitement evident and a hint of mystery in her voice.

The room is alive with Julie's energy as she eagerly awaits our guesses. In the impending silence, the morning light filters through the curtains, casting a warm glow over the kitchen.

"Alright, Julie, just tell us who visited you before you explode," Duncan urges.

With a burst of excitement, Julie announces, "Arabella—can

you believe that?"

"Oh," Duncan exclaims, his eyes widening with intrigue, "your little ghost friend."

"Yes," Julie replies, her voice brimming with enthusiasm. "That's her. We talked for what seemed like hours."

"Are you sure it wasn't just a dream?" Ryan interjects skeptically.

"No way," Julie retorts, her disbelief evident. "I was wide awake. Arabella came to thank us for getting rid of Ezekiel and Abrahim once and for all. Can you believe it? She told me how terrified she was of them. And get this—she didn't trust Isadora at all. Sorry, Duncan, those were her words."

"No problem," Duncan nervously chuckles, nodding in agreement. "I wholeheartedly agree with your little friend on that one."

Julie adds softly, a hint of sadness creeping into her tone, "She wanted to say goodbye. She knew I'd be leaving soon now that everything is right in the house. Arabella hates goodbyes—they feel too final to her."

"Sounds like you have made quite a special friend in Arabella," Rachael observes thoughtfully.

"Yes," Julie nods earnestly, a smile filled with mixed emotions spreading across her face. "I guess I have at that."

"You know," Rachael begins, her voice a blend of wonder and seriousness, "it is incredibly rare for a spectral being to form a bond of friendship with a human. The connection you have with Arabella is truly extraordinary."

Julie's eyes widen with hope. "Oh, I really hope she and I see each other again. I've grown so fond of her."

Rachael smiles gently, clearly moved by the depth of Julie's feelings. "As I mentioned, the bond you share with Arabella is unlike any other—it will endure throughout your lifetime."

"Oh, Rach," Julie replies, dabbing at her eyes as emotions well up within her. "You're going to make me cry."

Ryan chuckles softly. "Oh boy, here come the waterworks, and they haven't even started saying their goodbyes yet."

"Speaking of goodbyes," Rachael adds, "I'm releasing all of you from your promises to help me get the bed-and-breakfast up and running."

"But we promised to help," I protest.

"Look around you," Rachael smiles, gesturing to the many ghosts floating freely about the house. "I have all these ghosts who have nothing better to do. I will put them to work."

"Are you sure?" Julie asks. "We don't mind staying to help you."

"I will be fine, really I will," Rachael replies. "I have enjoyed having all of you as my guests, but you have your own lives to get back to."

After helping with the cleanup following breakfast, we all carry our bags downstairs into the parlor. The atmosphere is thick with the bittersweet feeling of our impending departures, and each of us is struggling with a whirlwind of emotions.

Julie's voice trembles with sincerity as she speaks, wrapping her arms around Rachael in a heartfelt hug. "Thank you for an unforgettable time," she says, her words reflecting the depth of her feelings and the strength of their new bond. "Sure, there were some rocky moments, but I feel fortunate to know you and to call you my friend."

Rachael, with a playful smile, dabs at her eyes with a tissue and replies, "If you keep this up, you are going to have me in tears." Her lighthearted banter provides a familiar comfort, adding a touch of levity to our emotional farewell.

Julie then turns her attention to me. "Taylor," she says, "whenever you find yourself in Austin, promise me you'll look me up? And you too, Giles."

"Absolutely," I respond, squeezing Giles's hand reassuringly. "Don't be surprised if we show up on your doorstep one weekend." The anticipation of future visits and the hope of reuniting fill the air, adding a hopeful note to our goodbye.

"That'll be a pleasant surprise," Julie beams as she wraps her arms around me and then Giles. Her warm embrace serves as a tangible reminder of the emotional bond we've formed and the many good times we've shared.

"Alright, troops, let's get a move on," Duncan urges, his voice brimming with enthusiasm. Turning to Giles, he adds, "It was truly a pleasure meeting you. Please take good care of our Taylor."

"I promise," Giles replies, shaking Duncan's hand firmly as if sealing a business deal.

With a grin that lights up his face, Duncan throws an arm around my shoulders and says, "Taylor, I'm really going to miss you, buddy." His warmth envelops me, making me feel like I'm part of something special.

My heart swells with emotion as I manage to say, "Right back at you," between breaths, feeling the warmth of Duncan's tight bear hug.

"Thank you so much, Rach," Duncan continues earnestly. "I'm truly sorry about Isadora and all the trouble she stirred up. You've been a rock star through everything. I'll never forget you."

"Do not give it a second thought," Rachael reassures him warmly. "Just know that my door is always open to you."

Meanwhile, Julie kneels down to give Beau a loving hug. He responds with a slobbery kiss that makes everyone chuckle. "You keep an eye on your daddy for me, okay?" she says playfully to Beau. He barks back enthusiastically, as if he understands every word.

All of us share a good laugh, savoring a moment of joy amidst the bittersweet farewells and raw emotions.

"Come on, Julie," Duncan calls out, his voice laced with urgency. "Goodbye, everyone," he adds over his shoulder, suitcase in hand, as Ryan and Julie trail closely behind him.

Suddenly, Ryan halts, as if he's forgotten something. He puts his suitcase down on the ground and walks back to the porch, where Rachael, Giles, Beau, and I stand frozen, curious to what is up with him.

"Taylor," Ryan begins, his tone serious yet earnest, as

Duncan and Julie look on from across the yard. "I can't leave without telling you something important." His words are heavy with emotion, his confession sincere, and its significance profound. "Last summer was a turning point for me—I made the biggest mistake of my life by letting you slip away." He then looks at Giles. "And Gill, I want you to know that you've got one of the great guys in Taylor. Don't make the same mistake I did—hold onto him with both hands."

With those heartfelt words lingering in the air, echoing both regret and hope, Ryan turns to rejoin Julie and Duncan, climbing into Duncan's SUV. Before closing the door, he waves one last time—a gesture that speaks volumes.

"That was a really nice of Rye," Giles says softly, squeezing my hand gently, grounding me amidst a whirlwind of mixed emotions.

"You'd have to truly know Rye to understand how difficult it was for him to admit he messed up," I reply, my voice trembling with emotion, swiping the back of my hand across my face as a wave of gratitude washes over me.

As Duncan's Land Rover pulls away from the curb and they drive into the distance, their figures fade into nothing more than a memory—a reminder that sometimes we must let go to appreciate what we had. And that's okay because change is a part of life.

"Then there were three," Rachael muses, her voice tinged with nostalgia.

"Actually, four," I gently correct, scratching behind Beau's ear. "Don't forget about Beau."

"How in the world could I ever forget sweet, adorable Beau?" Rachael smiles, glancing down at him as his tail beats against the porch floor, radiating pure joy.

"Rach," I say, my heart heavy yet grateful, "this reunion has been real. And if given the chance to do it all over again, I'd be the first one to come back here."

"I can only imagine how tough it must be to leave this house," Rachael replies thoughtfully. "I know I would struggle to walk away from it."

"Saying goodbye to this place is difficult, as it holds so many memories and has changed our lives in countless ways," I reflect, feeling a wave of shared experiences wash over me. The laughter, the late-night talks, and the joyful moments that seemed like they'd last forever all come flooding back.

"Leaving Lost Creek Junction the first time was for the better, right?" Giles interjects with a knowing smile, his eyes twinkling with shared memories.

"I can't argue with that," I admit, nodding in agreement. "Shortly after leaving here, everything changed for both Giles and me."

But the truth remains unspoken. This house is more than just stone and mortar; it's a repository of my heart, a place where memories are etched into every corner. I'm not ready to let go of these pieces just yet, but I know I must. I can't continue living in the past; the future beckons me.

"Do not be a stranger," Rachael whispers into my ear as she envelops me in a warm hug—the kind that lingers long after you part. Her embrace is filled with warmth and understanding. She then turns and hugs Giles tightly. "You and Taylor are always welcome here—come visit anytime."

"Thanks, Rach," Giles replies warmly, giving her back a reassuring pat.

"I suppose this is goodbye," I say, my voice tinged with a bittersweet note. The words feel heavy on my tongue.

"Let us leave it at *so long*," Rachael replies, her eyes reflecting the weight of unspoken words.

Arabella was right—*goodbye* feels far too final for this moment. It's not really the end; it's just another chapter waiting to be written.

As Giles and I load our luggage into the Jeep, I glance back at Beau. He stands immobilized in the yard, caught in an emotional tug-of-war between us and Rachael, his loyalty swinging like a pendulum. After what feels like an eternity, he finally makes his choice and hops into the back seat of the Jeep.

We wave goodbye to Rachael, who stands on the porch with a mixture of sadness and deep understanding as I back the Jeep out of the driveway.

As we embark on our road trip back to New Orleans, it feels like a significant moment. The open road stretches ahead, promising adventure and a few wild stories—I'm almost certain of that. As we drive away, a question lingers in my mind: what does the future hold? Will Rachael ever invite us all back for another reunion? It seems unlikely, unless Ezekiel or Abrahim decides to crash the party again. The chances of that happening feel as distant as a star in the night sky—like we're talking about two hundred years from now. By then, who knows which stories will have faded into oblivion? This uncertainty about the fate of our memories makes me feel introspective and contemplative. After we're dead and gone, will anyone even remember what happened in this house during the past two summers?

The memories I hold dear are filled with laughter and friendship, and they are firmly etched in my mind. No one can take them away from me. My visits to Lost Creek Junction brought many wonderful experiences. However, one thing that gives me a sense of closure is the relief that I won't have to witness the return of those two ghosts when they inevitably reappear. This thought brings me immense comfort.

For now, it's the three musketeers on our journey back home, welcoming the opportunity to create new memories while the old ones linger like shadows in the rearview mirror. Here's to the open road and the anticipation of new adventures!

The End. Period. Full Stop.
Do not pass go. Do not collect $200

Coming in 2026

It's a bird!
It's a plane!
It's Captain Merica to the rescue!

Rich Richards, the literary sensation, has set a high standard with his six New York Times Bestsellers, four of which have been adapted into blockbuster feature films with a fifth in production, and the Captain Merica franchise of action figures, clothes, toys, and more. His Captain Merica character has won over the hearts of both adults and children alike. Receiving a half-million-dollar advance payment for his seventh novel, the pressure is on to write another bestseller. However, Rich is facing a significant challenge: writer's block. With only six weeks left to submit a manuscript, time is running out, and he has nothing to show for it—except for a blank piece of paper. In a moment of desperation, he confides in his fictional character, Captain Merica, hoping for a miracle.

About The Author

Most of Dale Thele's life has been a lengthy series of compulsions strung together by atrocious acts of stupidity due to boredom. After raising heck in a sleepy oil town in north-central Oklahoma for eighteen years, he ventured to Oklahoma City University on a quest for higher education. He quickly learned "higher" education meant to "elevate" one's mind with the aid of either a reefer or a bong, and ample amounts of alcohol. Some years later destiny dragged him to Austin, Texas, where he currently lives vicariously through the fictional characters he conjures up, and the far-fetched adventures he writes.

Visit the Official Website:
www.DaleThele.com

"corrupting readers since 2008"
with LGBTQIA+ themed fiction

LGBTQIA+ RESOURCES

The Trevor Project – www.thetrevorproject.org
TrevorLifeline – 1-866-488-7386
A non-profit organization focusing on suicide prevention efforts among lesbian, gay, bisexual, transgender, queer, and questioning (LGBTQ) youth. They also operate The Trevor Lifeline, a confidential service that offers trained counselors.

National Suicide Prevention Lifeline –
www.suicidepreventionlifeline.org
National Suicide Prevention Lifeline – 1-800-273-8255
A suicide prevention network of over 160 crisis centers providing 24/7 service via a toll-free hotline:
1-800-273-8255 (TALK)
It is available to anyone in suicidal crisis or emotional distress.

It Gets Better Project – www.itgetsbetter.org
An Internet-based nonprofit founded in response to the suicides of teenagers who were bullied because they were gay or because their peers suspected that they were gay. Its goal is to prevent suicide among LGBT youth by having gay adults convey the message that these teens' lives will improve.

PFLAG – www.pflag.org
The United States' first and largest organization uniting parents, families, and allies with people who are lesbian, gay, bisexual, transgender, and queer. PFLAG National is the national organization, which provides support to the PFLAG network of local chapters.

Other Titles by Dale Thele

Chasing Unicorns

Masked Identities

Roadhouse Friday

Harvest Moon

Naughty Gay Adult Bedtime Stories

Clipped Wings

Blurred Lines

Ezekiel & Abrahim:
GHOST of LOST CREEK JUNCTION

Find these titles and more at:

www.dalethele.com